THE HALFADAY CREEK SERIES BY
JAMES B. HENDRYX

Skullduggery on Halfaday Creek
The Saga of Halfaday Creek
Adventures on Halfaday Creek

Visit www.jamesbhendryx.com for more information on
forthcoming installments in the Halfaday Creek
uniform matching series.

ADVENTURES ON HALFADAY CREEK

James B Hendryx

ADVENTURES ON HALFADAY CREEK

JAMES B. HENDRYX

ILLUSTRATIONS BY
PETE KUHLHOFF

ALTUS PRESS • 2013

© 2013 Altus Press • First Edition—2013

EDITED AND DESIGNED BY
Matthew Moring

SERIES EXECUTIVE CONSULTANT
Richard Hall

PUBLISHING HISTORY
"Black John Sells a Claim" originally appeared in the July, 1950 issue of *Short Stories* magazine (vol. 210, no. 1). Reprinted by arrangement with the Estate of James B. Hendryx.
"Corporal Downey: 'Suicide.' Black John: 'Maybe.'" originally appeared in the March 25, 1940 issue of *Short Stories* magazine (vol. 170, no. 6). Reprinted by arrangement with the Estate of James B. Hendryx.
"For Some Little Sacks of Gold" originally appeared in the September 25, 1933 issue of *Short Stories* magazine (vol. 144, no. 6). Reprinted by arrangement with the Estate of James B. Hendryx.
"Foreclosure on Halfaday" originally appeared in the October, 1949 issue of *Short Stories* magazine (vol. 208, no. 4). Reprinted by arrangement with the Estate of James B. Hendryx.
"All or Nothing" originally appeared in the August 28, 1955 issue of the *Boston Sunday Globe* magazine. Reprinted by arrangement with the Estate of James B. Hendryx.

THANKS TO
Theresa Burau Baehr, Deborah Fellows, Joel Frieman, Robert Loomis, Richard Moore, Rick Ollerman, Julie Rhodes, Garyn Roberts, Cynthia Whyte, & the Leelanau Historical Society

TABLE OF CONTENTS

BLACK JOHN SELLS A CLAIM 1

CORPORAL DOWNEY: "SUICIDE."

BLACK JOHN: "MAYBE.". 42

FOR SOME LITTLE SACKS OF GOLD 69

FORECLOSURE ON HALFADAY 161

ALL OR NOTHING 206

BLACK JOHN SELLS A CLAIM

BLACK JOHN SMITH closed the door behind him, stamped the snow from his feet and crossed to the bar as Old Cush, the proprietor of Cushing's Fort, the combined trading post and saloon that served the little community of outlawed men that had sprung up on Halfaday Creek, close against the Yukon-Alaska border, laid aside the newspaper he had been reading, and set a bottle, two glasses, and the inevitable leather dice box onto the bar.

Cushing won the drinks in straight horses, and when the glasses were filled, he glanced toward the folded newspaper. "I see a piece here in the *Nugget* where it claims they're aimin' to pull off a big celebration in Dawson around Chris'mas. They're a-goin' to set up a fifty-foot Chris'mas tree, all lit up, right on Front Street, an' give away candy an' presents to all the kids in town. The hotel's donated the dinin' room fer a dance, an' the wimmin's goin' to decorate the walls, an' they's goin' to be another dance over the A.C. Store. They's goin' to be big doin's in the church. An' on top of that Cuter Malone's got a big square advertisement in the paper about a big dance there in the Klondike Palace Chris'mas night, where everyone holdin' a ticket, him an' his lady will be entitled to three free drinks at the bar. He claims he's goin' to give away better'n five hundred dollars in prizes, fer the best man dancer, and the best lady dancer, an' the best-lookin' man, an' the prettiest gal, an' the best-dressed man an' lady—an' it says how them there Klond-ike Palace dance hall girls won't be wearin' no more clothes on 'em than what the law claims they gotta."

The big man nodded. "Yeah, I hear they were figurin' on pullin' off a big celebration at Chris'mas. Why don't you lock up an' we'll go down an take in the fun?"

Cush shook his head. "Nope. I don't figger it would be usin' the boys here on Halfaday right. Everyone likes to have a good time around Chris'mas. The Yukon wanted's wouldn't dast to show up in Dawson, an' if I was to lock up they wouldn't have nowheres to go. Cripes, we kin have a good time right here! They'll be a stud game goin' on, an' plenty to eat an' drink. What more would a man want?"

"Without any women on the crick, we couldn't pull off a dance."

"Huh. A hell of a lot you care about dancin'! An' you ain't goin' to draw no prize fer the best-dressed man, nor the best-lookin' man, neither. What I claim, a man would be a damn fool to hit a two-hundred mile winter trail fer to git three free drinks an' an eye-full of them half-nakid dance hall floozies!"

"Nevertheless Cush, the spirit moveth me to forsake this bucolic environment at Yuletide an' seek surcease from the humdrum in the giddy whirl of metropolitan festivities."

Cush emitted a snort of disgust. "Huh. Does that mean yer aimin' to go to Dawson fer Chris'mas?"

"That was the thought I endeavored to put across."

"You could of put it acrost better by sayin' so. We've got licker an' we've got stud right her on Halfaday fer to celebrate Chris'mas. The only thing we ain't got that Dawson has is wimmin—so it must be wimmin you want. So go ahead. Time you've got married four times, like I have, mebbe you'll learn not to fool around with no wimmin. Like I've told you before, sometimes some woman's goin' to git her hooks into you, an' then you'll wisht to God the sperit had movethed you to stay right here on Halfaday!"

"I've got just about time to make it if I pull out now. So, while

I get my outfit ready you weigh me out a couple of hundred ounces of dust; an' I'll be on my way."

IN THE late afternoon of the day before Christmas Black John halted his dogs before the door of the Mounted Police detachment in Dawson and stepped into the little office to be greeted by Corporal Downey. "Hello, John! Down for the big show, eh? Pull up a chair an' fill your pipe. How's everything on Halfaday?"

Drawing up a chair, the big man seated himself, lighted his pipe, tilted back against the wall, and elevated his heels to the officer's flat-top desk. "Everythin's okay on the crick," he said. "Thought I'd slip down an' see what's goin' on. Accordin' to the *Nugget,* you folks are pullin' off quite a celebration."

"That's right. An' it looks from here like we're goin' to have plenty to do, what with the town full of drunken chechakos."

"Yeah—an' that reminds me—what kind of a crime would you advise me to pull off? Not nothin' serious. How about tossin' a rock through a window, or maybe droppin' a chechako through a hole in the ice?"

"What the hell are you drivin' at?"

"I've got to get someplace to sleep—both hotels are full to the roof, an' folks sleepin' in the halls an' the office. I figure if I could pull off some pifflin' crime—one that would entitle me to be locked in a cell—it would sort of solve my lodgin' problem Of course, I'd want it fixed so I could sleep daytimes, an' bail myself out evenin's so's not to miss the fun."

Downey grinned. "Where's your outfit?"

"Out in front."

"Turn your dogs into the corral an' fetch in your pack. We've gut a bunk you can use. I'd hate to have to arrest you—it might give you a bad reputation."

Black John returned the grin.

"Much obliged. A man's got to watch his reputation," he replied, and stepped out to return a few minutes later to resume his seat.

"Any newcomers showed up to Halfaday in the last six weeks?" Downey asked.

"Nope. Why? Has someone broke a law?"

"Yeah. Two laws. Murder an' robbery. Along about the first of November the Consolidated Dredge Company sent fifty thousand dollars in paper money by a messenger to Mortimer P. Featherstone who was actin' as their agent in the purchase of a couple of claims up on the Bonanza. The messenger started with the money as soon as the bank opened in the mornin' an' that evenin' Burr MacShane an' Moosehide Charlie found him layin' in a gully off to one side of the trail. They hustled him to the hospital an' he died the next mornin'. He'd be'n whammed

over the head with somethin' heavy—a rifle barrel, or a piece of pipe, or maybe a crowbar. Before he died he come to long enough to mention the name of Ben Hambly. The fifty thousan', of course, was gone."

"Who's Ben Hambly?"

"He's a chechako that come this spring with his boy, a kid about eighteen, nineteen. They filed a location on a feeder that runs into Ophir an', accordin' to the kid, they was doin' all right.

"Moosehide showed me where they found the messenger, an' I hunted around there but didn't find anything, so I went to Ophir. The kid was there on the location an' he told me his dad had gone to Dawson for some supplies a couple of days before, an' hadn't showed up yet. I told him about the robbery, an' that the messenger had mentioned his dad's name. He took it mighty hard. I hunted around the place. The kid showed me their cache, but the money wasn't there. Later, I learned that Hambly had be'n seen in Dawson the night before the robbery. He hasn't be'n seen since. I hoped he'd hit for Halfaday. Was figurin' on swingin' up that way as soon as the Chris'mas rush was over."

"You can save yourself the trip, Downey," Black John said. "I'll give you my word this Hambly ain't on Halfaday—or he

wasn't when I left there—an' he'd shore had plenty of time to get there since the robbery. How about this agent—Mortimer P. Tailfeathers—or whatever his name is? Looks like he'd be the only one outside of the Consolidated office, an' the bank, that would know about that deal, him an' the ones that was sellin' the claims. An' why did the Consolidated send cash instead of a draft?"

"Mortimer P. Featherstone hit Dawson in July. He seems to have plenty of ready money. He's be'n speculatin'—buyin' an' sellin' claims, right an' left. I checked on him, an' as far as I can see, he's in the clear. I asked him why the bank sent that fifty thousan' in cash, an' he told me that's the way the men he bought the claims from wanted it. He said they told him that a Siwash had put 'em wise to a crick that runs into a river that runs into the Mackenzie, way over acrost the divide. An' they aimed to hit out an' locate there. That's why they sold out on Bonanza.

"I hunted them fellows up, an' they told me the same thing— they wanted the money in small bills that they could spend over in the Mackenzie country. They said they saved this Siwash from drownin' an' that's why he put 'em wise to this crick, where accordin' to him gold lays butter-yellow amongst the rocks of a shallow rapids. They came down here about a week after the robbery, an' got their cash an' hit out fur the Mackenzie country."

"H-u-m. That's a hell of a trip to make on the word of a Siwash. What's young Hambly be'n doin' since his dad disappeared?"

"He's be'n stickin' right there on the location. Seems like a nice kid. Works like hell, an' minds his own business. It's too damn bad the way folks treat him on account if his dad—like he was a crook, or an outcast of some kind. No one will have anything to do with him. An' that ain't good. I feel sorry for him. That kind of treatment will get any man's goat in time. I'm wonderin' how long he can take it. The sourdoughs—Bettles, Swiftwater Bill, an' Burr MacShane, an' Camillo Bill—are all right. The kid only comes to Dawson when he has to, for supplies, an' the sourdoughs go out of their way to show him they've got no hard feelin's. Their intentions are good. But damn it—they overdo it! The kid's no fool. He can see they're doin' it out of pity. An' that makes it hard to take. It's about as bad as shunnin' him."

Black John nodded. "Yeah, you're prob'ly right. I get shunned myself, by the sanctimonious—but it don't irk me none. Don't know's I've ever be'n pitied, so I ain't really competent to form an opinion. Well—guess I'll loaf over to the Tivoli, an' see if I can't persuade the sourdoughs to donate me a Chris'mas present over the stud table. Where's this bunk, you're lettin' me use? I'll throw my pack on it to sort of preempt it—like stakin' out a claim."

II

AT THE DOORWAY of the Tivoli saloon he met Bettles and Camillo Bill who were just about to enter. Camillo grinned broadly. "Speak of the devil, an' up he pops! We was jest wonderin' if you'd be down fer Chris'mas. Yer goin' to have a hell of a time findin' a room, though. Every damn bed in town is taken."

The big man grinned. "Downey's goin' to lock me up, daytimes. He's promised to let me out nights, though—so I can sort of keep an eye on you birds."

"What are we waitin' for?" Bettles asked. "Come on in. I'm buying a drink." As he turned to enter the doorway, a young man hurrying past caught his eye. "Come on, kid, an' join us. We're jest about to wet our whistle."

The lad hesitated a moment, then shook his head. "No thanks. I—I'm heading for home," he said, and hurried on.

"It's a damn shame," Camillo Bill growled, "the way folks treats that kid. Cripes—think of it. Chris'mas time, an' him hittin' out to Ophir to spend Chris'mas alone in his cabin!"

"Shore it is," Bettles agreed. "It's got so he thinks everyone's agin him." He turned to Black John. "That's Ben Hambly's kid. His dad knocked off a bank messenger that was hittin' for

Bonanza with fifty thousan' in bills, a month or so ago, an got away with it. An' ever sence then, folks treats the kid like it was him done it."

At the bar they joined Burr MacShane, Moosehide Charlie, and Swiftwater Bill. Bettles glanced at the three and jerked his head in the direction of Black John. "Look what we found wanderin' around altogether loose."

"He's only goin' to be loose nights, though," Camillo added. "Downey's promised to keep him locked up daytimes. We was jest talkin' about young Hambly. He passed jest as we was comin' in, an' Bettles asked him to jine us. He looked like he wanted to, all right. But he said he was hittin' fer home, an' hustled on. That's a hell of a way for a kid to spend Chris'mas—alone in a damn cabin up a feeder."

A tall man with a high forehead and slate blue eyes, approached along the bar. "Ah, gentlemen—will you join me in a bit of Christmas cheer?"

"Why, shore." Bettles accepted for the group, and glanced at Black John. "Featherstone, this is a friend of ours. John, meet Mortimer P. Featherstone."

The man glanced into the big man's face. "Ah—pleased to meet you, I'm sure. I—er—I'm afraid I did not catch the name."

"Don't be afraid," the big man replied. "It ain't as hard to catch as yours—Smith is the name, John Smith."

The man regarded him with a trace of annoyance. "You are a prospector, I presume, in town for the holidays?"

"O, shore. I don't get to town often. I've got a little claim up the White a ways."

"Doing well?"

"Only fairly well. It's hard work. I can't kick, though. I manage to take out a little better'n wages." Bettles made a strangling sound in his throat, as the big man continued. "But things might be lookin' up pretty quick. I struck another location on a crick that might pay out big."

"Ah! In case you find this property worthwhile, I may be interested. My business is the buying and selling of claims."

"If this here's as good a proposition as what I figger it is, it would cost you quite a bit, Mort."

The man flushed. "Featherstone, to you—Mr. Featherstone, please."

"Okay, okay, Mr. Featherstone. I didn't mean no harm. Back there in Ioway, where I come from, we figger it's kinda friendly like to call one another by our front name. That's one reason I hope this here proposition turns out good—so I can sell it, an' go back an' buy me a farm. Old Gabe Williams might sell me his farm. It's right acrost the road from pa's place. I hope this proposition turns out good so I can sell it to you. I've shore got a longin' to get back amongst them horses, an' chickens, an' pigs, an' cows. I don't s'pose you ever done no farmin' Mr. Featherweight?"

"Featherstone! Featherstone! No, I never did any farming."

"Ort to try it, sometime. Do you good. Ain't nothin' makes a man feel so good as gittin' up around four o'clock in the mornin', milk thirty, forty cows, slop a couple of hundred hogs, then go in an' eat breakfast an' jump into the day's work."

WITH A snort of disgust Featherstone turned to the others. "I saw young Hambly on the street a short time ago. There's a young man that'll stand watching."

"Why?" Burr MacShane asked.

"Well—because. Look what his father did. Like father, like son. And there's an old Hebrew saying: 'We may not expect a good whelp from a bad dog'."

"Admittin' that his dad did knock off that messenger an' got away with the cash the kid ain't to blame for it," MacShane retorted.

"Yer damn right he ain't!" Swiftwater Bill agreed. "It's tough enough on a kid if his old man did pull off that job, without folks rubbin' it in on him."

"He's good hard-workin' kid," Moosehide Charlie added. "I stop in to his place now an' then, an' he's allus workin'."

"He might have a damn good proposition there, too," Bettles opined. "A lot of them feeders on Ophir panned out big."

"Nevertheless," Featherstone argued, "you can't expect a well-ordered community to accept the son of a murderer and robber as an equal."

"It couldn't be possible, could it?" MacShane asked, "that you figure that if folks keep on treatin' him like a crook he'll break down an' hit for someplace he ain't known—an' you could buy his location cheap?"

Featherstone grinned, and winked at Bettles. "Well—business is business, you know. I'm always on the lookout for a good buy. If it should happen that way, I'd be conferring a favor on the community by ridding it of a potential criminal. You can't make a silk purse out of a sow's ear, you ought to know."

"Speakin' of sows," Black John cut in, "my pa had an ol' black and white sow one time, an' she—"

Featherstone interrupted with a scowl. "Nobody gives a damn about your father's sow! Why a yokel like you ever left the farm is more than I know!"

"Well it's like this, Mr. Featherbed, our ol' white mare—"

"Hurrumph!" with a snort of disgust, Mortimer P. Featherstone turned on his heel, and strode from the room.

When the door banged behind him the sourdoughs roared with laughter. Bettles thumped the big man a resounding whack on the back. "Go to it, John! You shore got his goat!"

MacShane nodded emphatically. "That was a swell build-up, John. Any coot that would deliberately heap misery onto a kid that's already got more than his share of it shore might to get what's comin' to him. We're with you. If it's of any interest to you, I happen to know that Featherstone's liquid assets run right around a hundred thousand. He considers himself quite a financier."

"W-e-e-l-l, the amount is worth contemplatin'," the big man admitted. "An' Mort ain't no one I could ever learn to like. But don't you boys go layin' no bets. Them big financiers is smart folks—prob'ly a damn sight too smart fer an Ioway farm boy to get the best of."

Swiftwater Bill chuckled. "There's be'n a hell of a lot of these smart guys that's run up against you John. But I never heard of any of 'em gettin' off with a profit."

"Profit!" Moosehide exclaimed. "They was lucky to get off with their pants!"

The shrewd blue eyes above the black beard widened. "But you boys got to remember that every one of them scoundrels was dishonest. An' you also know that, bein' as my pa was a preacher I can't abide dishonesty in any way, shape nor form."

Camillo Bill interrupted with a chuckle. "I thought you jest got through tellin' Featherstone that yer pa was a farmer."

"That was on week days," Black John replied. "On Sundays he preached. But, as I was goin' on to say—of course, if Mort should turn out to be dishonest, that might be somethin' else again. How about startin' a game of stud."

III

EARLY ONE AFTERNOON late in January, the door opened and a young man stepped into the saloon on Halfaday, interrupting a cribbage game between Cush and Black John. The newcomer paused beside the bar.

"Is this Cushing's Fort, on Halfaday Crick?" he asked.

"This is the place," Cush replied, and stepping to the back bar, picked up a glass which he placed beside the two glasses and the bottle on the table. "Fill up," he invited. "The house is buyin' one."

"Where's your outfit?" Black John asked.

"Just outside the door."

"Better unharness your dogs an' chain 'em. The shelters are around back."

Ten minutes later the lad returned, drew off his heavy parka, beat the snow from it and threw it over a chair near the stove. Then he seated himself at the table, and the three filled their glasses.

"Here's how!" Cush said, and as the three glasses were raised, Black John noted, out of the tail of his eye, that the young man downed his drink with a do-or-die air and strangled slightly as he returned the glass to the table.

A moment later he found his voice. "Hambly's my name. Bill Hambly. I suppose you are Black John Smith?"

"That's right. An' this is Lyme Cushing, the proprietor of this place."

"I remember of seeing you in Dawson. It was the day before Christmas. You were standing in front of the Tivoli with Bettles and Camillo Bill."

The big man nodded. "That's right. An' you were walkin' past, an' Bettles invited you in for a drink, an' you refused, claimin' you were headin' for home."

The lad nodded. "Then you know who I am—that is you know about my father—that he is accused of killing that messenger on the Bonanza trail and robbing him of fifty thousand dollars?"

"Yes, son. That's the talk in Dawson. I heard it."

"At first I refused to believe that my father was guilty. I'm not so sure, now. More than two months have passed and he hasn't showed up. I've thought it all out a thousand times. As far as I can see, there are three possible answers. Of course, only one of them could be right. Dad may have come along just as the crime was committed, and the robber may have knocked him off and succeeded in hiding his body. Or Dad could have committed the robbery, then someone else killed him and made off with the money. Or he may have pulled off the robbery and got away with it. I don't want to believe he was guilty. I was so sure that he'd really reformed."

"Reformed?"

"Yes. He and two other men robbed a train in Minnesota and Dad did a ten-year stretch in the Stillwater Penitentiary. My mother died while he was in prison. The disgrace killed her. When he got out Dad said he'd learned his lesson, and promised me he'd go straight.

"We heard about the gold strike and came up here, to get away from everyone who knew us. We located on a little crick that runs into Ophir and we were doing all right there. We panned out anywhere from three to seven ounces a day all summer, but we couldn't go down very deep on account of seepage. When we'd get a shaft down to where we couldn't keep the water bailed out, we'd start another one. The men on Ophir told us about winter mining—waiting till the ground froze, then building a fire in the shaft, thawing out the top gravel and throwing it onto a dump, and building another fire, and so on down to bedrock. Then in the spring they sluice out the dumps.

"In October Dad and I went into the hills where a fire had swept through, and cut a lot of fire-killed spruce and dragged it down to be used this winter. Then early in November he went into Dawson for supplies. I haven't seen him since.

"A few days after he left Corporal Downey came to the claim and said that a messenger had been murdered on the Bonanza trail, and that before he died, he had mentioned Dad's name. Downey looked all around and asked me a lot of questions. He asked me whether Dad had ever been in any trouble with the law, and I told him about his doing time in Minnesota for that train robbery. He was mighty fine about it. He didn't make it any harder for me than necessary. If everybody was like Corporal Downey I'd have stayed on the claim. But there on Ophir, and in Dawson, and everywhere I'd go, people would look at me and I could see them talking to one another. I knew what they were saying—there's that Hambly kid—his Dad knocked off that messenger and got away with fifty thousand dollars—but they wouldn't speak to me—just look at me as if I were a criminal, or a curiosity of some kind.

"The sourdoughs were different. They went out of their way to be nice to me—but that was almost as hard to take as the other. I didn't want their pity. I stuck it out as long as I could—there on the claim. But all alone that way—thinking and wondering—wondering and thinking. It got to where I just couldn't take it any longer. I don't know—maybe I'm yellow. Maybe if I had more guts I could have stuck it out. But I was afraid to. Afraid I'd go nuts and maybe kill somebody. So I decided to quit.

"I've always wanted to be a doctor. I finished high school, last year, and I figured that if we made good up here, I could go back and go to college. I've got some dust—but not enough. Several times since Dad—disappeared, a man named Featherstone in Dawson has offered to buy our location. But he only offered two thousand for it. Two thousand isn't enough, even with what dust I've got, to see me through college, and I know that location is worth a lot more than that, so t turned him down."

THE LAD paused, and Black John nodded. "You done right to turn him down, son. If a location is worth anything at all it's worth more'n two thousan'. But—that don't put you up here on Halfaday."

"What?"

"I mean, why did you come here? Were you figurin' on sellin' your location to me, or to Cush?"

The boy shook his head. "No. I came up here because I heard in Dawson that you're all outlaws up here."

"Figured that if your pa did pull that robbery, he might have hit for here?"

"No—it's not that. I—I couldn't stay there on the claim and go crazy. I can't do the thing I've always wanted to do—go to college. Everyone treats me as if I were an outlaw—so I decided

I'd be one! I heard that you are the captain of the outlaws here on Halfaday Crick—so I came up here to see if you would take me into your gang."

The big man stroked his heavy black heard. "H-u-u-m. So you want to be an outlaw, eh?"

"It isn't a question whether I want to be an outlaw or not. It seems to be about the only thing I can do."

"The outlaw business is mighty tough sleddin', son—especially here on Halfaday."

"I'm not afraid of tough sledding. I'll promise to do my best."

Black John shook his head. "Your best might not be quite good enough."

"Then you mean, you wouldn't have a place for me?"

"Yeah. Yeah, we'd have a place for you, son—if you're plumb set on being an outlaw. Pull on your cap an' I'll show you. You won't need your parka. It won't take but a minute." Leading the way to the rear of the building, Black John paused and pointed. "See them little white oblong mounds—with the wooden slabs at the heads of 'em?"

"Why—yes. They're graves, aren't they?"

"Yup. That's the place we've got for outlaws—when they show up on Halfaday."

"But—I—don't understand."

"Perusal of the check letters on them slabs will help out your onderstandin'. M is for murdered. H is for hung. You'll note that there's quite a few more H's than M's. That's because a good many other forms of skullduggery than murder are hangable on Halfaday. Them few Ds can be ignored. They're for the pitiful minority that died natural, here on the crick. It all adds up to this—on Halfaday an outlaw either mends his ways, or he earns himself a slab. So you see, son, there's no gang of outlaws on Halfaday—an' I ain't captain of nothin' but my soul."

"Well," the boy said, "so—that's that. I guess I might as well harness my dogs and hit back to Dawson."

"You can't start back till mornin'. We'll pack yer outfit over to my cabin. I've got an extry bunk there. I'm gettin' kind of hungry. S'pose you an' me slip over there an' see what we can do about a couple of big thick moose steaks."

THE MEAL over, Black John leaned back in his chair and lighted his pipe. "You spoke of hittin' back to Dawson, son. What do you aim to do when you get there?"

"Why—nothing. That is—I don't know. Go back to Ophir, I guess, and take a chance on wintering through without losing my mind."

"Well, that would be one way. But what we want to get at—is it the best way?"

"What do you mean? What else can I do?"

"Why not stay right here? I don't know much about psychology. But I do know that in winter the days are short, an' the nights are long. An' them long nights, with nothin' to do but think, ain't goin' to do you no good—after what you've be'n through. Even men without brains enough to do much thinkin' have gone crazy livin' alone through them long winter nights. Folks ain't goin' to treat you any different than they have be'n. An' a thing like that is cumulative, you might say. It keeps buildin' up in a man's brain till finally there's an explosion. When that explosion comes—you'll be through."

"But—what could I do here?"

"You can do what looks to me to be damned important for you to do right now. You can live a normal life until spring. After that we can prob'ly figure out where to go from there. You can mix with the boys at Cush's. None of them will give you the brush-off, an' whisper behind your back. They'll take you at your face value. I don't say they're all good men. A lot of 'em are, an' them that ain't are good by proxy—or else. You'll hear a lot of cussin', an see a lot of stud playin' an' drinkin' in Cush's. But you don't need to take part in it if you don't want to. An speakin' of drinkin'—I noticed when you downed that drink Cush bought, you did it because you thought it was the proper thing to do—not because you wanted it. I ain't no temperance lecturer, but I wouldn't see the sense in a lad's deliberately cultivatin' the liquor habit. Of course, both Cush an' I do considerable drinkin'—but it don't seem to bother us none, our guts bein' enameled, or annealed, or somethin'. Anyway—that's up to you. Aside from that, we can hunt moose, cut firewood, an' manage to keep busy durin' the day. In the evenin' you can read. I've got a few books here, an' chances are I'll be slippin' down to Dawson in a month or so, an' I'll fetch up some more. You say you want to study medicine. That's a damn good profession. When I'm down to Dawson, I'll sort of look around an' see if I can't find someone that would pay you a decent price for your location there on Ophir. You ort to get enough out of it to see you through college, an' get you set up in practice somewheres. I might even be able to persuade Mort Featherstone to pay you a decent price. But we can talk about that, later."

"You mean—you'd go to all that trouble for me—keep me here with you all winter—and—and help me sell the claim?"

"Why—hell, son—why not? There's be'n times when I've needed encouragement myself."

IV

LATE ONE AFTERNOON toward the middle of February an Indian stepped into the saloon and approached Black John who stood at the bar shaking dice with Cush for the drinks. "Iss dead mans in cabin got de door lock."

The big man filled his glass from the bottle and eyed the Indian sharply. "Where is this cabin? An' if the door's locked, how do you know there's a dead man inside?"

"Me, I'm look in de window. De dead man she sit by de table."

"Sittin' by the table! How do you know he's dead if he's sittin' by the table?"

"Got to be. Got no fire. Got no stove. Got no grub on de table. Got no pack. Got no grub on de shelf. Got no blanket on de bunk. Got nuttin'. Me, I'm look in de window good."

"Where is this cabin?"

"Cabin on leetle bit crick ron in Ladue Crick. Wan tam—long tam 'go, man nem Joe Nakish go pelton—w'at you call crazy, an' he keel he's 'oman wi't hax. An' Sebastian say tak heem 'way an' build good stout leetle cabin an' lock heem in dere, so he no keel no more peoples. So we go down Ladue Crick an' fin' de leetle crick an' we build de good stout cabin, an' mak' iron bars on de window, and we push Nakish in dere an' lock de door, an' we tak' heem grub an' shov t'rough de window, an' Nakish she live 'bout wan year, an' den she die, an' we tak' him out an' dig de hole an' bury heem. An', no wan go to de cabin no more. Iss *kultus tamahnawus* in dere—w'at you call de bad luck."

"You live in Sebastian's village?"

"Yes—me Pete Wolf Nose."

"When did you find this dead man? An' how come you was prowlin' around this cabin, if it's bad luck?"

"Me, I'm go moose hont, an' I'm com' down de leetle crick, an' I'm go fas' pas' de cabin, an' I'm see de lock on de door—"

"Lock on the door!" Black John exclaimed. "You mean the door is locked on the outside?"

"Yes. Got de lock on de door. Me, I'm t'ink dat dam' fonny—got de lock on de door, 'cause I'm trap down dere 'bout mont' 'go, an w'en I'm pass de cabin den, no lock iss on de door. So I'm look in de window an' see dead mans sit by table."

"This dead man—is he a white man, or a Siwash?"

"Is w'ite mans. An' w'en I'm tell Sebastian 'bout dat he say you go Halfaday Crick an' tell Black John."

THE BIG man glanced across the bar at Cush. "There's somethin' queer over there—damn queer. It's a cinch no white man got up there alone in the middle of winter with no grub, no blankets, no pack, an' holed up in a cabin with no stove. An' it's shore as hell he never locked himself in from the outside. You're the coroner, Cush. Looks like you an' me are goin' to take a trip. This set-up needs investigatin'."

Cush scowled at the Indian. "Mebbe the damn cuss is lyin'," he hazarded, hopefully. "Cripes, it's a hell of a trip over there with the strong cold on, an' mebbe no corpse when we got there. Even if he is there, what with the weather like it is, chances is he'd keep till spring."

"If it's like the Siwash says, we're up against a murder—an' a damn dirty one, too. Unnecessary delay might give the murderer a chance to get clear out of the country. An' damned if I'll ever give a murderer a break."

"Even if it is a murder," Cush persisted, "what the hell we got to horn in on it fer—way over on Ladue Crick?"

"Ladue Crick is a tributary to the White River, same as Halfaday, and you know damn well I've repeatedly held that our jurisdiction includes—"

"Oh, shore!" Cush interrupted, "you an' yer jewishdiction! By God, if someone done somethin' to someone clean over to Chiny, an' you wanted to hang him fer it, you'd claim it was subterainian or contigulus territory that made it in our jewishdiction! But I'm tellin' you it ain't goin' to be no fun sloggin' clean over there, cold as it is."

Black John grinned. "Yeah, it does look like Downey had sort of overlooked the humorous angle when he had you app'inted coroner. But after all, Cush—a coroner's business ain't supposesd to be uproariously hilarious."

"I don't see why the hell the Siwash couldn't of found him on some closter crick," Cush grumbled.

"Dead men are like gold—they're where you find 'em."

"This un ain't goin' to be much like gold. If he ain't got no pack, chances is we ain't goin' to find enough dust on him to pay us fer our trouble."

"Nevertheless, the fact remains that you are a duly constituted public official, an' I deeply deplore the mercenary attitude with which you—"

"I don't give a damn what you explore, nor how deep! So if you got any more big words, you kin keep 'em swallered. If we gotta go, we gotta go. The Siwash kin bed down here on the floor tonight. I'll git One Armed John to run the place till I git back. We'll pull out in the mornin'. An' if we find out when we git there that the Siwash lied, he's goin' to be huntin' somethin' soft to set on fer about a month after I git through workin' on him with the toe of my boot."

EARLY THE following morning the three hit the trail, and late in the evening of the second day reached the Indian village, where Black John and Cush put up for the night with old Sebastian, the chief. The old Indian confirmed the story told by Pete Wolf Nose of the cabin with barred windows that had been built years before for the incarceration of the murderous lunatic, Nakish. He said that Pete Wolf Nose was a reliable man, and that when he returned to the village from his moose hunt and had reported seeing the body of a white man in the locked cabin, he had told Pete to hit for Halfaday and report the matter to Black John.

"Why didn't you send him to the police?" Cush asked.

The old Indian shrugged. "Poliss too mooch far 'way. Poliss got to hont roun' too mooch for fin' w'at you call de hevidence. If a man iss lock in cabin, den som'wan keel heem—w'at you call de murder. By Gos', Black John he no fool roun' 'bout de hevidence. He ketch de man an' hang heem dam' queek."

The big man grinned. "Thanks for the vote of confidence, Sebastian. But you've got to catch a murderer before you can hang him. An' in this case, catchin' him might turn out to be quite some chore. Has anyone seen any white men along the crick in the past month or so?"

The Indian shook his head. "No. W'en Pete Wolf Nose tell me 'bout fin' de dead mans, I'm ask all de peoples if dey see anyone 'long de crick. No wan see nuttin'."

Shortly after daylight the following morning Black John and Cush, accompanied by Pete Wolf Nose and Sebastian, arrived at the cabin. As the Indian had reported, the door was secured on the outside by a padlock. Through the heavily barred window the body of a man could be seen seated at a table, his face buried in his folded arms. An exposed hand left no doubt that the body was that of a white man. After some difficulty Black John succeeded in prying the heavy staple loose and, pushing the door open, the four stepped into the room which was absolutely bare of any furnishings except a bare pole bunk, the rude chair upon which the dead man was seated, the table upon which he leaned, and an empty whiskey bottle on the floor beside him. As Pete Wolf Nose had said, there was no food, no blanket and no pack.

Stepping to the dead man's side, Black John stared down at the table top. The covering of cheap oilcloth that had been tacked to the table had been torn loose and reversed, and upon its surface pencil writing showed indistinctly in the dim light. Also the big man noted that the stub of a lead pencil was firmly grasped in the fingers frozen to the hardness of iron. He turned to Cush. "As coroner you will pronounce this man dead?"

"Why shore he's dead! Any damn fool would know that."

"An' the manner of his death?"

"I don't know nothin' about his manners."

"What in your opinion caused his death?"

"Looks like he froze to death. There ain't no grub in here, but he don't look skinny enough to starved. He prob'ly drunk that bottle of licker, an' went to sleep an' froze stiff."

"Okay. Go ahead an' swear us three in as a coroner's jury. I'm foreman, an' I'll report that the deceased came to his death at the hands of a party or parties onknown. Jury dismissed. Give me a hand, an' we'll move him back from the table. Leave him in the chair. We can prop him against the wall so he can't slip off. Now we'll take this oilcloth where the light's better, an' read what he's got to say about it."

Carrying the oilcloth outside, Black John spread it on the snow and knelt down beside it. The pencil writing was easily legible. He read aloud:

"My name's Ben Hambly. Once a crook, always a crook, I guess. Anyway, that's the way it's worked out for me. I done a 10-year stretch in Stillwater for train robbery. When I got out I aimed to go straight. Me an' my boy Billy come to the Klondike and located on Ophir. We was doin' all right. Then in Dawson I run onto Slim McCune. He was going by the name of Mortimer P. Featherstone, and claimed he was speculating in locations. He's a hard guy—works all the rackets, from the con game to robbery, arson and murder. He put a proposition up to me—acting as agent for a dredge outfit, he gets fifty thousan' in bills sent to him on Bonanza by a messenger, an' I knock off the messenger an' we split the fifty thousand. I says I don't want nothing to do with it. I'm goin' straight. He jest laughs. He know'd of a job me and another guy pulled, before I done time. A man was killed. He says how murder never outlaws—an' I'll rob this messenger, or he'll slip word down to Minneapolis. I could be identified, and murder don't outlaw. He had me. I lays for the messenger and raps him on the head with my rifle barrel, and Slim says we better hit out in the hills till the stink dies down. We hit out, go up the Yukon, and up the White River, and up a smaller river till we come to this cabin which Slim had found last summer on a prospecting trip. He says we'll hole up for a while. He pulls out a bottle of whiskey and we have some drinks. I go to sleep. When I wake up I'm alone in the cabin. Slim's gone, so is the grub and the blankets and the little Yukon stove. There's only the bottle left. It's half full. I'm locked in. I find a pencil. I rip the cover off the table and start to write. It's so cold I know I ain't got long before I freeze. My fingers are stiff, I keeping taking a pull at the bottle. It keeps me going. If it'll last till I finish this maybe if someone finds it Slim will get what's...."

The script broke off abruptly in the middle of the sentence. Cush was the first to break the silence. "Ben Hambly—why that's the kid's dad! Then he did pull that murder an' robbery!"

Black John nodded. "Y-e-e-a-h," he said, drawing the word out slowly. "He pulled it, all right. But—the kid must never know."

"But hell, John—how kin he help but know? If you take that writin' to Downey, he'll arrest this here Mortimer P. What's-his-name, an' it'll come out at the trial."

"That's right, Cush. Downey is a very estimable person, an' a damn good policeman. If Mort's case went to court, the kid would know—he'd know that his dad not only pulled this job—but that he'd pulled another murder, a long time back. That kid's be'n through enough hell already. Somehow, this don't look like a case for the police. It's got complications the police wouldn't onderstand."

"You mean yer figgerin' on gittin' this here Mortimer up to Halfaday an' hangin' him? Cripes—if you do that the kid would find out jest the same. We'd have to call a miner's meetin', an' we'd have to give the guy a chanct to try an' lie out of it—an' he'd be shore to spill his guts."

"I wasn't figurin' on a miner's meetin'," the big man replied. "Sebastian'll fix you up with a dog outfit, an' you hit hack to Halfaday. If the kid asks why I didn't come back, tell him I hit on to Dawson to fetch up them books I promised him I'd get. I know a shortcut by way of Miller's Crick an' the Sixtymile that'll get me there in a week."

"You hittin' fer Dawson? What are you goin' to do when you git there?"

"Yeah, I'm hittin' for Dawson. But first I'm goin' to stake out my claim."

"Claim!"

"That's right. It looks to me like this might be a good location. It ain't often a man gets the chance to file on a new location with a cabin already built. I'll set my stakes right now." He turned to Sebastian. "Has this creek got a name?" he asked.

The Indian shook his head. "No, no nem."

"Okay we'll call it Sucker Crick then. This will be a discovery claim an' I'm entitled to stake a thousan' feet."

Cush eyed the big man sourly. "You crazy, er what! You know damn well you'll never take an ounce of dust out of this location."

"Probably not," Black John replied. "I'm concerned only with its sale value. I've got a customer in mind. That's why I'm hittin' for Dawson. But first we'll take this tablecloth back an' fix it just like it was when Featherstone left. An' we'll move Hambly back like he was when we found him. Then we'll drive the staple back in place." He turned to the Indian. "An' you see to it that no one bothers this cabin while I'm gone."

Sebastian nodded. "No wan com' here. All mens 'fraid of *kultus tamahnawus.*"

V

IN THE TIVOLI SALOON in Dawson Black John joined Swiftwater Bill, Burr MacShane, and Bettles at the bar. He ordered a drink and as the glasses were being filled, Mortimer P. Featherstone stepped in with a stranger and, nodding to the sourdoughs, took his place a few feet down the bar.

Bettles raised his glass. "Well, here's lookin' at you, John. I s'pose you've come back to get revenge for the trimmin' we gave you at stud around Chris'mas time."

"Speakin' of a trimmin'," Burr MacShane said in an undertone with a glance toward the man who had entered with Featherstone, "I'll bet there's a sucker that's in for a trimmin' of some kind."

"Seems like you boys allus beats me playin' stud," Black John said, in a loud tone of voice. "Trouble is I can't never remember that a flush beats a straight, an' I keep fergettin' that two pairs don't beat three of a kind. But I didn't lose no more'n about two thousan' dollars, an' I don't care about that, now. That there claim of mine on Sucker Crick is comin' along even better'n what I figgered. I just come down to record it. Yes sir, I'm gittin' quite a big dump throw'd up. An' every day I pan a few pans to see how she's comin', an' seems like the deeper down I git the more gold is in the pan."

Bettles grinned and winked at MacShane. "I believe you're right, Burr," he said in an undertone. "About a sucker bein' in for a trimmin'. But I'll bet you've picked the wrong sucker."

"Showin' up pretty good, eh John?" Swiftwater Bill asked.

"You bet it is!"

"Every pan showin' colors, I s'pose," MacShane said.

"I don't know about no colors. But there's gold in every pan. Sometimes an ounce, sometimes more, an' sometimes only about half an' ounce. But sometimes they's quite a big chunk. An' cripes, is them chunks heavy fer the size of 'em!"

"You mean," cried Bettles, "you're takin' out better'n an ounce to the pan! Man—that sounds like them early days on Bonanza!"

The sourdoughs noticed that Featherstone had edged a little closer and that he seemed to be paying no attention whatever to what his companion was saying, but stood with his attention apparently fixed upon the row of bottles on the back bar.

"I don't know nothin' about Bonanza," Black John replied to Bettles, "but I be'n doin' some figgerin' on a piece of paper. A man had ort to pan out twenty-five pans a day, an' if gold is sixteen dollars a ounce, an' it run right around a ounce a pan, then he could make four hundred dollars a day. That's damn good money— if a man would like gold diggin'. But I don't like it. I don't like a country where it's so damn cold, an' where the days is so short in winter, an' where the mosquitoes is so thick in the summer, an' where you got to go so damn far to git anywheres. I like Ioway better, an' I like farmin' better'n what I do gold diggin'."

"That there farm of ol' Gabe Williams's lays right acrost the road from pa's. Gabe, he's got a hull section of damn good corn land—six hundred an' forty acres, an' he's holdin' it at four hundred dollars an' acre. Accordin' to the way I figger it, that's twenty-five thousan', six hundred dollars. It looks like a sight of money, bein' as his house is kinda old an' needs fixin'. But the land's good, so I figger if I kin sell my claim there on Sucker Crick fer fifty thousan' dollars, I could buy Gabe's farm, an' have enough left over to put up a new house, an' a new backhouse, an' git the barn shingled to boot, an' buy a good team of horses, an' some cows an' hogs.

"But the way I figger it, if I only make four hundred dollars a day, it would take me a hundred an' twenty-five days to git fifty thousan' dollars saved up. It's damn clost to the first of March, an' a hundred an' twenty-five days would be better'n four months—an' the hull damn summer would be wasted. I want to git back so's I kin git in a crop this spring."

"You mean," MacShane asked, "that you want to sell for fifty thousan'?"

"Shore I do. The quicker I kin git back to Ioway an' git to farmin', the better I'll like it."

"Tell you what," Bettles said, "fact is, we might be interested in this proposition. Of course, we'd have to go up to Sucker Crick an' look the location over before we made a deal. We'd have to see the bank about gettin' the cash, too. We might even have to pay, say half of it down, an' send you the rest later. It would take us mebbe a couple of days to get ready to make the trip." He turned to the others. "Aint' that so, boys?"

Swiftwater Bill nodded. "Yeah—an' I was jest thinkin' maybe we better hunt up Moosehide Charlie an' let him in on it. Moosehide's generally got some cash on hand, an' we're goin' to need all we can get hold of."

"That's right," MacShane agreed, "let's go see Moosehide, right now. He's over to the blacksmith shop gettin' some new runners on his sled." He turned to Black John. "You wait here.

It might be a couple of hours or so—but we'll be back."

NO SOONER had the door closed behind the three sourdoughs than Featherstone, forsaking his companion, edged along the bar to Black John's side. "Hello, Mr. Smith!" he said heartily. "Don't you remember me?"

The big man nodded. "Oh, shore. You're Mr. Featherrock, ain't you?"

"Featherstone—Mortimer P. Featherstone."

"Yeah—'bout the same thing. You got kinda mad at me one day when I called you Mort. An' you wouldn't listen when I was goin' to tell you about that ol' sow of pa's."

The other laughed. "Forget it, old timer!" the man replied, heartily. "I remember—I had a toothache that day and felt sort of grouchy. Suppose we let bygones be bygones. Let's see, I believe I heard the boys call you John. Okay—you call me Mort, and I'll call you John. How about a little drink?"

"Well, I had one a while back. But mebbe another one wouldn't hurt. My pa, he didn't never hold with drinkin' licker. He's kinda temperance, like. But I claim one er two drinks don't hurt none when a man gits to town."

"Let's see," Featherstone began, when the glasses were filled, "I believe you mentioned, that day, something about a proposition you had on some crick, that you thought might turn out pretty well. Did you ever do anything about it?"

"Shore, I done sometin' about it. I be'n workin' it every day. It's a damn good claim. I git about a ounce of gold out of every pan. But I don't like diggin' gold. I'm goin' to sell out to Bettles an' Swiftwater Bill an' Burr MacShane, an' mebbe Moosehide Charlie. I told 'em I'd take fifty thousan' fer the claim. They gone right now to see if they kin git holt of the money. They said they might have to pay part down, an' send me the rest. They're goin' back with me in a couple of days an' look at the claim."

"Listen," Featherstone said, "what you want is a quick cash deal, isn't it?"

"Why shore. I want to git back to Ioway an' buy Gabe Williams's place an' go to farmin'. I want to git there in time to git in my spring plantin'."

"That's right. Now listen to me. Why wait for those fellows to rustle around and try to raise the fifty thousand? If you do, you'll probably only get maybe half of the money down. Then maybe they'd gyp you out of the rest of it. I've got the cash to pay you the fifty thousand right now. That is, just as soon as I go up with you and look the proposition over. If it's as good as you say, we can come back here to the bank and I'll lay the money right on the barrel head. That's the way I do business— no part payment, no delay—you deed the location to me, and put the cash in your pocket. Not only that, but what's the use in waiting a couple of days to get started up there? Let's go today—right now. I've got a stampeding outfit—six good dogs. Always keep it ready. Never can tell when I'll want to hit out to look some proposition over. You can leave your outfit here till we get back. Come on. Let's go!"

"You shore you got that much money?"

"I've got twice that much."

"How kin you prove it?"

"I can prove it, all right. Come on—we'll step over to the bank."

Pausing before the cashier's window a few minutes later, Featherstone asked, "Will you give me my cash balance, please."

The cashier stepped to a file, and returned. "One hundred and one thousand, six hundred and seventy-one dollars and seventy cents."

Featherstone turned to Black John. "Satisfied?" he asked.

The big man nodded. "Yes, sir. That's shore a sight of money. Yeah—I'm satisfied. Let's go."

VI

THE GOING WAS good. Leaving the well beaten Yukon sled trail, they headed up the Sixtymile, following Black John's back trail. Crossing the divide at the head of Miller Creek, they struck the Ladue Creek valley at the head of the little creek upon which Black John had staked the claim. Rounding a bend, Black John pointed to a newly faced stake protruding from the snow. "That's my upper stake," he explained. "The lower one's below the cabin yonder. These discovery claims are a good proposition—a man gits four times as much for his money when he stakes the first claim on a crick."

They proceeded, with Featherstone in the lead. As they drew opposite the cabin, Featherstone halted abruptly and stared wide-eyed at the iron barred window. Suddenly he whirled to face the big man who had dropped behind on pretense of adjusting a snowshoe. "What—what the hell is this?" he demanded, in a voice that seemed high-pitched and unnatural.

"Why, that's a cabin, Mort," Black John replied. "It's built good an' stout. See them bars on the winder. Can't no one break into that cabin, Mort—nor out of it."

Featherstone reached the sled at a bound, and jerking the rifle from beneath the lashing of the load, cocked it, threw it to his shoulder, and leveled it at Black John's chest. "What's the meaning of this? Talk, damn you! And talk fast!"

The big man grinned into the blazing eyes. "Why—there don't seem to be much to say, Mort. Just pull out your key an' unlock the door an we'll go on in. There's a friend of yours in there, Mort. He's be'n waitin' quite a while for you to come back."

There was a sharp metallic click, as the hammer of the rifle struck the firing pin. The man worked the action, took point-blank aim, and again the metallic click sounded sharply on the keen air.

The smile widened on Black John's lips. "I forgot to mention it, Mort," he said. "But I took the shells out of your rifle last night while you were asleep—just in case."

With a snarl of rage the man leaped toward the speaker, his rifle barrel upraised, only to bring up sharply beside the loaded sled as his narrowed eyes focused on the muzzle of the .45 six-gun that the big man held in his hand. "Better just toss the rifle into the snow, Mort, before you get hurt. I didn't take the shells out of *this* gun." When the man had complied, Black John continued. "Even when it ain't loaded a rifle's a sort of dangerous weapon. Fella got bashed over the head with one a while back, down on the Bonanza trail, an' it killed him. But cripes, Mort, you know all about that! Come to think of it, this guy was the messenger that was supposed to deliver fifty thousan' in bills to you to pay for a location you bought for the Consolidated Dredge outfit. Before he died the messenger mentioned the name of Ben Hambly, an' the police have be'n lookin' for him ever since. They ain't be'n able to locate him—but I did. He's in that cabin. He'd be'n in there quite a while when I found him, Mort—waitin' for you to show up with his cut of that fifty thousan'. So if you'll unlock the door we'll go on in."

"What the hell are you talking about!" Featherstone cried. "What do you mean—Hambly's a friend of mine? I never saw the man! And what do you mean—his cut of that fifty thousand? If Hambly killed that messenger he got it all! I don't know a damned thing about it! And how the hell do you expect me to unlock that door? I never saw this place before!"

"I didn't figure you'd recognize it till you got right to it. That's why I steered you in the back way. If we'd come up the White, an' up Ladue Crick, the way you an' Hambly got here, you'd have got suspicious, an' I'd had a hell of a time gettin' you up here. If you never saw this place before, why did you whirl around an' crack down on me with your rifle. Or, is it just an idiosyncrasy you've got, Slim—to shoot someone every time you see a strange cabin?"

"Slim! What do you mean—Slim?"

"I mean you—Slim McCune. Cripes, you don't s'pose I fell for that fancy moniker you sported around Dawson, do you?"

THE MAN'S face was livid. His shoulders drooped perceptibly, and the belligerent tone was gone from his voice as he asked: "Who—who are you? Iowa farmer—hell! You talk altogether different now from what you did there in the Tivoli. By God— you never saw Iowa!"

"Well, I ain't missed much, at that. Smith is the name—John Smith, just as I told you there in the Tivoli. I'm known, here an' there, more or less favorably, as Black John—on account of my whiskers bein' that color."

"Black John Smith!" the man cried, his eyes suddenly widening. "You mean you're Black John Smith, the king of the gang of outlaws that hang out on Halfaday Crick? I've heard all about you from Cuter Malone, there in the Klondike Palace!"

"Cuter mentioned nothin' detrimental to my character—I hope."

The man's lips smiled, and his voice again held a note of confidence. "Well, believe me, I'm glad to know you, John! God—when you sprung that 'Slim McCune' on me, I thought for a minute you were some damned dick that had trailed me up from Minneapolis! Okay, I'll unlock the door. I guess you and I can dicker. I'm quite something of an outlaw, myself." Producing a key, the man stepped to the door, unlocked it, and threw it open.

"Go on in," Black John said, following close behind him. "Go on over an' sit on the bunk yonder. I'll stand here by the door. Ben's usin' the only chair in the place."

The other shot a contemptuous glance at the frozen figure sprawled over the table. "Nothing but a damned punk," he said. "Shot a bartender in a saloon holdup on Washington Avenue. He got away with that one. Then later he and a couple of other punks tried to pull an express car job on the Oriental Limited near Anoka. Hambly did ten years in Stillwater for that. I never saw him after he got out till I met him there in Dawson.

"I'd doped out this Consolidated job, figuring to pull it myself, but when I ran onto Hambly I changed my plans. Why should I take the risk when I could get a punk to do it for me? I put it up to him and he turned it down. Claimed he was going straight on account of his boy. But he changed his mind when I reminded him of that bartender he shot and that the saloon porter and a couple of customers could identify him, and that murder never outlaws, and that it would be a cinch for me to slip the word to Minneapolis that he was here in Dawson.

"So he pulled the job, and I told him we'd better hit out in the hills for a while, and lay low. I brought him here. I'd happened onto this cabin last summer on a trip I made up Ladue Crick to look over a proposition a guy wanted to sell me farther up the crick. When we got here, I uncorked a bottle and it wasn't long before Hambly got a snootful and went to sleep. I slipped out and left him here. Took the fifty thousand and every damn thing in sight—except the quart bottle of liquor that was about half full. Pretty neat, eh?"

"Yeah," Black John replied, his glance shifting to the dead man, "yeah—pretty neat. You mentioned a while back, about you an' me bein' able to dicker. What sort of dicker did you have in mind?"

"Well—you know, of course, that I got away with the fifty thousand. I'd promised Hambly a fifty-fifty cut on it. But seeing he won't be able to use it—how about me slipping you, say, about half of what I promised him. After all, you didn't take any risk. And twelve thousand five hundred would be damn good pay for the time you've put in. How does that strike you?"

"Not very forcible."

"You mean—you want a bigger cut?"

"No. No, Slim—I don't want any cut of that fifty thousand."

"What do you want? What did you get me up here for, if it

wasn't to put the bug on me for a cut?"

"Why—just like I told you there in Dawson—I got you up here to sell you my claim. It's this location we're on—cabin an' all. I showed you the upper stake. The lower one is down the crick a piece."

The man laughed a short, nervous laugh, and winked knowingly. "That claim stuff was okay to get me up here, John," he said. "And I'll admit you pulled a fast one. You had me fooled with that farmer gag, and I fell for it. I didn't know who you were, then. But since I've found out, I know damn well you've got your eye on that fifty thousand. What's on your mind?"

"My mind's partly on that boy of Ben Hambly's. You rec'lect him, Slim—he's the kid you said there in the Tivoli would stand watchin'. I remember that when the sourdoughs claimed he was a good, hardworkin' kid, you quoted an old sayin' to the effect that folks couldn't expect a good whelp out of a bad dog, an' another one about not bein' able to make a silk purse out of a sow's ear, an' I rec'lect you said society couldn't be expected to accept a murderer's son as an equal. Later, you tried, I believe, to buy the Hamblys' location on Ophir from the kid."

"That's right. Offered him a couple of thousand for it."

"Figured on makin' a profit, eh?"

"Sure, I did. I talked to some of the sourdoughs, and they figure it might go thirty or forty thousand before it was cleaned out."

BLACK JOHN nodded. "Yeah, it might, at that. You never can tell about a location till you get clean down to bedrock. Take this location of mine right here. It might go two hundred thousan' for all anyone knows. Maybe I'm a fool for lettin' it go cheap—but I'm willin' to gamble."

"You still kidding about this location?"

"No. No. Slim—I ain't kiddin'. I'm sellin' it to you, lock, stock an' barrel. I'm sellin' it to you dirt cheap—at a hundred an' one thousan' dollars, cash on the barrel head—that's the way you claimed you do business. You can keep the six hundred an' one dollars an' seventy cents your bank balance calls for. It will just about get you out of the country."

The man's face flushed, and his eyes glared into the cold blue eyes above the black beard. "Look here, Smith," he said, in a low, gritty voice, "if you think you'll ever get your hands on a damn cent more of that dough in the bank than I want you to have, you've got another guess coming. Like I said, you pulled a fast one when you got me up here. But don't let that go to your head. You ain't dealing with any damn punk now. I'm a guy that knows all the answers. I've heard how you've hung men up there on Halfaday Crick. I know you've got the drop on me now, and could shoot me down. But what the hell would it get you? Not one damned cent! That dough is right there in the bank where no one but me can get it out. And don't try to tell me to write out a check for it, or you'll knock me off. I couldn't do it if I wanted to. Plenty of folks around Dawson know I've got money. I'm dealing in mining propositions all the time. And just in case some smart Joe cracked down on me off on some crick and tried to force me to write a check, I never carry my checkbook with me. I leave it in the bank with the cashier, and he's got his orders not to deliver it to anyone but me—even if some guy pulls a signed order from me to hand it over. How do you like that?"

Black John shrugged. "Seems like a kind of a clumsy way of doin' business. But I like it, all right. If you don't carry a checkbook, how were you goin' to pay me the twelve thousan' five hundred?"

"Why, we'd go to Dawson and I'd draw the check right there in the bank where I write all my checks, and hand you over the money."

"Yeah—but when we got there, how do I know you wouldn't hand me a laugh, instead of the money?"

"You've got my word for it, haven't you?"

"Oh, shore. Just like I had your word that you'd never seen

this cabin before. Fact is, Slim, your word ain't worth two whoops in hell."

"Okay. So what? Where do we go from here?"

"From here we go down to the bank. When we get there you'll write a check for a hundred an' one thousan', an' cash it, an' hand over the money to me. Then if you're smart you'll draw out the six hundred an' one dollars and seventy cents that's left, an' buy you a sled load of supplies an' hit for the outside as fast as God will let you. Or you can stay in Dawson an' get hung."

"Hung? Hung for what?"

"Murder. Couple of murders, in fact. You an' Hambly murdered that messenger. Then you murdered Hambly. You might not know it, Slim—but murder's a pastime that's frowned on here in the Yukon. There's a law agin it."

"Who says I was mixed up in knocking off that messenger? And who says I murdered Hambly?"

"I do."

"Yeah? Well, listen to me, wise guy. As far as anyone in Dawson knows, I'm a reputable business man. No one knows I ever saw Hambly. On top of that, everyone in the country knows you're an outlaw. Who the hell do you think would take your word against mine?"

"Corporal Downey would—an' the judge, an' a jury."

The man laughed—a short, sneering laugh. "You're dumber even than I thought you were when you pulled that Iowa farm stuff on me! Listen—if it comes to a showdown I'll swear that I never saw Hambly in my life and never saw this cabin—and there's not one damn bit of evidence to show that I did."

"How about you havin' the key to this cabin? Men don't go around carryin' keys to cabins they never saw before."

"The key's there in the lock. There's nothing except your unsupported word to prove that I ever saw that key."

"That's so," Black John admitted. "I hadn't thought of that."

"There's a hell of a lot of things you hadn't thought of when you got me up here on this wild-goose chase," the man sneered. "I don't know what it takes to get the reputation of being an outlaw, in this country—it sure as hell ain't brains. Trouble with you, Rube—you picked the wrong guy. I know every racket that was ever pulled—and when they invent new ones, I'll know them, too. I'm the baby that knows all the angles. But even at that—you can't blame a man for tryin'. And just to show you there's no hard feelings, let's hit back to Dawson and I'll buy a drink."

"I've gone to quite a bit of trouble just for a drink. How about that twelve thousand five hundred, you promised me?"

The man laughed. "You can forget that twelve thousand five hundred. You doped it out right when you said, 'once we got to Dawson, I'd hand you a laugh instead of the money'."

BLACK JOHN shook his head slowly. "Tch, tch, tch, it's just like I figured—you're thoroughly ontrustworthy. You know, Slim, sometimes it grieves me to contemplate the depths into which human depravity can sink. In this case, however, the grief is somewhat mitigated by the amusement I got out of hearing you extol your erudition concerning the intricacies of the realm of sin."

The man's eyes widened as he stared into the face of the speaker. "What the hell are you talking about?" he interrupted.

"About you, Slim. I can't seem to figure you out. Why would a man that knows all the angles, pull a damn dirty murder up here in this cabin, an' then walk off an' leave evidence layin' around that would give the first rooky policeman that came along an iron-clad case against him?"

"What do you mean?" the man's voice sounded suddenly harsh, as his eyes darted about the cabin. "It's just like I told you! When I left this cabin I took every damned thing with me that could possibly be used as evidence!"

The big man shook his head. "That's what you think, Slim. An' it just goes to show that you ain't very well equipped for thinkin'. When you left here you thought you took everything with you—but you overlooked three items. From your angle, it was an expensive oversight. Those items are goin' to cost you just exactly thirty-three thousan', six hundred an' sixty-six dollars an' sixty-six cents apiece."

Something in the quiet, assured tone of the big man's voice, struck sudden terror to the heart of the other. There was a shrill note in his voice—a note of fear. "What do you mean—three items?"

"I'm referrin' to that piece of oilcloth that covers the table, to the stub of a lead pencil that is still gripped by Hambly's frozen fingers, an' to the quart bottle that sets there on the floor beside him." Stepping to the table, he slipped the oilcloth from beneath the dead man's arms and returned with it to the doorway. "When Hambly woke up an' found you gone, an' the grub an' blankets along with you, an' the door locked, he knew that for him, the jig was up. He found that stub of pencil—might have had it in his pocket—might have found it there on the shelf—it don't matter. He rips the oilcloth off the tabletop, reverses it, and starts to write. But the strong cold was on. His fingers began to stiffen before he got through, so he took a pull at the bottle there that you'd left half-full. The liquor kep him goin', Slim. Every time his fingers would start to stiffen, he'd take another drink, an keep on writin'. The bottle lasted till he finished. It's quite an interestin' document, Slim. I'll read it to you." Holding the cloth to the light, Black John read the penciled script. When he finished, he eyed the man who sat on the edge of the bunk as though in a trance. "So you see, Slim, if you'd have be'n smart enough to have taken any one of those three items along with you, you might have got away with this murder—but to leave all three of 'em! Such stupidity is almost onbelievable."

The man leaped suddenly to his feet, but sank back on the bunk at the sight of the muzzle of Black John's six-gun. "It's a damn lie!" he cried, hysterically. "You wrote that stuff, yourself and planted it here!"

"There were three men with me when we found Hambly. I pried the hasp loose, and we all stepped in here. They can swear that the writin' was there when we found him."

"Someone else could have written it! Anyone who came along could have written it. You can't prove that's Hambly's writing!"

"It won't take long to prove it, Slim. His written description of his claim is on file at the recorder's. An' his boy has letters he saved that his dad wrote him from the pen. You claim to know all the angles—you should know that it won't take Corporal Downey long to prove that this writin' is Hambly's after I give him this oilcloth."

The man sat in silence for several moments. When he finally spoke, it was in a low, toneless voice. "All right. I guess you've got me. How about a fifty-fifty split on that hundred thousand?"

BLACK JOHN shook his head. "No. It wouldn't be right. If I was to split that money with you my conscience would never quit botherin' me. I'd be connivin' in a crime. If I take it all, there's no connivin' about it. That kid of Hambly's—I've got pretty well acquainted with him. He's a fine boy. Wants to go to college an' study medicine. I figure that fifty thousan' will see him through college an' give him a good start in his profession. The other fifty thousan', I'll take care of personally. It ain't that I want the money, Slim. But the fact is, I abhor crime. It's born in me, I guess. My pa was a preacher. He battled crime from the pulpit. I hold that such method is ineffective, because damn few crooks go to church. So I lock horns with crime wherever I find it. An' experience has taught me that the surest way to make a crook see the error of his ways, is to deprive him of the emoluments of crime. Once he gets it through his head that crime don't pay, he'll quit committin' crimes. So you see, Slim, I'm doin' this for your own good. That accounts for a hundred thousan'. That extra thousan' I'll use to defray any incidental expense I've incurred in teachin' this lesson—it's like passin' the plate in church."

"You sanctimonious skunk!" the man exclaimed in a low, gritty voice. "No wonder Cuter Malone claims you're the damndest outlaw in the Yukon! You've got me. I'll pay. I've got some other irons in the fire that will pay out. There's just one condition—when I hand over the money, you give me that oilcloth."

"The condition is turned down. If you've got other irons in the fire, the fire better be a hell of a long ways from the Yukon. When you turn over that money, you're goin' to hit the trail for the outside. Hit it quick, an' travel fast. Three days to the minute from the time you turn over that money to me, I'll turn over this oilcloth to Corporal Downey—an' from that time on the police will be huntin' you. With three days start you ought to keep ahead of 'em—if you step lively. We don't want any such disreputable characters as you in the country. While I'm in Dawson I'll fix up some sort of a deal with the bank where they'll pay young Hambly regular installments of the fifty thousan' till he comes of age—then give him the rest of it. He's a good kid—be'n livin' with me up there on Halfaday for couple of months."

THE RETURN trip to Dawson was made without incident. The two proceeded directly to the bank where, white-faced and tight-lipped, Featherstone drew out his entire deposit, and counted out one hundred and one thousand dollars which he handed to Black John who in turn handed him a folded document. "Here's the grant to your claim, Mort," he said. "I figured you'd grab it—onct you'd got up there an' looked it over. I shore like to deal with a man that lays the cash right out on the barrel head."

Without a word the man turned on his heel and strode from the room as Black John crossed the floor and tapped on the door of a room marked PRIVATE, and entered the office of the manager of the bank.

A couple of hours later he strolled into the Tivoli Saloon where he was greeted by Bettles, who stood at the bar talking with Burr MacShane and Swiftwater Bill. "Hi, John!" he grinned.

"You're a hell of a fella to sneak off the way you did when us boys was out tryin' to raise fifty thousan' to buy that Sucker Crick claim off you!"

The big man eyed the three gravely. "Well, I tell you, boys, the fact is Mortimer P. Featherstone must have sort of overheard what we were talkin' about, because no sooner'n you'd gone than he edged over an' wanted to know about that location. He said he'd go right out an' look it over, an' if it suited him, he'd take it, an' lay the cash right on the barrel head. He said the chances was that you boys wouldn't be able to raise only part of the money, an' would promise to send the rest down to Ioway to me—an' that's the last I'd ever hear from you. So, lookin' at it that way, I figured it was better to do business with him."

MacShane grinned. "Did he buy the claim?"

"Oh, shore."

Swiftwater Bill's brow drew into a frown. "What I can't see—if he went out an' looked the location over—why the hell would he buy it? You know damn well you ain't got no such location as you was talkin' about!"

The door opened and Moosehide Charlie crossed to the bar. Pausing before Black John, he jerked off his cap and bowed low.

"What the hell's eatin you?" the big man asked.

"I was over to the hotel when Bill Emmet, the bank cashier come in fer his lunch an' we got to talkin'. He told me that you an' Featherstone come into the bank an' Featherstone draw'd out every damn cent he had an' handed you over a hundred thousan' dollars! By God, my hat's off to anyone that can take a guy like him fer a hundred thousan' cash money!"

"The cashier was in error," Black John corrected. "The amount was one hundred an' one thousan'."

Bettles' jaw dropped, and Swiftwater Bill's eyes widened. MacShane was the first to find his voice. "But Cripes, John—he heard you offer it to us for fifty thousan'!"

"Oh, shore. But when he got up there an' looked it over he realized that takin' that claim for fifty thousan' would be practically stealin' it—so he doubled the price. Not only that but he insisted on payin' the expenses of the trip—that's where that extra thousan' comes in. An' believe me—if you boys know what I know, you'd realize that Mort made a damn good deal. I'm buyin' a drink an' then I'm pullin' out for Halfaday. But first I've got to hunt up a bunch of books for that kid of Ben Hambly's to read. He's be'n stoppin' with me fer the past couple of months. When the break-up comes he's goin' outside on the first boat—goin' to some college an' study medicine." When the drinks were poured Black John raised his glass. "Here's how. So long. Be seein' you in the spring."

CORPORAL DOWNEY: "SUICIDE."
BLACK JOHN: "MAYBE."

AS BLACK JOHN SMITH entered the barroom of Cushing's Fort, the stalwart log outpost of civilization that served the requirements, spirituous and temporal, of the little community of outlawed men that had sprung up on Halfaday Creek close against the Yukon-Alaska boundary line; Old Cush, the proprietor, set out a bottle, two glasses, and a worn leather dice box.

"Where an' the hell you be'n fer the last week?" he asked, as the big man picked up the box, rattled the dice noisily, and rolled them out onto the bar.

"There's three fives in one. I'll leave 'em. I've be'n over on Willow Crick attendin' to some ecclesiastical matters."

"You mean some kind of prospectin'?" Cush asked, as he gathered the dice and shook them. "There's three big sixes to top them three little fives you left. An' here's right back at you with four sixes more."

"Three of which," growled Black John, "I mistrust was the ones you rolled out the other time. I can't prove it—but after this when you shake, you set that bottle off to one side so I kin see what yer doin' with them dice!"

"Looks like I done pretty good with 'em," Cush grinned, as he glanced at Black John's three deuces, made an entry in his day book, and reached for the bottle. "Willer Crick is a hell of a ways from here, an' it ain't nothin' but a moose pasture when you git there," he observed, "an' besides, I heard some Siwashes was plantin' gardens over there. It looks like anyone would have more sense than to prospect on it."

"Well, Bonanza wasn't nothin' but a moose pasture when Carmack made his strike. All the wise ones had passed it up. It took a squaw-man to find out what it was worth."

"Yeah—but there ain't no more Bonanzas. An' besides, you ain't no squaw-man, if there was. Onlest," he added, "that big word you used is some kind of a nickname fer gittin' married."

"No," grinned Black John, "I didn't git married. I went over to call on a priest."

"I heard there was a priest over there. It was him got them Siwashes to plant them gardens. But I didn't know you was so religious you'd go sixty, seventy mile jest to call on a priest."

"I don't claim to be no more religious than the average husky dog," Black John replied. "My pa was a preacher, an' from what I could see, he worked damn hard at it with little er no visible results. So I sort of devoted my life to other pursuits."

"A little religion don't hurt no one, though," Cush opined. "My fourth wife was religious as hell—an' she had my first three ones beat a mile. Trouble is, outside of preachers an' wimmin, there ain't no one else got no time to monkey with it.

"I was off moose huntin' the day you pulled out. One Armed John claimed a Siwash come in here an' bought five, six ounces worth of supplies, an' you got to talkin' to him, an' then you ordered a hull canoe load of supplies, an' draw'd a hundred ounces out of the safe, an' went off with this Siwash. I figgered he'd put you wise to some crick an' you paid him the hundred ounces."

"IT WASN'T exactly that way," Black John explained. "The Siwash come in, jest as One Arm said, an' he bought a little grub, an' one cheap blanket, an' paid fer 'em with bills. I got to talkin' with him, an' he told me the stuff was fer Father Duchene. He's a damn fine old man. Most of the missionaries do more harm than good to the natives, what with makin' 'em change their ways of livin' to conform to the white man's notions. But not Father Duchene. He's one priest that's got sense enough to look after the physical needs of the natives before he worries about their hereafter. The Siwash told me things hadn't be'n goin' so good on Willow Crick. The gardens the good Father had 'em plant was comin' along fine till that cold spell we got a couple of weeks ago, when they froze black, right down to the ground.

"Trappin' had be'n pore last winter, an' the Siwashes didn't have no credit, an' they was mighty short of supplies to face the winter on—an' no chanct to better themselves till the Chris'mas tradin' time. There'd be'n sickness amongst 'em, an' Father Duchene had got a doctor up there durin' the summer, an' had used up the money the church sent him, payin' fer medicine an' what-not, till them few dollars was all he had left. He'd paid the doctor out of his own pocket because he knew that if he waited fer the Indian Department to git around to sendin' one it would be too late.

"I know the old Father likes his little nip, now an' then. An' I know he loves his pipe. But there wasn't a bottle on that Siwash's list of supplies—nor a damn ounce of tobacco. So I loaded up the canoe with stuff—all it would hold. An' took a hundred ounces out of the safe, an' went over to Willow Crick with the Siwash, an' seen to it that the old priest got a few bottles of licker, an' some tobacco, an' enough grub to last him a while. I shore had to talk turkey to the old fella because he wanted to give out most of the stuff to the Siwashes. There's about forty of 'em, an' they'll need plenty more supplies to carry 'em on to the Chris'mas tradin'. I told Father Duchene to keep them hundred ounces fer an ace-in-the-hole, in case he run into more sickness, er some-thin', an' made him promise to send three canoes over here fer more supplies. So when they come, you give 'em whatever the priest's list calls fer, an' charge it to me."

"I will like hell!" growled Cush.

"What do you mean?"

"I mean—who the hell do you think you be, hoggin' all the expense of them damn Siwashes? They'll git the supplies all right, but by God, I've got as much right to git in on this as you have!"

"Oh, all right!" replied Black John. "Have it yer own way. But, tell me, has anything portentious transpired in the haunts of the iniquitous?"

Cush scowled. "If that's somethin' you want to know, you

better say it over. I wouldn't have no time to look up all them big words even if I had a dictionary, an' they prob'ly wouldn't mean nothin' if I did."

"I was merely inquirin' how things has be'n goin' on Halfaday."

"'Bout the same like always. Feller drifted in an' located in Whiskey Bill's old shack. Draw'd the name of Dan'l Hayne outa the name can. Set in the stud game t'other night an' won him a few ounces."

"Yukon wanted?"

"He didn't say. He's a damn chechako. Mightn't be wanted nowheres. Might jest be prospectin', like he claims."

"If he ain't wanted, why should he draw a name out of the can? Did he claim his name was 'John Smith,' like all the rest?"

"No. He didn't claim it was nothin'. I was here alone when he come in, an' we had a couple of drinks, an' you know how chechakos is—like puppies, allus into everythin.' He seen the name can settin' there on the end of the bar an' he looked in it an' seen them slips an' wanted to know what they was. An' when I told him, he draw'd one out an' claimed he'd use it instead of his own, which he claimed didn't make no different to no one, nohow."

Black John glanced toward the open doorway through which streamed the golden sunlight of late autumn. "Look who's comin'," he said. "I predict we'll presently hear news of sorts. When One Arm picks 'em up an' lays 'em down like that, he's got some information to onload."

II

ONE ARMED JOHN burst into the room as Cush spun a glass across the bar. "There's a feller," he gasped, as he reached for the bottle, "in Olson's old shack!"

"Well," grinned Black John, "s'pose there is? What does he look like?"

"He looks dead as hell, to me."

"Dead!"

Old Cush glowered. "Damn if you ain't the worst corpse hound in the Yukon—bar none! But why an' the hell do you allus have to be findin' 'em on Halfaday? Cripes—the country's full of other cricks!"

"Well—hell—Cush, Halfaday's where I'm at. An' it's where the corpses is at. So I got to find 'em here. A corpse ain't no different than anythin' else—you got to find it where it's at."

"The statement savors of sound reasonin'," Black John grinned. "But tell us more about it."

"There ain't no more to tell. I come past there fishin', an' I seen how the door stud open a little, an' I went over to shet it so the rain er snow wouldn't pile inside, an' there he laid spraddled out on his back on the floor. I give the door a yank an' got to hell outa there as fast as I could leg it. Fishin' ain't no fun if you've got to keep runnin' onto dead folks. I wisht someone would die sometime where I wouldn't have to find him!"

"Me an' you both," agreed Cush. "Did he look prosperous?"

"I don't know how he looked! Jest like I said—I seen him, an' run."

"A mercenary attitude in a public official is deplorable," grinned Black John. "As coroner, Cush, it's your duty to hold an' inquest to determine the manner of his death, be he prince er pauper."

"Oh, shore. I was jest wonderin'. It ain't nothin' agin a man if he'd like to turn a profit, now an' then. Anyways, it's a nice day fer an inquest, an' the ground ain't froze yet, an' he's bound to be middlin' fresh, what with the cold nights. I swung around that way huntin' only three, four days ago, an' there wasn't no one in Olson's shack, then."

"We might's well go on down," Black John said. "You kin leave One Arm to tend bar."

A JURY was drafted on the way from among those citizens of Halfaday whose claims lay down the creek from the fort. The big man, together with Cush, and the five others who made up the jury, filed into the little cabin and stood looking solemnly down at the corpse.

"Cush, as coroner, pronounces this man dead," Black John announced. "An' it now devolves upon us, as the jury, to try an' determine the cause of death."

"That ain't goin' to be no hell of a chore," opined Pot Gutted John, pointing to the .38 calibre nickel-plated revolver lying on the floor close beside the man's outstretched hand. "You kin see the powder burns on his skin where he helt the gun practically agin' his right temple."

"Don't no one touch that gun!" Black John ordered. "This

looks like a suicide. But it might be a murder. An' if it is, it might be that the one that done it left his fingerprints on the butt, er the trigger, er somewheres."

"How the hell could you tell whose they was, if he did?" asked Long Nosed John.

"This here fingerprint stuff is a lot of damn nonsense," opined Short John, as he watched the big man pick the gun up by the barrel and carefully wrap it in an old newspaper.

"Yeah?" retorted Black John. "Well, it might be comfortin' fer you to know that that same opinion has be'n expressed by several gents right up to the time they was hung—fer leavin' their fingerprints around where the police could git holt of 'em."

"What's the police got to do with it?" questioned Red John. "We handle our own murders on Halfaday."

"Prob'ly nothin'," the big man admitted. "But I'm keepin' the gun as it is—jest in case." He paused and allowed his glance to travel searchingly about the room. "I don't see nothin' that would indicate that anyone besides the dead man has be'n in here. The stuff shows a one-man outfit. An' it looks like he ain't be'n here long." He paused, his eyes centering on the dead man. "I don't s'pose any of you ever seen him before?"

ALL DENIED ever having seen the man, and Black John stooped and began methodically to remove the contents of the pockets— a long-bladed clasp knife, a pipe and tobacco pouch, a blue bandana handkerchief with two holes cut near the center, about an inch and a half apart, a gold hunting case watch attached to a heavy gold chain bearing a Masonic emblem, and a leather wallet containing two ten dollar bills in United States money. The wallet was removed from the hip pocket of the man's trousers, and the bills were stained by the leather for about one-third of their length, as though he had waded in water, wetting the lower end of the wallet, which also contained a penciled note. Placing the collection on the table, Black John stepped to the doorway and, holding the paper to the light, began to read it carefully. When he had finished, he glanced at Red John.

"You was askin' a few minutes ago what the police had to do with this case," he said. "Well, I'm bettin' it'll be plenty. I'm predictin' that Corporal Downey'll be showin' up here before very long. An' after he goes back it might be that we'll have a chore of our own to do."

"What do you mean—a chore of our own?" Cush asked sourly. "Ain't it enough we should come clean down here to set on this corpse, an' not enough on him to pay fer three rounds of drinks?"

"Accordin' to this, he had plenty on him when he come here. He claims his cache was robbed."

"Robbed!" exclaimed Pot Gutted John. "How much does he claim he had in it?"

"He says here it was twenty-five hundred ounces."

"Twenty-five hundred!" cried Red John. "My God, that's forty-thousan' dollars! An' him a chechako! It don't sound reasonable. Where does he say he got it?"

"He says here that on September the tenth he laid fer the manager of the Detroit-Yukon outfit an' a packer comin' down the Klondike trail with the clean-up an' he shot 'em both with his revolver, an' packed the dust to the Yukon, an' loaded it in his canoe an' hit fer Halfaday. He says he got here on the twenty-third, an' cached his dust an' throw'd his stuff into this shack. On the mornin' of the twenty-fourth he claims he went to his cache to git some dust to go on up to Cush's an' buy some supplies an' he found the cache empty. He says he ain't only got twenty dollars left, which ain't enough to buy supplies that would take him anywheres, an' he wouldn't know where to go if he had the supplies. He says he's afraid to go back to the Yukon an' face a hangin', so he's takin' the only way out. He asks whoever finds his body to send the watch an' chain to the manager's wife, as her picture is pasted in the back. An' he winds up by sayin', 'So long, world—to hell with you! Here goes nothin'!' That's all. There ain't no name signed to it."

Cush shrugged. "Well," he said, "I guess that finishes the case. What'll we do, John—go ahead an' bury him? Er leave him here fer Downey to see?"

"We better take him up an' bury him in the graveyard. It might be quite a while before Downey gits here. We'll take all this other stuff along, too. We won't sink him very deep, in case Downey would want to dig him up."

"That'll give us a new kind of a check letter on his slab," Cush said. "We've got D's fer died natural, an' H's fer hung, an' M's fer murdered. But we ain't never had no suicides before. At that, a S is so damn crooked it'll be hard to make. But I wonder who in hell robbed his cache?"

"That," replied Black John, a grim set to his lips, "is what I meant a while back, when I said we might have a chore of our own to do."

III

ONE BLUSTERING DAY of alternating sunshine and snow squalls, some three weeks after the inquest, Corporal Downey stepped into the barroom at Cushing's Fort to find Black John and Cush facing each other across the bar, the inevitable dice box between them.

"Hell of a day fer anyone to be out," greeted the big man, as Cush slid a glass across the bar and shoved the bottle. "What you doin'—huntin' moose, er probin' into the machinations of the sinful?"

"I'm huntin' a murderer," replied the officer, as he poured his drink. "A bird knocked off a packer for the Detroit-Yukon outfit, an' shot the manager in the head. When I left Dawson ten days ago the doctors at the hospital give him about a twenty-five percent chance of pullin' through."

"H-m-m. Was the venture successful, from a financial standp'int?"

"He got away with twenty-five hundred ounces."

"He did, eh? You got any specifications on him? Er are you goin' it blind?"

"The manager regained consciousness several times an' he was able to give a sort of description of the robber. Said he looked like a chechako. Stood about six foot, and would weigh around a hundred an' seventy-five er eighty. Said he had his face masked with a blue bandana with white dots an' a couple of eye-holes cut in it. He used a nickel-plated revolver. That's about all we could get out of him. He only stayed conscious a few minutes at a time."

Black John nodded approval. "He done pretty well, as fer as the description goes."

"You mean the man's here—on Halfaday."

"Yeah, he's here."

"Where 'bouts?"

"Out back. We didn't plant him only about two foot deep, figurin' you'd be along an' might want to look him over."

"You mean he's dead?"

"That's what Cush claimed, an' he's the coroner. We took his word fer it an' buried the man. He's in that new grave, this way from the others. It's the one with the S fer a check letter. Cush got the letter headed the wrong way—but so was the fella—so I guess it's O.K."

"What do you mean 'S'?" asked Downey. "An' how come he's dead?"

"The word 'suicide' answers both questions."

"You mean, he killed himself?"

"That's what it looks like. An' that's what he claimed in his note." He turned to Cush. "Hand out that package of junk we fetched up with the corpse, an' Downey kin see fer himself."

The officer read the note through twice and looked up with a frown. "Who robbed his cache?" he asked abruptly.

Black John shrugged. "If we knew the answer to that one

there'd be a new H grave alongside of his."

Downey pried open the back of the watch and glanced at the photograph. "That's her," he said, "the manager's wife. She'll prob'ly be glad to get this back. An' the D-Y outfit would be damn glad to git their twenty-five hundred ounces back, too."

"Who the hell wouldn't!" remarked Black John. "I'm glad it's them an' not me that's got to worry about it."

"You never did worry very much over any big outfit's loss."

"Well, I ain't begun to git gray over 'em."

"I see you wrapped the gun up separate. Did anyone handle it?"

The big man shook his head. "Nope. One Armed John found the corpse. He was fishin' along there an' seen the door of Olson's old shack was open, so he went to close it, an' when he seen the body sprawled out on the floor he pulled the door shet an' legged it fer here an' told me an' Cush about it. So we gathered a coroner's jury an' went down an' set on the case. I picked up the gun by the barrel an' wrapped it up in that paper, an' it's be'n here ever sense. I figgered you'd want to look it over for fingerprints."

"That's right," Downey approved. Unwrapping the gun, he picked it up by the barrel, turning it this way and that to catch the light. "An' it looks like we might get some, too." He examined the other objects, one by one, and returned them to the package. "We'll go out, now, an' dig up the body. I want to photograph it an' git his fingerprints fer the file. It might be we can get plain enough prints off the gun to compare 'em here an' find out if it was him that handled it last. If not I'll have to wait till I get to Dawson where we've got better equipment."

THE BODY was disinterred, photographed and its fingerprints taken. Stepping into the saloon, Downey dusted some fine powder onto the butt, trigger, and trigger-guard, and with a pocket magnifying glass compared them with the dead man's prints. "I'm almost positive they're his prints," he announced, after several moments of close scrutiny. "I make out some islands an' whorls that seem to jibe, all right. I can't tell for sure till I get back to detachment."

"I s'pose we kin go ahead an' rebury him, then," Black John said.

Downey shook his head. "Not yet. Even if I can prove that he was the last man to handle this gun, an' that his finger was the last finger to pull that trigger, an' that the gun was held close enough to his head to leave powder marks on his skin—that don't prove that it was this gun that killed him. He might have fired a shot at someone else, an' someone else might have held some other gun to his head an' knocked him off."

"It could be that way," Black John admitted, "but it ain't likely."

"No, it ain't likely. But in police work a man wants to be sure. The bullet that killed him is still inside his skull. I'll borrow a hand-saw from Cush an' get that bullet, an' compare it with a bullet fired from this gun. If they match up, I guess the case will be closed—except fer recoverin' them twenty-five hundred ounces. The D-Y's sure goin' to put up a squawk."

"Well, a good squawk won't hurt 'em none. We'll keep our eyes open fer the one that robbed that cache, an' if we find him he'll meet up with what the newspapers call 'summary justice'— you kin bet yer last stack of blue ones on that."

"An' the twenty-five hundred ounces—I s'pose you'll turn them over to me, when you find 'em?"

"I wouldn't like to make no rash promises till I find 'em," Black John replied gravely. "Ounces like them is apt to be damn hard to locate. 'Specially when the one that's got 'em knows they've already be'n stole out of one cache. He's likely to hide 'em pretty good."

"But," persisted the officer, "you'll return 'em if you do locate 'em?"

"Hell, Downey, what you quibblin' about? Cripes sake! We

returned that watch, didn't we? An' them two ten-dollar bills? If we'd wanted to be onderhanded we could of held 'em out on you an' claimed there worn't no sech items in his inventory. It shore pains me to feel that you'd entertain even a breath of suspicion agin my integrity."

"Well," Downey replied dryly, "jest to keep the pain from gittin' too bad fer you to stand, I'll buy a drink. An' then I'll be hittin' back. If I hurry, an' have good luck, I can make it back to Dawson before the freeze-up."

IV

A FEW DAYS later, as Black John stepped into the saloon, Cush addressed a tall, well set-up newcomer who faced him across the bar.

"You was askin' about Black John—there he is. I'll make you acquainted with him." As the big man took his place beside the other, Cush said, "John, this here's Dan Hayne. He's the fella I was tellin' you about that's located up on Whiskey Bill's old claim."

There was a look of frank admiration in Hayne's eyes as he extended his hand. "I'm sure glad to meet up with you," he said. "I've heard quite a bit about you, here an' there. Have a drink?"

The big man shook the proffered hand. "Yeah, I take an occasional drink, jest by way of passin' the time."

"I be'n tellin' Dan about that fella that shot hisself down in Olson's shack," Cush said, as he set out the bottle and glasses.

"Yeah—the damn cuss!" Hayne exclaimed. "Knockin' them two fellas off the way he done. Served him damn good an' right that someone stole that dust on him. It's too bad the law couldn't of hung him, though—fer a kind of a sample of what happens to folks that carries on like that. Cush tells me the case is closed, an' this Corporal Downey has went back to Dawson."

"Yeah, the case is closed all right, as fer as the law's concerned."

"It's funny he wouldn't of stuck around a while an' tried to locate that dust."

"It wouldn't of done him no good," Black John explained. "On Halfaday we don't never hinder the police, but likewise, we don't never help 'em, neither. Downey ain't no fool. He knows that if he hung around here, the one that had the dust would slip acrost the line with it—an' he couldn't do a damn thing about it. How you doin' on Whiskey Bill's claim?"

"Not bad. I'm takin' out a lot of dust there. I figger if I work it all winter I'd ort to have right around forty er fifty thousand dollars in dust, come spring."

"You do, eh? Well, when a man kin do that good he'd be a fool not to stay with it."

"That's what I claim." The three emptied their glasses, and Hayne drew a paper from his pocket and laid it on the bar. "I made me a list of stuff I've got to git. I ain't got no dog outfit, an' I figger I'd better lay in my winter's supplies while I kin pole 'em up the crick in my canoe. The still places'll be freezin' over one of these nights, an' then I'd have to back-pack 'em."

Glancing down at the paper, Black John's eyes narrowed, slightly. "That's right," he agreed. "Fill up. We'll have another, an' then I'll git the stuff out fer you so Cush kin be gittin' on with his bar chores."

As the three filled their glasses Cush frowned across the bar. "Cripes—here it's ten o'clock in the mornin'! The bar chores has—"

"Shore, I know!" Black John interrupted hurriedly. "The bar chores has be'n kind of botherin' you, hangin' along like they are. But I'll git this stuff out myself so you kin git at 'em. That back bar looks like hell, the way it's messed up. An' the floor don't look like it's be'n swep' fer a week. If you git slip-shod, Cush, you'll begin losin' trade."

CATCHING THE big man's eye, Cush curbed an acid retort and even managed a mumbled thanks for the proffered assistance.

The drinks were had, and Black John headed for the storeroom.

"Fetch yer list along, Dan," he called, "an' we'll be gittin' at it!"

Behind the bar Cush eyed the two with a puzzled frown, and as they disappeared through the storeroom doorway he took a month-old newspaper from the back bar, spread it out upon the bar, adjusted his square, steel-rimmed spectacles, and proceeded to laboriously devour its contents. An hour later, as the two returned to the barroom, he folded the paper and set out the bottle and glasses.

Black John cast an approving glance about the room. "Got through, eh? Looks about a hundred percent better in here. You ort to keep it lookin' like this all, the time, Cush. A little extry work, now an' then, would do the trick. Folks likes to do their drinkin' where it's tidy. I got Dan all fixed up. I've got the list here. It figgers up to six hundred an' twenty-four dollars."

Cush made a penciled calculation as Hayne tossed a pouch onto the bar. "It figgers jest thirty-nine ounces," he announced, picking up the pouch and shaking the dust onto the scale. He emptied the pouch and peered at the scale. "You ain't only got thirty-one ounces here," he said.

Hayne laughed. "Hell, that's all right! There's plenty more where that come from. I kin pay you now," he offered, producing a wallet from his pocket and drawing some bills from it, "er if you'd ruther have it in dust, I kin leave part of the stuff here an' come back fer it when I fetch down the dust. I never thought about not havin' enough in the poke."

"Put up yer wallet," Black John advised. "Cush, he don't like to take in bills when he kin git dust. You kin take the stuff along with you an' fetch the dust down later."

"All right. But there's a little more'n that owin'. It's fer them two boxes of .30-40 ca'tridges. There wasn't no price mark on 'em, an' you didn't know how much they was."

"That's so," the big man agreed, consulting the list. "It's a good thing Dan's honest, Cush, er you'd of got beat out of them shells."

"I figger honesty pays a man, in the long run," Hayne said. Then, with a quick glance of apology toward Black John, "Not meanin' no slurs agin you! I heard how you held up an army er somethin', somewhere over in Alasky. What I claim—that takes guts!"

"No offense," reassured the big man. "The incident has on-doubtless be'n greatly exaggerated. Anyhow, I always regarded the event as more of a sportin' proposition than a dishonest transaction. Drink up, an' I'll buy one."

"I've got to figger on layin' me in some meat," Hayne said, as he filled his glass and shoved the bottle. "I ain't never hunted no moose. Use' to hunt deer, back in Michigan. But I s'pose moose huntin' is different."

"Yeah, it's a lot different than deer huntin'," Black John said. "Fact is, moose huntin's a kind of particular business. Take deer, now—if a man's got a rifle an' sort of pokes around in the woods where the deer is, an' kind of keeps an eye on the runways, he's damn near shore to git one. But a man could hunt moose fer a month, right where they was thick, an' never see one, if he didn't know how to go at it."

"There's plenty of moose around here, ain't there? I seen some tracks when I was comin' down."

"There used to be," Black John explained, "but lately they're gittin' kind of scarce. It's got so a man's got to go quite a ways back to git him a good one. Of course, he could knock off an old bull, er a lean, leggy cow right here on Halfaday. But chances is he couldn't eat the meat after he got it. Young stuff—two an' three year olds is what a man wants. I've be'n figgerin' on layin' in my winter's meat, myself. This snow we got last night is all right fer trackin', an' it's good enough fer the sled, with a light load. I know a place, quite a piece back from here, where there's a lot of young moose hangin' out. I'll be pullin' out tomorrow mornin', an' you kin go along, if you'd like. We'll take a couple of weeks' grub along an' kill plenty of meat fer both of us."

"That would be fine!" Hayne exclaimed. "It's damn good of you to take me along. I'll be glad to furnish the grub fer the trip, if you'll furnish the sled an' the dogs, an' show me about the huntin'."

"We'll go fifty-fifty on the grub," Black John replied. "You better git this stuff up to yer shack now, an' then come on back an' fetch yer rifle an bed-roll along. You kin sleep in my extry bunk tonight, an' we'll git an early start in the mornin'. You kin take all the stuff up with you—like I said, Cush'll trust you fer them other nine ounces."

Cush nodded assent. "Shore, take it along. An' you better git goin if you figger on gittin' back here 'fore dark. It's quite a piece up to Whiskey Bill's."

Black John obligingly helped the man carry his supplies to the creek and load them into the canoe. As the other stepped into the craft, the big man pointed to his hip pocket. "I see you've got a pistol in there. Are you any good with it?"

The man looked a trifle startled. "Well—not so bad, I guess. Why?"

Black John grinned. "Nothin', except that if you kin hit anything with it, it would be a damn good thing to have along on the moose hunt. We'll be runnin' onto a lot of Ptarmagin on the trail, an' if we had a light gun to knock 'em off with, we'd save rifle ammunition an' not waste no meat."

"How's this?" laughed the man, and picking up an empty tin from the bank, tossed it into the water and drilled it twice before it sank as it drifted past.

Black John voiced approval. "I'll say you ain't so bad! Fetch it along. Them Ptarmagin's damn good eatin'."

WHEN HE returned to the barroom Cush regarded him with a frown. "Seems like yer gittin' damn thick with chechakos all of a sudden," he growled, as he filled his glass and shoved the bottle across the bar.

"Oh, Dan seems like an up-an-comin' young fella."

"Huh—what's so damn up-an'-comin' about some chechako which he ain't got no more brains in his head than to figger he could take forty, fifty thousan' dollars out of Whiskey Bill's old claim in one winter?"

"Well—he's a trifle optimistic, mebbe. But it shouldn't take a man so long to pan out forty, fifty thousan' if he's spry."

"You talk like a damn fool!" Cush growled. "An' besides, what was the idee in you claimin' I didn't have my bar chores done?"

"An', waitin' on him yerself, an' then claimin' the place here looked a hundred precent better, when I never done nothin' to it whilst you was in the storeroom but read in that paper? An' you claimin' I'd ruther take in dust than bills? An' then claimin' there worn't no moose on Halfaday except old an' pore ones, an' offerin' to take him off to hell an' gone on a two weeks' huntin' trip. You know damn well you could git any kind of a moose you want right here, in a day's hunt."

"Answerin' all them queries to onct," grinned the big man, "I will state that assumin' the population of New York City to be rapidly approachin' the four million mark, taken together with the fact that scientists have calculated the distance between here an' the sun to be somethin' over ninety-two million miles, as the crow flies, might have some bearin' on the subject—but I doubt it. I'll be biddin' you adieu, for the nonce, as a poet would say. I have a certain matter to attend to."

"Huh—an' if Downey was here I'd shore as hell loan him that hand-saw agin, so he could lift off the top of yer head an' find out what's wrong in there! I s'pose this here matter you've got to 'tend to ain't got nothin' to do with you knowin' Dan Hayne has got to go to his cache to git out some dust?"

"I detect, in the tone of your voice, a ring of irony which should nettle me. However, as the supposition is your own, you may have it for what it's worth. I'm wastin' time here, I'll be seein' you later."

Hayne returned just on the edge of darkness, and a few minutes later Black John entered the saloon, yawning prodigiously.

"Back already, eh? I had me a good nap. Come on over to my cabin an' we'll eat supper, an' then come back an' set in the stud game fer a while. We want to git an early start in the mornin', so we won't play very late."

ONE EVENING, after five days of steady traveling toward the northeast, Black John halted on the bank of a frozen river. "We'll camp here," he said. "Last time I was here the moose was good an' thick. An' there's plenty of sign around."

"Seems to me we've be'n seein' a lot of tracks ever sence we started," Hayne said as he helped remove the outfit from the sled.

"Oh, shore, there's be'n plenty of tracks. But you must of noticed they was all big ones. Them old moose travels further'n what the young ones do. That's what makes 'em tough. When a man tries to eat one it's like chawin' a chunk of rubber."

"Seems like a hell of a ways to come fer meat, though."

"It's kind of far, all right," Black John admitted, "but what's a few miles, if a man gits the kind of stuff he wants?"

"Oh, I don't mind it! Fact is, there ain't be'n a day but what I've learnt somethin' about winter travelin'. An' now I'll learn about moose huntin'."

"That's right. In the mornin' you hit out along the river, an' I'll swing inland, an' that way we'll keep 'em between us, an' one of us'll be bound to git a shot."

On the afternoon of the second day, with three moose down, Black John said, "That's about all the meat we kin handle. I'll slip upriver to that Siwash village an' git 'em to help us haul it in. I figger it'll take five more sleds."

The cutting up and loading of the meat took all the next day, and the following morning the six sleds pulled out, following down the river. On the third day thereafter they pulled out onto a broad expanse of snow covered ice.

"Why—what's this?" cried Hayne, in evident surprise. "It—it looks like the Yukon!"

Black John grinned. "That's prob'ly because it is the Yukon. It's a damn sight easier haulin' the stuff down the Sixtymile, like we done, an' up the Yukon to the White, an' up that to Halfaday, than it would of be'n to haul it cross country through them damn mountains. Besides that, we've got more meat than we need. Them was all big three year olds we got, an' they dressed out right around a thousan' pounds apiece. We don't need more'n a thousan' pounds between us, an' that leaves us a ton to sell."

"Sell? Where?"

"Dawson, of course! When Downey was up on that D-Y murder case he told me moose was scarce this fall along the river, an' meat was fetchin' a dollar a pound. So what's the matter with me an' you sendin' two of these sleds on up to Cush's, an' slippin' the other four down to Dawson? There's anyways a couple of thousan' dollars in it fer us—plenty to finance a damn good bust. I sort of feel a jamboree comin' on. It's be'n a hell of a while sence I've flung them gals around a dance hall floor, an' took a whirl at a wheel, an' had an all-around, bang-up good time. We've got a long winter ahead of us. Cush's is all right, fer as it goes, but a man gits tired of it after a while. He likes to git out an' see the sights. An' besides, Downey was tellin' me there was a lot of new gals come in on the last boat. It looks like we'd ort to go down an' kind of look 'em over." As he talked, he noted that the other showed increasing interest, especially at mention of the girls.

"Well," Hayne said, after a few moments of hesitation, "it is kind of lonesome up there on Halfaday. We could do it all up in a few days."

"Shore we could!" Black John agreed. "I wouldn't figger on stayin' no more'n three er four days at the outside. I ain't no hand to let frivolity interfere with business."

"All right—let's go!"

Two days later the outfit pulled into Dawson. Black John disposed of the meat, handing Haynes a thousand dollars for his share.

After a few drinks together in the Tivoli, Hayne headed for Cuter Malone's notorious Klondike Palace, where Black John looked in a couple of hours later to find him hilariously drunk, whooping it up with the dance hall girls. Then he headed for the detachment headquarters of the Northwest Mounted Police.

V

CORPORAL DOWNEY LOOKED up from his desk as the big man stepped into the office. "Hello, John!" he greeted. "Did you ever find the bird that robbed that cache?"

"Not yet, I ain't."

"Pshaw! I was hopin' you'd step up here an' plunk them twenty-five hundred ounces down on the desk."

"You was, eh? Well, hopin' don't hurt a man none. An' it's about the only pastime there is that don't cost money."

"The D-Y outfit has be'n raisin' hell about that dust."

"They have, eh? Well, well! Take me, I can't seem to work up no agony over their loss. If it was some private prospector I might mourn a bit—but not fer no corporation."

"It's a cinch someone on Halfaday got it."

"D'you reckon?"

"Sure! The fella cached it there, an' it was lifted."

"What fella?"

"Why, the suicide, of course!"

"Oh, him. Hell, I don't believe he ever had a cache."

"Never had a cache! Then why would he kill himself?"

"He wouldn't."

"What! What do you mean? That was as clear a case of suicide as I ever seen!"

"Yeah? Well, how many suicides have you ever seen?"

"Not very many," Downey admitted. "But there ain't a chance in a thousan' that wasn't one. When I got back here I checked his fingerprints with those on the gun, an' they matched to a T. An' the bullet I took out of his head was fired from that gun. Then I showed the photograph I took of him to a lot of folks here in Dawson an' learnt that he was a chechako by the name of Jack Lewis. When his claim on Squaw Crick petered out, he done odd jobs here an' there, an' hung out mostly around Cuter Malone's. He got to drinkin' pretty heavy, an' several times he pawned his revolver—that nickel-plated one—fer a few dollars. But he always paid up the loan an' got it back.

"One night there was a stick-up right here on Front Street. A chechako was stood up at the point of a nickel-plated gun an' robbed of a hundred an' fifty dollars in United States bills, an' six ounces of dust. He reported it an' said the robber had his face masked with a blue bandana with white dots on it, an' that he stood about six foot, an' was well set-up. I put a rookie constable on the case, an' mebbe he give his hand away an' scairt the fella out of town—because the next day the D-Y job was pulled off on the Klondike trail. An' the description the manager gave of the robber checked exactly with the description of the Front Street robber. This Lewis had be'n goin' from bad to worse, an' when he come to the end of his rope, he shot himself."

"Kind of looks like that, don't it? That's what Cush thought, an' the jury, too—an' they didn't have as much to go on as you have. But it's like I always claim, Downey—folks hadn't ort to jump at conclusions."

"Jump at conclusions! Good God, John—with all that evidence you couldn't call this case, 'jumpin' at conclusions'!"

"No? Well, let's kind of run over the facts. In the first place, where in hell would a chechako git forty thousan' dollars to cache?"

Downey looked astounded. "Are you drunk, er crazy?"

"Nope," grinned the other, "an' if I was, I wouldn't incriminate myself by admittin' it."

"Why—he got it out of the D-Y robbery, of course! His own confession shows that. It detailed the crime exactly. He had the manager's watch in his possession. An' he tallied to a hair with the manager's description of the robber, blue bandana an' all. An' it's a double murder, now. The manager died the day before I got back to Dawson."

"Too bad. The damn skunk that done it ort to be hung."

"Hung! Hell, he's dead!"

"Dead, eh?"

Downey scowled; then grinned. "I don't know what you're stringin' me along fer, John. But if he ain't dead he damn well ort to be. I sawed his head in two goin' after that bullet."

"Oh—you mean that fella! So you figger he's the one that done it, eh?"

"Hell—no!" Downey exploded in wrathful irony. "It couldn't have be'n him; I've jest got through provin' to you why it couldn't! He never robbed anyone! He is not even dead! That shot he fired at himself in Olson's old shack missed him a mile! An' that hand-saw I used never even gave him a headache! I closed the case jest because I like to see a murderer have a good time! He's right now down in Cuter Malone's celebratin'!"

"Well," grinned Black John, "you got that part right, anyhow— even if yer argument ain't quite logical."

Downey subjected the big man to several moments of search-ing scrutiny. Then he shrugged. "I quit," he said, with an air of resignation. "Out with it! You've got somethin' on yer chest. Spill it!"

"YOU CLAIM you've got this case closed. There ain't no law agin reopenin' it, is there?"

"Of course not! I thought it was closed—all but the recovery of them twenty-five hundred ounces."

"We kin fergit about them ounces. This here's a murder case. Them ounces is incidental an' trivial. Now when you close a case, you still keep yer file of the evidence, don't you? Like the note the fella had in his pocket, an' his wallet with them stained bills in it, an' the gun, an' the bullet you dug out of his head?"

"Yes, that's all right here." The officer stepped to a cabinet, returned with a packet done up in heavy brown paper, and untied the string.

Black John tossed a crumpled piece of paper onto the desk. "See anything peculiar about that?" he asked.

Downey scrutinized the paper for a moment, then extracted the suicide note from the packet, and placed it beside the other. "It's the same handwritin'," he said.

"That's right. An' not only that, the word 'cartridge' is spelt 'caterige' in each one."

"The murderer wrote 'em both, all right. But what's that got to do with the case? This is prob'ly a list of supplies he'd made out to git the first time he went up to Cush's."

"Yeah, that's the way I figger it—the murderer wrote 'em both. An' the only thing it's got to do with the case is that the list of supplies was wrote about ten days ago."

"What!" cried Downey, half-rising from his chair, his eyes on the other's face.

"Yeah. There's a couple of more things, too, that sort of casts a doubt on yer deductions. Fer instance, the fellow that wrote it is packin' around a few ten-dollar bills that's stained jest like them bills in the wallet, there. I seen 'em when he pulled 'em out up to Cush's. That sort of ties him in with Olson's old shack and the dead man you say was a suicide. On top of that, he's packin' a revolver—an' he's a damn good shot with it. Did you git the bullets that killed the D-Y packer an' the manager?"

Downey shook his head. "No. The packer was shot through the heart, an' the bullet went on through him. The doctors didn't dare to operate on the manager to remove the bullet from his head. An' by the time I got back here I thought I had the case cleared up anyway. So I never give no thought to the bullet."

"Kind of slip-shod, ain't you—fer an up an' comin' young

policeman?" grinned the big man.

Downey shrugged. "Go ahead—rub it in. I've got it comin'. It sure looks like I fell down hard on this case."

"I was only kiddin'," Black John hastened to say. "Hell, anyone else would of thought the same thing. If ever a case looked like it was all sewed up in the bag, this one did. But—kin you git that bullet?"

"Sure I can! I'll get in touch with the doctors, an' get permission from the manager's widow to open the grave. I'll have the bullet within a few hours."

"Okay. I'll be down to the Tivoli tryin' to teach Bettles, an' Swiftwater Bill an' Moosehide Charlie some of the rudiments of stud."

Slipping into the Klondike Palace to make sure that Hayne was still there, Black John proceeded to the Tivoli and was soon deep in a stud game from which Corporal Downey summoned him shortly after midnight.

"I've got the bullet," the officer said, as they reached the sidewalk.

"A thirty-two, ain't it?"

"Yes."

"All right. The gun you found in Olson's shack was a thirty-eight. Yer man's down to the Klondike Palace. He's got the gun on him that killed that manager. You better go git him. An' watch yer step—he's a good shot. Now mind you, Downey, I would do nothin', one way nor another, to help the police, but we don't want no sech bird on Halfaday as this Dan Hayne!"

VI

THE ARREST WAS made without incident, and the man locked in a cell. He made a complete confession the following morning when confronted by the evidence which included the stained bills, and the easily demonstrated fact that the manager had been killed by a bullet fired from the revolver he had in his possession at the time of his arrest. He told of witnessing the hold-up on Front Street, and of slipping the robber the word that the police were looking for him, and of advising him to skip to Halfaday Creek.

Noting that the man was about his own size and build, he procured a blue bandana with white dots, and slipping out the next day, pulled the D-Y job, then fled with the dust to Halfaday, to find that the man, Lewis, had not arrived there yet.

Drawing a name from the can, he learned of Whiskey Bill's abandoned shack and moved in. Then he watched the lower creek and when Lewis arrived, a few days later, he steered him into Olson's old shack.

The man told him he had been delayed by heading up Ladue Creek until he met an Indian who set him right.

Hayne said he watched his chance and shot the man with his own gun, holding it close against his head to make sure of leaving powder marks. Then he carefully wiped the gun and pressed the man's hand upon the butt—his finger upon the trigger. He then wrote the suicide note, left the manager's watch in Lewis's pocket, robbed him of all but twenty dollars of the fruits of the Front Street robbery, leaving two tens in the wallet, so no robbery would be suspected. Then he returned to Whiskey Bill's claim, confident that he had cleared himself of all suspicion.

HE SAID that the twenty-five hundred ounces of dust was cached near Whiskey Bill's shack, and drew a detailed map of the location of the cache.

The following morning, accompanied by Black John, Corporal Downey set out for Halfaday.

Proceeding directly to Whiskey Bill's claim, they located the cache without difficulty. It was empty?

Downey eyed Black John sternly. "You would have made a wonderful policeman, John—except for one thing. Whenever a corporation happens to be the victim of a robbery—you are never able to locate the loot!"

Black John grinned broadly. "Oh, hell, Downey—don't let that worry you none! Cripes—you're a damn good policeman! An' I kin rec'lect quite a few times, like this one here, when you ain't be'n able to locate the loot, neither."

FOR SOME LITTLE
SACKS OF GOLD

I

A PARTNERSHIP DISSOLVES

YOUNG STEVE BLAINE pouched his share of the day's clean-up and added a figure to a long list of figures in a little black notebook.

"Not so bad," he approved. "This brings it up to four hundred an' fifty-two ounces—a little better than thirty-one hundred dollars apiece."

Across the table Sam Buckley snorted contemptuously, causing the candle flame to flare smokily and send wavering shadows playing about the interior of the little pole shack. "Thirty-one hundred for five months of the hardest work I ever put in my life! Five months living like a damn Siwash—chopping and hauling wood, tending fires, cranking a windlass, shoveling mucky gravel! They're paying an ounce a day for labor around Dawson. Any damn bum that was sucker enough to work, could have earned twenty-four hundred in the same length of time—and you say it's not so bad because we've made a lousy seven hundred dollars more than wages."

Steve's gray-blue eyes narrowed slightly at the sneering words. "If you knew more about prospectin'," he said curtly, "you'd realize that anything better than wages is not so bad for a new proposition on a new crick. We haven't got down into the good stuff, yet."

The other flushed angrily. "I know all I want to know about prospecting—and it's a damn sight more than I wish I knew. And I'm good and tired of listening to that bunk about not being down into the good stuff—and what we'll strike on bedrock. To hell with bedrock! To hell with prospecting! And to hell with you! I'm through! I'm pulling out for Dawson in the morning. Now that the crick's open I can make it in the canoe."

"Quittin'?"

"Yes—quitting! What of it?"

Steve shrugged. "Nothin'. I think you're a damn fool, that's all. What you goin' to do in Dawson?"

"Do! Play stud—throw monte—roll the ivories! There'll be plenty of easy pickings this spring in the big camp, with a flood of chechakos boiling into the country on the break-up. Hell— give me a month's time among 'em, and I'll make the sixty-two hundred we've rooted out of the gravel look like chicken feed."

"Thirty-one hundred," reminded Steve. "Only half of it's yours."

"One of the claims is mine. I'll take the dust, and you keep the claims. You'll get a good bargain, at that—you say there's so damn much more in the gravel than we've taken out."

Steve grinned. "Yeah? Don't play me for a chechako, Sam. Remember, I was born north of sixty."

"What do you mean—chechako! Ain't that claim of mine worth thirty-one hundred?"

"Maybe. Fact it, I believe someone'll take a hell of a lot more than that out of it. But I ain't buyin' claims—that's all."

"Ain't buyin'?"

"Why should I? The law says a man can locate another claim on the same creek sixty days after he has recorded a claim. I recorded Discovery, an' filed you on No. 1 Below, because you grubstaked me for the trip. When I get to Dawson, I'm going to locate No. 1 Above for myself. I'd be a sucker to pay you thirty-one hundred for a claim when I can get one just as good for the recording fee."

Buckley glared. "What the hell will I do with my claim, then?"

Steve shrugged. "Work it. Sell it. Abandon it—"

"Yes—and let you file on it!"

"Maybe," grinned Steve, "when the year's up. There wouldn't be anything to prevent me. Tell you what I'll do—write out an assignment, an' I'll give you a hundred dollars for the claim—not a cent more."

"Like hell I will! I'll sell it in Dawson!"

Steve laughed. "Try it. Who's goin' to pay out good dust for a claim on a crick that ain't even on any map?"

"Give me the hundred," growled the man, as he scribbled an assignment and tossed it onto the table.

"That's a hell of a way for a man to use his pardner!" he added, as he slipped the dust from the scales into his pouch.

Steve laughed shortly. "And a hell of a pardner you've be'n! It was your own proposition—this partnership. I didn't want any of it. I saw that I'd do most of the work—an' believe me, I haven't be'n disappointed! Why—you can't even go out an' kill meat without gettin' lost!"

"I grubstaked you when you were broke," retorted the other. "Hadn't been for me, you'd never found this crick."

"Yeah," agreed Steve bitterly, "an' why was I broke? Because I got a little tight down in Dawson an' run up aginst you in a card game. Old Bettles, an' Camillo Bill, an' Moosehide Charlie, an' all the rest of the sourdoughs was out in the hills, so when you offered to grubstake me, I took you up. Any one of the old timers would have let me have all I wanted, but I didn't want to hang around the camp like a bum till some of 'em showed up. I'd had my spree, an' I was anxious to get out into the back country. That grubstake didn't cost you much. You've be'n well paid."

"Well paid workin' like a nigger fer a lousy thirty-one hundred in dust!" interrupted Buckley. "Hell—I could make more than that in one night, if the cards were running right! I've got better'n twenty thousan' in Cuter Malone's safe, right now."

"Yeah—an' you'd see that the cards ran right! Yer nothin' but a tin horn gambler, Buckley—an' a damn crooked one. As fer workin' like a nigger—there ain't be'n a day since you've be'n out here that you've done a man's share of the work!"

"Whose fault was it I stayed out in this damn hole all winter? Ten or fifteen days of it was enough for me! If I thought I could have made it back to Dawson alone, I'd have hit out when winter clamped down on us. I've told you a hundred times to take me out!"

"An' I told you I was too busy," grinned Steve. "I offered to let you have the dogs any time you wanted 'em."

"The dogs! I can't even hitch 'em up, an' I couldn't handle 'em if they were hitched. They hate me—an' you know it. The damn wolves! They'd eat me up on the trail, or else run away an' leave me to starve or freeze to death in the snow! Why didn't you go with me? You could have come right back. Ten days is all you'd have lost. I even offered to pay you for your time."

THE BLUE-GRAY eyes hardened between the narrowed lids. "I'll tell you why, Buckley. It was because I was havin' too much fun seein' you suffer—seein' you tryin' to do the only real man's work you ever tackled, an' fallin' down on the job! Makin' you stick out here where you didn't want to be for five long months. Remember that pot where you hooked me for my pile—sixteen hundred dollars, it was—an' you took your time, skinnin' your cards over careful—stringin' me on. I'm no gambler, Buckley, an' I suffered while that pot was bein' played—five minutes, it prob'ly took, five minutes that you gloated while I suffered. You've paid for that five minutes; paid with damn good interest, Buckley—five months for five minutes. Put that in your pipe and smoke it!"

Buckley was on his feet, white with rage. A hand flew to his armpit and the yellow candle light glinted on the blue black barrel of a six-gun. A sharp crack sounded, and another, as Buckley's finger worked the trigger.

Across the table Steve Blaine laughed sneeringly as Buckley sank trembling onto his bench. "Better stick to chechakos, Buckley. The sourdoughs'll outguess you. I moved your coat, one day after we'd be'n up here about a week, an' that holster was under it. I figured you'd be damn fool enough to try to use the gun some time, so I drew the powder out of the shells an' filled 'em with flour, an' reloaded the gun. Then I found part of a box of shells in your war bag, an' done the same with them. You ought to thank me, Buckley. I saved you from committin' a murder."

II

ON FRENCH CREEK

OLD JIM ADAMS looked up from his sluice box as a shadow fell athwart his shoulder. "Hello, Stevie!" he greeted. "How's things over on Deep Crick?"

To the sourdoughs Steve Blaine was always "Stevie," or "Young Steve" to distinguish him from his father, "Old Steve," who had been killed two years before in a slide on Forty Mile.

"Hello, Jim! Everything's fine an' dandy. I busted down into the real stuff, yesterday. Old gravel—plumb heavy with coarse gold."

"How far down?"

"Ten foot. There's a lot of seepage. I'm headin' fer Dawson to get me a pump."

"Goin' it alone?"

"Yeah. Buckley quit a couple of weeks ago. Figured he could make Dawson in the canoe without gettin' lost."

Old Jim grinned. "Pulled out on you, eh? Well, if it was me,

I wouldn't be mournin' his loss none. Each one of them three times you an' him come acrost here to French Crick durin' the winter, he got me off to one side whilst you was talkin' to Sally, an' offered to pay me to take him to Dawson. Claimed he didn't dast to tackle it alone in winter. But I laid off. I figgered you had some reason fer keepin' him there, er you'd of took him down yerself. But what a man would want a pardner like him fer is more'n I can figger."

"It wasn't that I wanted him fer a pardner. He grubstaked me, an' when I made the strike he wanted to go partnership. I knew he was a gambler, but hell, I've known gamblers that were square, an' damn good men, so I took him on. But it wasn't a week before I found out what he was—just a crooked tin horn that bragged how he rooked the chechakos. When I found out how he hated the work, I kep' him at it to pay him back fer the trimmin' he gave me when he took me for my roll."

"He sure got a bellyful," grinned Adams. "You be'n up to the shack?"

"No, crossed the ridge below here."

The older man's grin broadened. "Sally, she'll prob'ly light into you. We went to Dawson early, an' when we was comin' back we met Buckley below the forks comin' down. It was evenin', an' we camped—an' believe me, he spilt us an earful. He's a good talker, Buckley is, an' if a man didn't know him, he might be convincin'. Accordin' to him, you worked hell out of him all winter, an' then beat him out of his claim to boot. Come on up an' we'll see what Sally's got fer dinner."

SALLY ADAMS, at the age of nine losing her mother by a plague of smallpox that swept the country, had for the succeeding ten years shared the vicissitudes of the Northland with her father, the redoubtable old Jim Adams in a hundred stampedes that had carried them half across Alaska and the Canadian Yukon. In vain had old Jim tried to persuade her to remain at some school or mission. Once, when she was ten years old, he asserted his authority and placed her under charge of the missionaries at Fort Yukon while he joined the Koyukuk stampede. Fifteen days later, driving five stolen dogs, and an outfit she had pledged his word for at Rampart, she overtook him at Coldfoot, three hundred miles within the Arctic Circle. The sourdoughs remember that the day she arrived at the new camp it was fifty below. After that Old Jim gave it up, and her name became a byword for trail mushing in the high North. How she acquired an education was a mystery even to Old Jim, himself a man of no mean schooling. But acquire one, she did—an education that included not only the three R's, but more than a smattering of the classics, and a dozen Indian dialects for good measure.

SALLY TURNED from the stove and slipped an extra plate onto the oilcloth covered table as the two appeared in the doorway. "Hello, Stevie! I've been wondering when you'd show up. How's the slave driver?"

"Fine," smiled Steve, uncomfortably conscious that his heart had stepped up a few beats under the level gaze of the liquid brown eyes.

"Oh, I wouldn't grin about keeping a man prisoner for five months. Don't you know that a man like Sam Buckley isn't used to hard work?"

"He ain't yet," laughed Steve. "He never done none."

"He told us you beat him out of his claim—after he'd grubstaked you," persisted the girl.

For the first time Steve realized that there was no answering smile on the full red lips, and that there was a disapproving frown on the brow beneath the high piled mass of raven hair. The smile died from his own lips. "He lied," he said shortly. "I bought his claim."

"For how much?" taunted the girl.

"For a hundred dollars in dust. An' I hope I take out a million. The way things look now, I might. Did he bother to tell you how come he grubstaked me?"

"Because you were broke. Because you got drunk and blew in your dust on the dance hall girls in the Klondike Palace—and especially on one girl."

"Did Buckley tell you that?" interrupted Steve, in a dry, hard voice.

"No, he didn't. Not in so many words. But I gathered it from what he did say—little things he let slip. But—you needn't think I care! It was your dust. You had a right to spend it where you wanted to."

Behind the girl's back Old Jim winked and, with obvious effort, suppressed a grin. But there was no mirth in Steve Blaine's heart. That the girl had believed Sam Buckley's insinuations about the dance hall girls, and had sided with him, struck Steve with the force of a blow. He had loved Sally Adams for two years—ever since he had first known her on Forty Mile. Since he had located on Deep Creek, eight months before, he had come to look upon her as his own. Between them they had worn a well defined trail across the rough twenty miles that separated Steve's shack on Deep Creek and the Adams claim on French. And on the crest of a high ridge, midway between was the "post-office stump," a hollow wind-fallen spruce that had served as the repository for numerous letters of inconsequential detail, but of vast import to both.

STEVE BROKE the long moment of silence that followed the girl's words. "I guess you didn't gather nothin' that Buckley didn't want you to," he said bitterly. "I mistrusted somethin' was wrong when I come by the post-office stump an' found it empty. I'm talkin' now—an' see what you can gather from this. Sam Buckley's a damn liar, an' you're a fool to believe him! Not only I never had anything to do with any dance hall girl in the Klondike Palace, but I don't even know any of 'em by sight. The gettin' drunk part I ain't denyin'. I did get drunk an' set in a game with Buckley in the Palace, an' he trimmed me good an' proper. It served me right fer playin' with a crooked tin horn. Next mornin' I was ready to hit fer the hills, but was broke, an' there wasn't a sourdough in Dawson. Buckley come along, an' offered to grubstake me fer a trip, an' I took him up. I've spoke my piece. You can take it, or leave it."

The girl turned away. "Dinner's ready," she said. "You better eat it before it gets cold."

"I ain't hungry," answered Steve, and turning abruptly on his heel, he disappeared rapidly down the creek.

III

DOMINION DAY

SPRING SLIPPED RAPIDLY into summer. Alone on Deep Creek Steve Blaine worked as he had never worked before, and as never before was his work rewarded. And as the yellow gold piled up in his cache, the weeds and the wild flowers and the bakneesh vines obliterated the trail to French Creek.

In Dawson things were lively. To the thousands of chechakos who had swarmed down the Yukon, was added a goodly sprinkling of sourdoughs in from the hills. Canadians and Americans were foregathering in the big camp for the double celebration of Dominion Day and the Fourth of July. From the First till after the Fourth, high carnival would wage, and the saloons and the dance halls would reap a golden harvest.

Far and wide word of the big Dominion Day dance had penetrated the wilderness—by poling boat, by canoe, by moccasin telegraph. And lone miners on far creeks threw down their shovels, laboriously shaved before dim little mirrors by the light of wavering candles, donned their best, and forsook the high hills for the bright lights of Dawson.

Young Steve Blaine stood in the doorway of the Tivoli and with jaundiced eye, watched the crowds surge past toward the big open air pavilion that had been erected on a vacant lot at not too great a distance from the saloons.

All day long the valley of the Yukon had sweltered under a broiling sun. Even now, with the long shadows tempering the heated air, women in low necks and short sleeves were walking the street carrying only the lightest of wraps on their arms.

Steve scowled as his eyes swept the faces of the passing throng—holiday faces all. Eyes bright, lips smiling—faces bent on fun. Men in blacked boots and clean new overalls, men in moccasins and overalls not so new or clean, men in dress suits with silk socks showing above the tops of buckle trimmed pumps, men in cotton shirts, flannel shirts, and men in sweaters mingled on the sidewalks with women in flaming squaw cloth, women in calico prints, women in Yarmouth druggets, and women in silk finery purchased at The Mode, a new emporium.

"Hello, Stevie! Ain't you goin' to the dance?"

From his elevation of two steps, Steve looked down into the bearded face of Old Jim Adams smiling up at him from the sidewalk. The man had paused, and at his side, a woman had paused also, a hand resting on Old Jim's arm. Steve's eyes strayed to the bare, finely rounded arms, and beautifully turned shoulders of the woman who had stooped to make some trivial adjustment of the hem of her silk skirt. A gay old dog, Jim Adams, when he was on the loose, thought Steve, as an answering grin twisted the corners of his lips. Well, with his dust he could afford the pick of the camp, and—again Steve's eyes dwelt on luscious curves of bare arms and shoulders and back—it looked like he'd got it. And Sally, who didn't like the big camps, was probably back in the cabin on French Creek in flannel shirt and trousers, reading a book in the last light of the gloaming. Steve wondered whether this girl's face could possibly be as beautiful as it should be—with arms and shoulders like those. Then, suddenly she straightened and liquid brown eyes were gazing up into his own.

"Sally!" Involuntarily the name leaped to his lips, from which the smile had vanished.

Something—the startled tone, the instant disapproval that registered in the blue-gray eyes that looked down into her own, brought a taunting smile to the red lips. "How do you like it, Stevie—my new gown?" she asked.

"You look like hell!" blurted out Steve viciously. "Like—like one of them!" His arm raised, and his pointing finger indicated a group of demi-mondaines who, in tawdry finery, were proceeding noisily toward the pavilion.

"Thank you," she answered sweetly. "I thought you'd like it."

A tug at the arm of Old Jim, and she was gone—swallowed up in the throng that was crowding toward the huge dancing platform.

STEVE BLAINE stepped into the Tivoli, walked to the bar and ordered a drink. The saloon was all but deserted, most of the patrons having gone to the dance. Steve emptied his glass at a gulp, and refilled it from the bottle that stood before him on the bar. Again he refilled it and again. Curley, the proprietor, a friend of the sourdoughs, noted the procedure out of the tail of his eye. Casually he sauntered along and paused facing the younger man across the bar. "Why, hello, Stevie! Ain't you goin' to the dance?"

"No," answered Steve shortly, and poured another drink.

Curley, with all the sourdoughs, liked Young Steve. He knew that, with everyone else in Dawson hilariously gay, it was not so good for Stevie to be standing there drinking moodily and copiously—alone. He strove, by light banter, to rouse him out of his mood. "Someone steal yer best gal?" he grinned.

Steve ignored the question. Without even raising his eyes, he traced patterns in some slopped liquor with the bottom of his glass.

Curley gave it up, and passed on.

Sally. Sally Adams. Rigged out like a dance hall girl! Old Jim ort to have his neck broke for lettin' her do it. What was

Jim thinkin' of, anyhow? But—maybe Sally wouldn't listen to him. Steve remembered the story of the Koyukuk stampede. Sally was hard to handle. She done as she damn pleased, an' to hell with 'em! By God, Sally could out-mush, an' out-shoot, an' out-paddle any damn sourdough in the North! An' she could Siwash through a country that would starve a wolf. He bet she could out-dance any of 'em, too.

Steve poured and downed another drink. She might be dancin' right now with Sam Buckley. Sam, the damn crooked tin horn, with his smooth, lyin' tongue. Sam better not open his head to him, or he'd get it knocked clean off his neck.

Steve suddenly remembered that he was some dancer himself. He used to whoop 'er up pretty good, back in Forty Mile. Bet she would be dancin' with Sam Buckley. Rigged herself all up so Sam would pick her to dance with. He poured another drink, slopping liquor liberally upon the mahogany. A bartender mopped it up and Steve regarded him with owlish gravity. He swallowed the liquor, and tossed a well filled pouch onto the bar. "I didn't keep track of 'em," he uttered thickly. "Maybe a dozen or so. Take what you want. By God, I'm goin' to the dance!"

Determinedly, if a trifle unsteadily, Steve left the saloon and headed for the pavilion. "If Shally's dancin' with Sam Buckley," he muttered aloud, "I'll knock her head off—his head off," he corrected. "An' see how she likes that."

Suddenly, a thought struck him and he paused to ponder it. People jostled him passing to and fro on the sidewalk, and he couldn't think straight. With a frown of annoyance he cast about for a quiet spot in which to ponder his problem. Several chairs placed invitingly just beyond the inner edge of the walk caught his eye, and making his way to them he sat down in one heavily.

"Hey, there!" growled a voice in his ear. "Them chairs is fer players."

"What kind of players?" asked Steve, eyeing the other empty chairs. The man, who lolled against a rude counter upon which stood several baskets of cheap baseballs and an open box of cigars, pointed down the narrow alley between two buildings. Squinting his eyes, Steve made out a row of grotesque objects ranged before a white sheet that blocked off the end of the alley. "Knock down a nigger baby, an' git a seegar. Three ball fer half a dollar. One baby; one seegar."

"A man can't throw worth a damn settin' down," opined Steve, gravely.

"Hell—you stand up to throw. The chairs is fer them that's waitin' their turn."

Steve rose and tossed a silver dollar on the counter. Selecting six balls he proceeded to heave three of them down the alley. Two hit the sheet high above the row of babies, and the other ricochetted from the wall of one of the buildings and rolled along the ground. Then he seated himself in the chair.

"You got three more," grinned the man. "Maybe you'll have better luck next time."

"I'm settin' here till, it's my turn again," retorted Steve. "An' if you don't shut up an' leave me think, you won't have no luck at all. I'll knock one of yer nigger babys' head off, an' see how you like it."

The man grinned, and sauntered off to retrieve the three balls, leaving Steve in silent contemplation of his problem. "Shally made me mad, an' I'm goin' to make her damn good an' mad," he muttered. "If I bust Sam one in the head, she might not get so mad at me as she would feel sorry fer Sam—an' that would be worse'n ever. She might take his head in her lap an' get her new dress all bloody. Back there on the crick, that day, it seemed like it wasn't so much what I done to Sam made her mad, as thinkin' I was blowin' my dust on them Klondike Palace girls. If that made her mad, she's goin' to get damn good an' mad. They're all over to the dance, an' I'm goin' to dance with the whole kaboodle of 'em, an' blow my dust on 'em, too—a whole damn sackful! I'll get 'em all soused, an' I'll take 'em all down to The Mode an' buy 'em a new dress, jest like Shally's—

an' see how she likes that!"

Abruptly he rose from his chair just as the proprietor of the nigger baby game returned with the balls.

"Yer turn come 'round agin?" grinned the man.

Steve glanced from the grinning face to the three baseballs in his hands, and then to the line of grotesque nigger babies. "They're too damn little," he said. "You can't hit 'em." And as the man stared wide-eyed, he drew back his arm and hurled the balls. One after the other, they sailed high above the heads of the pedestrians on the sidewalks, and squarely into the middle of the raised dancing pavilion, nearly half a block down the street. A chorus of loud, angry cries reached Steve's ears, and he grinned happily as the strident music wavered and the dancers surged from the floor. Solemnly he reached over and took three cigars from the box, and crowding them into his pocket, tossed another silver dollar onto the counter. "That's for good measure," he chuckled. "It sounds like I made a good score." And the next moment he had merged with the crowd.

BUYING A handful of tickets, Steve ascended the steps to the platform just as order was being restored and the orchestra was striking up a new tune. Sure enough—just as he had anticipated, Sally Adams whirled past, dancing with Sam Buckley! Catching his eye as she floated past, her lips curved into that taunting smile.

With set lips and gritted teeth, Steve slipped his arm about the waist of one of the most notorious demireps of Dawson, and whirled her out onto the floor. From that moment on it was one dance after another with the girls from the Palace, the Tivoli, the Antlers, and between dances he invited them in droves to drink at the Klondike Palace bar. Not once did he dance with Sally Adams. In fact, with the exception of that one glance he had caught of her flashing past in the arms of Sam Buckley, Steve couldn't remember seeing Sally Adams at the dance.

Early next morning, sick and disgusted, with his head throbbing unmercifully, he turned his back on the flesh pots of Dawson and struck out for Deep Creek. Toward noon he crawled into the shelter of a spruce thicket and slept for hours. In the evening he pushed on toward the little pole cabin nestling in the shadows of the high hills.

IV

OLD BETTLES GETS AWAY WITH A BLUFF

ON THE AFTERNOON of the Fourth, three days after the Dominion Day dance, Sam Buckley swaggered up to the bar of the notorious Klondike Palace, and passed a slip of paper to the proprietor.

Glancing at the slip, Cuter Malone rolled his fat cigar to the opposite corner of his mouth and favored the gambler with a thick lipped grin. "Drawin' out all yer dust, eh? What you aimin' to do—pull yer freight?"

"Listen," said Buckley, stepping closer and resting his elbows on the bar, "there's a big game on over at the Tivoli—a damn big game. It's been running for two days, and I've been watching it, off and on. There's a killing there—for a man that knows his stuff."

"Yeah," agreed Cuter dryly. "An' a killin', sure as hell, fer one that don't know his stuff. Who's settin' in?"

"They come an' go. Lay off to eat and sleep a while, then go at it again. When I left a few minutes ago there was Moosehide Charlie, Camillo Bill, Stoell, Burr MacShane, Swiftwater Bill, and Ace-in-the-hole Brent. With most of the sourdoughs in the Yukon looking on. Stoell is the only professional gambler in the game."

"Yeah, an' he plays 'em square."

"Maybe," admitted Buckley. "If he does, he's a damn fool. Hell—none of those others are professionals."

Cuter Malone shrugged his thick shoulders. "Mebbe not—but they've played a hell of a lot of poker."

"I'm taking a chance," retorted Buckley. "A man ain't necessarily so damn smart just because he's a sourdough. It would be a crime to pass up that heavy dust."

Cuter stepped to the safe and returned with numerous heavy little sacks which he passed across the bar. He watched Buckley stow them into his pockets. "Good-by, dust," he said lugubriously. "I got a hunch you ain't comin' back."

Buckley smiled. "Well—when I came back from Deep Crick and started in on the suckers, I had less than twenty-four thousand. It's thirty-six thousand now, and by this time tomorrow it'll be better than a hundred thousand. It's the big play I've be'n waiting for. I knew it would come, sometime. Don't worry about me, Cuter. I know my stuff. No one yet has ever been able to call my play—to come right out and say I'm not on the up-and-up."

"That's right," admitted the burly proprietor. "An' that's why I'm advisin' you to stick to drunks an' chechakos. Them sourdoughs is a different breed of cats."

AN HOUR later, in the Tivoli, Ace-in-the-hole Brent rose from the stud table, cashed in twenty-odd thousand dollars worth of chips and markers at the bar, and Sam Buckley slipped into his vacated chair, and ranged several goodly stacks of chips before him.

A supercharged atmosphere permeated the room—a tenseness manifested in the grim silence of the spectators that rimmed the table, and in the expressionless faces of the players who sat with hat brims drawn low over their eyes to protect them from the glare of the acetylene lamp that threw a bright light onto the green table. One or two of the players nodded curtly at Buckley; the others, apparently, unaware of his presence, studied their exposed cards, and made their bets in short clipped monosyllables, accompanied by the soft rattle of chips.

Glancing up while waiting for a new deal, Buckley encountered the eyes of Old Bettles, dean of the sourdoughs. The leathern faced old hero of a hundred anecdotes and ten thousand miles of trail mushing, stood with one foot on a rung of Moosehide Charlie's chair, which was the next chair on Buckley's right. The rheumy old eyes that regarded the gambler were diamond bright, and slightly bulging the front of his checked shirt, just above the waistline of his trousers Buckley could trace the outline of a six-gun. A tough old hombre, Old Bettles. Tough, and square, and—hard. Buckley dropped his eyes, pulled down his hat brim, and shifted a bit uneasily in his chair. Then a pot was raked in, someone gathered the cards, riffled them expertly, dealt—and Buckley's attention riveted upon his hole card.

Half a dozen times during the next hour Buckley glanced up to find the keen, smoke-gray eyes of Old Bettles upon him. They reminded him of an eagle's eyes, as Old Bettles' face with its thin hooked nose, reminded him of an eagle's—an eagle watching with never tiring vigilance for the chance to swoop down upon his prey.

Be it here stated to Buckley's credit, or discredit, according to the point of view, that he was an artist in deft manipulation of the cards. And being an artist, he was imbued with an artist's arrogant confidence in his own ability. Nevertheless, that persisting presence behind Moosehide Charlie's chair began to wear upon his nerves.

Cautiously, steadily, Buckley was winning—not too often on his own deal. He fidgeted uneasily, and glanced up more often—always to meet for a fleeting instant the steady stare of the smoky unwinking eyes—always to drop his own to the checked shirt front with its ominous bulge. God, was the old man going to stand there forever? Wouldn't he even shift so much as a hand or a foot? Buckley's attention wavered from the cards and he turned down a hand that might well have won a considerable pot.

Across the table, Burr MacShane withdrew from the game leaving an empty chair. Nobody claimed the seat. The game was too steep for any but the most seasoned. Buckley estimated the chips stacked before him at nearly thirty thousand. He had bought ten thousand to start with. Why didn't Old Bettles take Burr MacShane's seat? He was a big money player—to hear some of the yarns that floated around the camps, he was the best of 'em all. Best of 'em all! Well, what if he was? What did that mean when it was all said and done? Best of a lot of damn amateurs! What did the old fool expect to see—standing there staring by the hour?

It was Buckley's deal. He picked up the deck—riffled the cards. He'd show him something! He'd set up a hand right under the old fool's nose—and he'd never be any the wiser. Moosehide cut the deck, and deftly Buckley flirted off the hole cards and the first round of faced cards. Bets were made, and again he dealt. Pairs showed in one hand on the second exposed deal, and in two others on the third. On the next deal Swiftwater Bill bet three tens, and was raised by Buckley, whose hand showed a pair of fives and a king. Two others trailed, and Swiftwater raised. So did Buckley. One man dropped, the other met the raise. Again Swiftwater raised, and Buckley and the other called. Buckley dealt. Swiftwater caught a seven, and Buckley another king. The odd man, who failed to help an exposed pair of aces, dropped out on the third raise, and Swiftwater called a bet of ten thousand. Buckley flipped over his third king, and Swiftwater turned a seven. Buckley raked in the chips, and glanced up at Old Bettles. Was there a gleam of triumph in the rheumy old eyes? Hell—no! The hand is quicker than the eye—if it's the right man's hand.

Camillo Bill was gathering the cards for the next deal. Again Buckley glanced up. Old Bettles was gone. A moment later, the old man slipped into Burr MacShane's chair and was stacking chips before him in high, regular columns. Must have bought twenty-five thousand, thought Buckley, staring across at the array of chips. He aims to play 'em high.

Hour after hour the game progressed with varying fortune for most. Buckley consistently won. Then he dealt for a killing. It became evident on the second round that the deal would hold plenty of action. Bets and raises followed each other in quick, tense succession, with all players staying. And so on the next round, and the next. When the final card was dealt one player showed four hearts, another two pairs, and three others showed threes—Buckley, three kings, Stoell three eights, and Bettles three jacks. Buckley bet, and on his left Camillo Bill raised him five thousand on his four exposed hearts. Stoell folded his three eights, and Bettles raised ten thousand. Moosehide folded, and Buckley raised Bettles ten thousand. Camillo studied his four hearts for what seemed to the tensely staring onlookers like an eternity. Then he folded them and tossed the hand into the discards. Bettles raised another ten thousand, and grinning, Buckley counted in all his chips, then reached into his pockets and emptied them of dust. "I'm betting my pile, Bettles," he said. "The chips figure twenty-two thousand, and here's twenty-six in the sacks. Do you want it weighed?"

Old Bettles fixed his eyes on Buckley's three kings, and allowed them to rove over the chips and the little gold sacks heaped in the center of the table, and come to rest on the three jacks spread out before him.

"You mean, yer broke? You don't stand to play no more than that?" he asked.

Buckley's grin broadened. "I can't play any more than that, because I haven't got it. But I ain't broke, Bettles. At least, I won't be when you call."

"Ain't you got no more in Cuter Malone's safe? Is that all you've took off the chechakos. We could hold up the game till you send fer it. I've got a good hand, here, Buckley. I'd sure like a run fer my money. You couldn't hardly expect to make a king-full stand up every time, Buckley."

"I wish to God I had more in Cuter's safe, Bettles—or

somewhere else. But there's every damn cent I'm worth, right there. You going to call it? Or are you just stalling to kill time?"

"Oh, I'll call," answered Old Bettles, fumbling at his chips. "Let's see, what we be'n playin' these yaller ones at? Oh, yeah—a thousan'. Well, there you be—but they ain't only seventeen thousan', eight hundred in my stack. You said what, Buckley? Oh, yeah—twenty-two thousan' in chips, an' twenty-six in dust, didn't you Buckley? That's thirty-eight thousan'—no, twenty an' twenty's forty—forty-eight thousan' I've got to put in, ain't it? My marker's good fer the balance, Buckley? That'll be—let's see—it'll be—"

"Twenty-eight thousand, two hundred!" supplied Buckley in a tense, nervous voice. "Sure, your marker's good. And for cripes sake, get it in there! You're—you're holding up the game!"

Bettles fumbled in his pocket and produced the stub of a pencil and a bit of paper. "They ain't no hurry," he said. "That's the trouble with you young fellas—always in a hurry. Give a man time. What d'you say that was, agin?"

"Twenty-eight thousand, two hundred," snapped Buckley, as the old man bent forward and laboriously wrote on the slip with his stub of a pencil.

"There you be," he said, holding the result of his labor to his eyes. "Yeah, that's right. Taint no fancy writin', but Curley kin read it—he's read a lot of 'em, off an' on."

AS HE rattled on the bright old eyes once again focused on Buckley's as his fingers held the slip of paper above the pot.

Buckley's glance dropped involuntarily to the bulge that showed the outline of a six-gun just above the edge of the table, and as he did so the fingers of Bettles' other hand casually loosened two buttons on the front of his shirt!

Buckley felt himself grow suddenly weak. Could it be possible that Bettles had got onto his trick? Why had he stood there for two hours behind Moosehide's chair—staring with those unwinking eyes? Why had he suddenly decided to take a hand in the game, just after he, Buckley, had dealt that other set-up hand. Suddenly into Buckley's brain flashed the words of Steve Blaine—"better stick to chechakos, Buckley. The sour-doughs will out-guess you." Had Old Bettles out-guessed him? And then the same words of advice from Cuter Malone—"stick to drunks an' chechakos.... Them sourdoughs is a different breed of cats." And he remembered the sneering grin with which Cuter had said "an' a killin' sure as hell fer a man that don't know his stuff." Had the continued scrutiny caused his hand to lose its cunning, so that it betrayed him at the crucial moment—with the eagle eyes of Old Bettles upon him? The color receded from Buckley's face, leaving it ashy gray. His fascinated gaze remained fixed upon that bulge in the front of the checked shirt, and upon the hand that lingered close about the two loosened buttons. Buckley's hair roots prickled in an agony of terror. He could feel the hot, tearing stab of a bullet plowing through his lungs. And if Bettles should miss, there were the others—sour-doughs all—waiting to finish the job.

The slip of paper that was Old Bettles' marker fluttered from his fingers and dropped into the pot. For an instant Buckley saw it lying there on top of the pile of chips and the little sacks of dust—his dust—the dust that Cuter Malone had prophesied would never go back in his safe. Then the fingers that had held the paper flew swiftly to the hole card lying face downward in front of Old Bettles. They flipped it over—and again the voice of Bettles sounded across the table. A voice that sounded like the garrulous prattle of a senile old man—yet, somehow, seemed fraught with deadly menace:

"Four jacks! They're good, ain't they, Buckley? It ain't in the cards, Buckley, fer a king-full to stand up every time."

Sudden understanding flashed into Sam Buckley's brain. Old Bettles was giving him a break! He was cleaned, right down to his hide; but the old man was giving him a chance to get off with his life! He moistened his dry lips with his tongue.

"They're good," he repeated, in a voice that sounded in his

own ears like the voice of another—miles away. Mechanically his fingers gathered his exposed cards, turned them face down on top of the unexposed hole card, and slipped the hand into the pile of discards that were the abandoned hands of the other players. Then, abruptly, he got up from the table and passed swiftly from the room.

Old Bettles raked in the pot, tore up his marker, and began to stow gold sacks in his pocket. "Well," he asked, testily, "who's deal is it? What the hell's the delay? We won't never git no stud played at this rate."

The delay was that the other sourdoughs were sorting out the discarded hands which they had faced upward upon the table. Each man knew to a card what he had thrown away. When the hands were restored, five cards remained on the table face up in the glare of the acetylene lamp—Buckley's hand—four kings, and the nine of hearts!

The eyes of the sourdoughs sought the face of Old Bettles in silent query.

"Sure," chuckled the oldster. "I know'd he had 'em—the damn tin horn! I stud there back of Moosehide's chair an' watched him till I damn near dried up an' blow'd away fer the lack of a drink. Then I set in. An' I got him."

"What was his game, Bettles?" asked Stoell, the gambler. "How did he work it?"

AGAIN OLD Bettles chuckled. "Damn if I know. He's a slick one, all right. I watched him a good two hours, an' I couldn't find out how he done it. But you see he didn't know I didn't git onto his game. He thought I did!"

"My Gawd!" cried Moosehide, staring wide-eyed at the cards. "Bluffed him out *after the call!* It's the damndest play I ever heard tell of!"

Camillo Bill grinned across at Bettles who was still chuckling behind a mountain of chips. "But if you wasn't onto his game, what would you of done if he'd turned up his hole card?"

"Why—I'd of give him the pot, of course! Cripes—that's all they'd of be'n to do! I figgered he wouldn't turn it up though. Them tin horns ain't got no guts."

V

SAM BUCKLEY MAKES A DEAL

SAM BUCKLEY STEPPED hurriedly from the door of the Tivoli and headed directly for his shack, a one-room shanty near the edge of camp. Closing the door behind him, he lighted the oil bracket lamp, and glanced at his watch. It was nearly midnight. There was, he knew, a steamboat tied up at the wharf that was due to pull out for downriver points at daylight—and daylight was not far off. His sole and only thought was to put miles between himself and the sourdoughs of Dawson. If Old Bettles should reveal the trick by means of which he had won their dust they'd kill him sure, just as Cuter Malone had said. They might even call a miners' meeting and hang him—for the good of the camp! Hurriedly, he threw his belongings into the duffel bag that had served him on Deep Creek. Fastening the straps, he threw back a floor board and withdrew from a recess a flat wallet, and opening it, he counted the bills. Yes, they were all there—the five hundred dollars in currency that he had sagaciously cached for just such emergency. Get-away money, laid by in case the vicissitudes of his calling should demand hurried flight from Dawson.

Thrusting the wallet into his pocket, he picked up his duffel bag, blew out the light, and by a devious course reached the wharf and took passage for Eagle, that being a camp located on the American side of the International Boundary line.

Cowering in his tiny stateroom he leveled a pistol at the door each time footsteps sounded from the passage. Daylight grayed the small square of his window and it was with a sigh of vast relief that, at the end of what seemed an interminable period of loud-bawled orders the throbbing of the engines told him that the vessel was under way.

At Eagle, he secured a job tending bar, the previous incumbent having joined a stampede to the headwaters of Birch Creek. Buckley felt reasonably secure in Eagle. Such of the sourdoughs as might be interested in his whereabouts, were happily located at Dawson, and there was little travel from that point downriver.

His duties were not arduous, for Eagle was a dead camp, and the pickings in occasional poker games added but little to his modest salary.

He had been two months on the job when one day the door opened, a man stepped into the room and crossed to the bar. Buckley's casual glance froze to a stare of horror as he recognized Moosehide Charlie, then instantly dropped to the six-gun that lay at hand beneath the bar. Then the man was greeting him, and there seemed nothing homicidal in either the tone or the words.

"Hello, Buckley! What the hell you doin' here?"

"Working," answered Buckley, a grin of relief widening his lips. "Tending bar. Have one on the house!"

When the drinks were poured, Moosehide cast his eyes about the place. "This is a hell of a camp—always was. Shouldn't think it would pay a man to hang around here. Leastwise, not one that was pretty good with the cards."

So it was coming, then. Moosehide's good natured greeting had been assumed to cover his real purpose. Once again Buckley's glance rested on the six-gun, as he answered, "There's no play here to speak of. No one's got any dust."

"Not like Dawson," agreed Moosehide with a grin. "A man can git plenty of action there. You ort to know. Remember that game Fourth of July when Old Bettles cleaned you?"

"I ain't apt to forget it," replied Buckley. Why did Moosehide refer to that game? And why was he grinning?

"Gawd, that bluff he put over on you was the best I ever seen!

No one but Bettles could of got away with it."

"Bluff?" said Buckley dryly. "You saw him turn the fourth jack."

"Yeah," retorted Moosehide, his grin widening. "An' when you'd went out we turned over your cards. Four kings, an' the nine of hearts, Buckley—an' you turned 'em down, jest as Old Bettles figgered you would."

Buckley's lips moved mechanically. "Why," he asked, "did he figure I'd turn 'em down?"

"'Cause he figgered you'd figger he'd got onto your tricks whilst he was watchin' you from behind my chair. An' he figgered you'd turn 'em down ruther'n have him call the turn on you an' then kill you. 'Course, we all know'd you was crooked, Buckley—but long as we couldn't ketch you at it we couldn't do nothin'. Bettles didn't ketch you, neither. He tried damn hard, but you was too slick fer him."

"Do you mean to say—?"

"Yeah—I mean to say that if you'd guts enough to of turned up that king you had in the hole, you'd of raked in that pot; an' Bettles, nor no one else would of had a damn word to say to the contrary. Yer good with the cards, Buckley—but yer damn short on guts. That bluff's be'n the joke of the camp fer two months! Le's have another drink. The boat'll be pullin' out fer upriver pretty quick. I be'n down to Fort Yukon to see my brother. He's in the horspital there."

Buckley waved aside the gold sack Moosehide tossed onto the bar. "The drinks are on me," he said. "And, by God, my hat's off to Old Bettles! You can tell him I said so. Do you mean that—that if I showed up in Dawson, the sourdoughs wouldn't—er—I mean—they don't hold any—grudge?"

"Hell, no! They all know yer crooked—but they don't hold that agin you when they can't prove it. They'd prob'ly kid hell out of you, an' most likely they wouldn't set in no game with you no more. But you don't belong with the sourdoughs, nohow.

You ort to stick to chechakos."

"I guess you're right, at that," admitted Buckley. "Hold on, if you're going down to the boat. I'm pulling out on her, too. A man could be dead a year in this camp, an' never know the difference."

DESPITE THE assurance of Mooshide Charlie that the sourdoughs bore him no grudge, Buckley cut a wide circle when the boat tied up at Dawson. Tossing his duffel bag into his shack, he proceeded to the Klondike Palace by a circuitous route.

The scene, as he opened the door, was a familiar one. Bright lights flooded the interior. Chechakos lined the long bar, or played cards at the various tables. Other chechakos crowded the roulette wheel and the faro layout in the rear of the big room, and through the wide arch leading to the dance hall blared the incessant jangle of the tinny piano. Welcome contrast to the monotonous evenings of the dead little saloon at Eagle.

Buckley's glance took no note of the chechakos. Probably none of them would recognize him, anyway—and what difference if they did? Chechakos came and went; no one took them seriously. As he had anticipated, no sourdoughs were present. They rarely invaded the Palace, having small liking for the rococo dump.

In his accustomed place at the end of the bar Cuter Malone, the inevitable fat cigar protruding at an angle from the corner of his mouth and big yellow diamond flashing from the center of his flaming tie, surveyed activities with heavy-jowled complacency. Spotting Buckley before was half across the floor, the proprietor clamped his cigar between his teeth and greeted the gambler with a loose-lipped grin.

"Hello, Buckley," he greeted when the other paused before him. "Where the hell you be'n—off somewheres blowin' in the dust you took off'n them sourdoughs?"

"Never mind the kidding, Cuter," replied the other. "Let's go where we can talk."

Malone indicated a small door near the end of the bar, and as Buckley passed through, he followed, pausing to secure a couple of glasses, and a bottle of private stock which, he took from a tiny cupboard beneath the back bar.

"Well," he said, setting the bottle and glasses upon the table in the little back room, "you raised hell, didn't you? I told you you better stick to chechakos."

"Sure—I know," answered Buckley, slipping into a chair, and pouring himself a drink.

"You was good enough so they couldn't git onto yer deal—an' even then you couldn't beat 'em," persisted Malone. "I told you them sourdoughs was a different breed of cats."

"You did," admitted Buckley. "There's no argument. I'd have been better off to have listened to you."

"The way they tell it, Old Bettles spent the hull afternoon buildin' up that play."

"He did. He'd never have got away with it if he hadn't."

"Sourdough brains, an' sourdough guts to back 'em! All the tricks in the book can't beat that combination, Buckley. You was a damn fool to try." The man seated himself opposite and tossed off a drink. "Where you be'n?" he asked abruptly.

"Eagle. I lammed out that night, figuring Old Bettles had it on me. I didn't know till yesterday when Moosehide told me, that it was all a bluff. When I learned they weren't gunning for me I came back."

"What would a man do fer two months in Eagle?"

"I tended bar for Crump, and played a little stud for twenty-five cent chips."

"What you goin' to do now?"

"Why—go back to work. It looks like there's plenty of chechakos. You'll have to stake me for a while."

"How much you got?"

"About four hundred. I've got a little coming from Crump, but I didn't bother to get it. He wasn't there when the boat pulled out, so I locked the dump up, and came away."

"Fork it over," said Cuter, "an' then we'll talk about stakin'."

"What do you mean?"

"What I mean is that when you draw'd out yer dust fer to git into that game with, I was thinkin' about what a sucker you was to tackle them sourdoughs, an' I plumb fergot to look up yer bar tab. I run acrost it after you'd gone. Four-forty, it amounts to. If four hundred's all you got, I'll knock off the forty—ten per cent fer cash, as the feller says."

Buckley watched Malone fold the bills and put them in his pocket. "How about a stake?" he asked. "I've got to have some working capital. Say, two or three thousand."

"What security you got?"

"Why—none! Except that I'll be right here in the house—"

"Yeah—soakin' up my heat an' light! What the hell does that git me?"

"I'll pay you ten per cent on what you loan me. Hell, I'm not going to skip out!"

"You done so onct," reminded Cuter. "I felt like hell about that four-forty."

"You got it back, didn't you?"

"Part of it," admitted Cuter. "But if I was to hand you over two, three thousan' in dust I'd worry like hell, less'n I had good security. Tell you what I'll do—I'll loan it to you on yer claim. But I got to git fifteen per cent instead of ten."

"What claim? I haven't got any claim."

"Why, the one that Young Steve Blaine filed fer you on Deep Crick. You took thirty-one hundred out of it, last winter, didn't you?"

"Sure—but I sold the claim. When I quit up there I sold the claim to Steve for a hundred dollars. That's all he'd pay for it."

"Did you sign it over?"

"Sure. Prospectin' is too damn hard work to suit me, and as Steve said, who'd buy a claim on a crick that isn't even on any map?"

"What's maps got to do with it? Besides, if it ain't on no map, now, it damn soon will be:"

"What do you mean?"

"Young Steve come down this spring an' bought him a pump, an' filed on the next claim above the one he had. Then he come down agin fer the Dominion Day doin's an' he flung dust a-plenty. Guess he tipped off some of the sourdoughs 'cause, after the Fourth, a bunch of 'em went up an' filed the rest of the crick, which it ain't only a short one where it kin be worked."

"That's right," corroborated Buckley. "You couldn't get more than ten or a dozen claims on the crick."

"Yeah—an' they're all took."

"You mean—Steve made a real strike. And the sourdoughs are up there working the other claims?"

"Maybe one or two is. Most of 'em that filed has got goin' propositions on other cricks. They aim to clean them up first—except jest to work out their assessments on Deep Crick. But there ain't no doubt about Young Steve makin' a real strike. He busted into some old gravel that's lousy with coarse gold. An' he's shovelin' it out till hell won't have it! It sure looks like there's a jinx on you, Buckley—what with sellin' out a million dollar proposition fer a hundred—an' then not havin' guts enough to turn over that fourth king."

BUCKLEY COMPLETELY lost control of himself, and for the space of minutes, he cursed in wild, senseless rage. He cursed Steve Blaine, the cards, and Bettles, and all the sourdoughs. He cursed his luck, Malone, the Yukon, and all subtending terri-tory—but most of all he cursed Steve Blaine. When the spasm was over, he poured another drink and swallowed it at a gulp. Then he looked across at Malone. "You've got to stake me, Cuter," he said. "Hell, I've got to have dust to play on. I'll pay you fifteen per cent—twenty, if I have to. I tell you you've got to stake me!"

"I ain't got to do nothin'—but die," retorted that worthy. "An' you couldn't expect a man to stake no one with a jinx like yourn. Why don't you go git it off'n Young Steve? He's got plenty."

"Young Steve!" cried Buckley. "He hates my guts!"

"Well?" Malone was leaning back regarding the man with a grin.

"He wouldn't loan me a dollar at a hundred per cent interest if I was starving."

"There was a lot of express companies an' banks didn't loan Jesse James no money, neither. But he got it offen 'em jest the same."

"You mean—?" The man paused, and regarded the other, wide-eyed.

"I didn't mean nothin'," Cuter said with a shrug of his thick shoulders. "I ain't no accessory before no fact—nor neither after none."

Buckley shook his head. "Robbery isn't my game, Cuter. I probably couldn't get away with it. But if you won't stake me to the dust, I'll tell you what you can do—it'll be easier, and a hell of a lot safer than robbery. You give me a receipt for a good sized deposit of dust in your safe—something I can flash on Old Jim Adams and his girl, so they'll think I've got plenty. I'll stick it in my pocket and go up to French Crick and make a play for the girl. You've seen her—she was the best looking dame at the Dominion Day dance, by all odds. I wouldn't mind marrying her, and once I get her—well, you know Old Jim's got plenty."

"Yeah," admitted Cuter. "But you ain't Old Jim. An' marryin' his gal don't make you him, neither."

"Hell—that girl can have anything Old Jim's got."

"Mebbe."

"Then you'll give me the receipt? It won't cost you a damn cent—and it'll be safe."

"Safe fer who? Where the hell would I git off at if you was

to show up an' demand the dust that receipt called fer?"

"God—you don't think I'd doublecross you, do you?"

"Nope. I know damn well you won't."

"It's like this—all I want the receipt for is to show 'em I've got plenty. Quick as I get the girl, I'll tear the receipt up, and claim I lost the dust in a game. It wouldn't cost you a cent. You want to remember that the girl is Old Jim's only heir. He's lived quite a while. Something might happen to him most any time."

"What would I git out of it? How much would you figger the receipt ort to call fer?"

"Oh, forty or fifty thousand—it wouldn't matter, so long as it'll never be cashed. Might as well make it good and strong. Of course, I'd be glad to pay you for the use of the receipt, just as soon as I get the girl."

"Yeah," grinned Cuter. "An' if you don't git the gal, you sell the receipt to someone an' he comes an' presents it fer payment— an' where in hell am I at? It's a safe game from your slant, Buckley. But it ain't a-goin' to work—an' there's plenty reasons why it ain't. In the first place, I ain't goin' to give you no receipt. In the second place, Old Jim Adams wouldn't let no gal of his'n marry no tin horn gambler, like you. You couldn't fool him with no receipt. He knows Bettles cleaned you out, jest like all the other sourdoughs know it. An' in the third place, the gal wouldn't marry you nohow. From what I hear Young Steve Blaine's got the inside track with her."

"Not since the Dominion Day dance, he hasn't!" Buckley retorted. "When Steve got drunk and started swinging the dance hall girls high, wide, and handsome, she got so damn mad she quit the dance. And not only that, she hit out for French Crick, and wouldn't stay for the rest of the doings."

Cuter's grin was a sneer. "You better stick to the cards, an' leave women out of it, Buckley. It don't take no hell of a lot of thinkin' back to remember that Young Steve didn't show up none after the dance, neither. I s'pose you figger that she went on up to French Crick, an' him to Deep Crick, do you? Well—mebbe. Le'me tell you somethin' about women—they'll raise hell with a man if they like him, jest to git the chance to patch it up."

Buckley returned the sneer as his glance rested momentarily upon his own tailored clothing. "What the hell would a girl like her see in a damn boob like Steve Blaine?"

"She'd see a sourdough, Buckley," growled Malone, "an' not no damn tin horn. A man rigged out like a damn dude would have to mud up to go courtin' her."

THERE WAS a long silence, during which Buckley poured and swallowed another drink. "If I go up to Deep Crick, will you alibi me, Cuter?" he asked, leaning forward tensely. "Damn Steve Blaine! He's got it coming!"

"W-e-l-l." The man drawled out the word with frowning brow. "This here accessory business is damn risky. If some hitch come, I might find myself in a hell of a jam. But I'm always willin' to do a friend a good turn. Now this here alibi—I'd have to have a little commission—say, about twenty-five per cent. An' believe me—when you tap Young Steve's cache, you're goin' to get plenty. He don't bank his dust here in Dawson like most of 'em does. He caches it. Acccordin' to the talk, he's be'n takin' out at least twenty ounces a day fer the last four months. That's around twenty-four hundred ounces—a hundred an' fifty pound—damn clost to forty thousan' dollars."

"That's more than a man can carry."

"It ain't more'n a canoe kin carry. Or a man could cache part of it, an' go back after it when the excitement died down. You see, I know pretty clost to what's in his cache—so it wouldn't pay you to try to hold out on me. A hell of a fix you'd be in if I was to fergit about that alibi. I might even tip off Corporal Downey, er some of the police, if I don't git a square break on this. The play wouldn't hurt me none at that. I don't stand none too good with 'em."

VI

BUCKLEY GETS HIS STAKE

VERY EARLY THE following morning Sam Buckley, packsack on his back, slipped out of Dawson and struck up the Klondike on foot. A poor canoeman, at best, he had no wish to buck the current of the Klondike to the mouth of French Creek, which, he knew, together with its tributary, Deep Creek, would be unnavigable even for a canoe at this time of year. Another reason for eschewing water travel was the extreme likelihood of recognition by the occupants of Dawson-bound craft. On the foot trail that paralleled the river one could, by the exercise of caution, avoid embarrassing meetings by slipping into the bush. The success of the venture depended upon his ability to reach Deep Creek and return to Dawson unseen. This accomplished, Cuter Malone and his trusted minions could be depended upon to furnish an unshakable alibi to account for the ten or twelve days during which he would be absent from Dawson.

Buckley made good time, and on the evening of the fifth day he peered over the rim into the little valley of Deep Creek at a point just opposite the little pole and mud cabin in which he had wintered with Steve Blaine. There was the cabin, nestled snugly against the rock wall at the edge of a thicket of spruce. Buckley frowned and cursed softly under his breath as each familiar landmark brought vivid memory of those hated five months of toil and boredom. A cold, drizzling rain had been falling since noon and Buckley was wet to the skin, having forgotten to include a slicker in his outfit. He shivered as he drew the sodden collar of his coat closer about his neck. No smoke rose from the stovepipe that protruded from the dirt roof, and no light showed from the little window that overlooked the creek, though the gathering gloom would have rendered the interior of the cabin dark.

For a long time Buckley squatted among the rim rocks, his

eyes searching the floor of the valley for sign of life. Where the devil was Steve? He should either be sloshing about the shaft or the sluice box in gum boots and slicker, or he should be in the cabin on a day like this. With every branch and twig dripping cold rainwater it was no day for hunting, nor for the chopping of wood.

Gathering darkness and the sheer discomfort of squatting there in the rain decided Buckley's course. The little remaining daylight must be utilized in making the descent of the steep valley wall. If Steve was away, all well and good. He could locate and rifle the cache and maybe be back in Dawson before the theft was discovered. Buckley, however, found himself frowning at the idea. His hatred for the man who had virtually held him prisoner for five long months had flamed into a consuming rage upon learning that the claim the other had bought for a hundred dollars was, in all probability, worth a fortune. He regarded the deal as a robbery rather than a business proposition, and he had worked himself into a frame of mind where the murder of Steve Blaine assumed the aspect of a simple act of justice.

Revenge—that's what he wanted—revenge, that only the complete blotting out of Steve Blaine could satisfy. Grimly the man fingered the pistol in his armpit holster, and the leather padded slug-shot that Cuter Malone had left lying conveniently to hand on the table in the little back room. Cuter had, with apparent irrelevance, explained that, properly wielded such instrument could crush a skull noiselessly, and without leaving a mark. The advantage of silence was to be considered if other prospectors were on the creek.

From his position Buckley had not been able to pick up any sign of other workings though there might be several such, either above or below, as he had circled the rim rather than chance meeting anyone in the narrow valley.

RISING, HE made his way to a foot trail, hardly better than a cat climb, that he and Steve had used on various excursions after meat, and after a precarious twenty minutes on the slippery rocks in the uncertain light, found himself on the floor of the valley.

Crossing to the cabin he paused before the door and stared about him. Even in the half darkness that had settled upon the valley, the place had a strangely untenanted appearance. Withered birch leaves had drifted against the door, and lay in undisturbed heaps upon the path to the shaft. Following this path to the dump a few yards distant, Buckley noted that the sluice box was half filled with leaves, and that a thick coating of leaves lay upon the bottom of the shaft. Retracing his steps, he pushed open the door, and, striking a match, he held the flame to the wick of a candle thrust into the neck of a bottle that stood on the table. A pile of chopped wood with kindlings and birchbark was ranged against the wall, and it was but the work of a moment to build a fire in the stove. As the heat permeated the damp, chill air, Buckley surveyed the interior of the cabin. Here also appearances bespoke desertion. Dust lay thick upon the table top and the benches that served as chairs, and tiny sparks of glowing dust shot upward from the surface of the stove, beginning to show dull red in spots as the dry spruce roared in the firebox. A red and black checked mackinaw that he instantly recognized as Steve's hung from a wall peg, and a pair of pacs evidently worn but little, lay at the foot of the bunk. Steve's rabbit robe was spread upon the bunk, but a pair of heavy blankets that Buckley remembered was missing, as was Steve's packsack, and a compact stampeding outfit of cooking and eating utensils.

"Gone somewhere," the man muttered aloud. "Looks as though he'd been away a month or more. What's the answer? If he was doing as well as Cuter Malone claimed he was, what the devil did he pull out for? And where did he go?"

FINDING NO suggestion of an answer, he pulled off his wet coat, hung it up, and crossing to another bunk, once his own, now serving evidently as a catch-all for odds and ends of gear and clothing, selected underwear, shirt, and socks, and proceeded to strip himself of his own soaked garments.

"Good thing Steve and I are about of a size," he grinned. "Even his pacs fit me," he added as he laced the new pacs and regarded them approvingly. "First time I've been comfortable today. And now for a good feed."

With water aboil, a can of beans heating, and salt pork sizzling in the pan, he crossed to Steve's bunk, threw back the rabbitrobe, and clawing away the mattress of spruce boughs, peered into the narrow orifice formed by a section of hollow log ranged along the inside of the bunk.

"Changed his cache," he muttered, regarding the empty cavity. "Of course he wouldn't leave any heavy dust laying around the cabin. But where the hell is he? And where did he cache that forty thousand in dust that Cuter credited him with having? It sure won't be any forty thousand—he hasn't been working for a month or more."

DOG TIRED from the unaccustomed work of the trail, Buckley blew out the candle and retired as soon as he had finished supper. It was broad daylight when he awoke, and, after a hurried breakfast, he began a systematic and thorough search of the premises.

But though he searched until dark, no trace of a cache could he find.

"I might hunt a month, or a year and never find it," he muttered disconsolately, as he ate his solitary supper by the light of the guttered candle. "Steve's no damn fool. He might have cached the stuff a mile away. No use hunting any more. I'll hit back in the morning. By God, Cuter's got to stake me!"

His own clothing was still damp the following morning, so, crowding it into his packsack, he struck off down the creek, wearing Steve's. He didn't bother to climb to the rim on the return journey. His sole thought was to get back to Dawson and sell Malone the idea of staking him.

As he was cutting across a flat bend, a mile or so below the cabin, a shout reached his ears, and he whirled to see, across the narrow valley, almost against the opposite ridge, a man waving his hat. Words hurled across the intervening quarter of a mile by powerful lungs reached his ears:

"Hey, Steve! When d'ye git back?"

Buckley waved his own hat in return. "Yesterday," he shouted at the top of his voice. "See you later!" And, hurrying on, he plunged into the spruce and birch growth that lined the banks of the creek.

"This red and black coat of Steve's—everybody in the country knows it. I'll have to ditch it before I get to Dawson. I'd hate to be pinched for stealing a coat."

HE CAMPED that night on Deep Creek, just above ifs confluence with French Creek, and in the morning struck off down the larger stream. Toward noon, as he rounded a bend in the creek, his attention was attracted by a thin plume of smoke that rose from a copse close beside the creek at the next bend. Slipping into the scrub, he approached the smoke, the sodden ground, and litter of dead leaves and needles rendering his progress noiseless. From the distance of a few yards, he made out the figure of a solitary camper, evidently in the act of eating his midday meal. Further scrutiny gave a glimpse of the man's face.

"Old Jim Adams," breathed Buckley. "Hell—I don't want him to see me!" The gambler's muscles suddenly tensed, and his eyes narrowed as a sudden thought struck him. If not Steve Blaine—why not Old Jim? It was the old prospector's custom, he knew, to journey to Dawson every couple of months to foregather with his cronies, the sourdoughs, in the Tivoli, for a few days of good right and left handed drinking.

As a brazen excuse for these sprees, Old Jim was wont to carry several heavy little sacks for deposit in the Tivoli safe. The justification fooled no one, least of all Sally Adams, for whose benefit the fiction had been established, and who always gravely accepted it at its face value. She loved her daddy—did Sally Adams. And she understood his whys and wherefores.

It was of these little sacks that Sam Buckley was now thinking. Old Jim had a mighty good proposition on French Creek. He would be packing not less than a thousand ounces. A thousand ounces was sixteen thousand dollars on the scales in Dawson—with four thousand for Cuter for his alibi, that would leave twelve thousand—a good stake to go after the chechakos with. And—Buckley's eyes lit with a sudden gleam—Steve Blaine would get credit for the job! Hadn't the prospector on Deep Creek called Steve by name, and seen him hurrying down the creek yesterday—just in time to arrive here for the job? Even if Steve should be some place where he could establish an alibi, no one could suspect him, Buckley. Cuter Malone would attend to that. Cuter hated all sourdoughs because they avoided his place and spent their dust in the Tivoli and The Antlers. He would as lief alibi him for knocking off Jim Adams as Steve Blaine. The damned crook would alibi a man for knocking off his best friend for four thousand dollars.

SWIFTLY AND silently, Buckley circled the bend, and took up a position behind a tall rock fragment that reared close against the trail where Adams must pass within arm's reach. With his handkerchief he masked his face to the eyes, and slug-shot in hand awaited his victim.

Minutes passed, tense nervous minutes, during which Buckley suffered spasms of fear. What if his foot should slip? What if he should miss the man's head? Old Jim was a powerfully built man and strong as a bull, despite his sixty-odd years. Buckley shuddered at thought of his bones breaking and the breath being squeezed from his body in the grip of those powerful arms. Maybe he had better pass up Old Jim, after all. But suppose Cuter should persist in his refusal to stake him? What then?

And on sober thought Buckley believed that Cuter would refuse, would turn him down as he had turned him down on the receipt proposition. Cuter only risked money on a sure thing. Buckley knew that his roulette wheel was crooked, and that his faro dealer dealt the cards from a double-slotted box. No, Cuter wouldn't stake him. He had to go through with it! It was his only chance. Life was like that—made up of quick decisions and quick action. The man smiled, grimly—funny thing, life. Here a few days ago he was figuring on winning Old Jim's daughter for a wife, and now he was going to kill him. And Old Jim had no inkling of either. Cuter Malone was the deciding factor in the destiny of the old sourdough—Cuter Malone would be Old Jim's real murderer. If he had written out that receipt to show Sally, things would have been all right. It was through no fault of his own, argued Buckley, that he had to resort to murder rather than matrimony to acquire a stake—it was Cuter's fault.

FOOTSTEPS SOUNDED on the trail. Grasping his slug-shot, Buckley clenched his teeth and poised, every nerve in his body taut and tense as a pointer's.

Down came the slug-shot with a dull jarring thud. Old Jim grunted, staggered forward, and dropped to his knees. He turned as in a daze:

"Stevie!" he muttered thickly, and again, "Stevie!"

Buckley rushed upon the kneeling man and struck again. This time the massive form crumpled into a heap and lay very still. Working feverishly, Buckley tore into the man's pack and removed twelve little sacks of dust which he transferred to his own pack. Then he glanced down at the inert form at his feet. What should he do? Leave the body on the trail? Adams was a big man—upwards of two hundred pounds. It would be a job to get rid of him. But what if someone should come along? As he stood in a panic of indecision, the old man heaved a low, choking sigh. Buckley started nervously and raised the slug-shot.

He wasn't dead—he must finish him off! Then another thought flashed into his brain. Adams had recognized him as Steve Blaine! If he should live, he would openly accuse Steve—and with the corroborative evidence of the man on Deep Creek, Steve could never beat the rap!

On the instant, Buckley turned and fled. He hoped Old Jim would live! Maybe he wasn't hurt so bad. Felt hats are stiff—good padding—maybe he would come to. He was coming to, or he wouldn't have sighed! Jerking the handkerchief from his face, Buckley ran on for a piece. Then he turned from the trail, and in the niche of the valley he discarded Steve's clothing and drew on his own damp garments, tossing Steve's among the rocks.

He felt tired and weak from excitement and the packsack was heavy, but fighting off fatigue, he avoided the trail and headed down the creek for Dawson.

VII

IN MALONE'S BACK ROOM

IN THE LITTLE back room in the Klondike Palace, Cuter Malone accepted his cut of twenty-five percent, along with Buckley's story of the robbery of Old Jim Adams.

"It would of paid you better," he growled, "to waited till Young Steve come back to his claim. You'd got a damn sight more'n these here nine hundred an' sixty ounces that Old Jim had on him."

"Maybe," admitted Buckley, "but I wasn't going to stick out there in the hills till God knows when. I couldn't stay in the cabin, and have him walk in on me. I'd have had to Siwash it—and the nights are getting cold. This way it's safe. Old Jim will claim it was Steve that robbed him, and that lone prospector on Deep Crick will swear he saw Steve headed down the crick the day before. And with the alibi you've ribbed up, no one in the world will suspect me."

"It ain't so bad," admitted Malone. "I was jest sayin' it could of be'n a hell of a lot better. Yer sure Old Jim'll think it was Steve?"

"Dead sure. Hell—he couldn't think anything else! I had on Steve's coat—and there isn't another one like it in the Yukon. He couldn't see my face, and he called Steve's name twice, looking right at me, before I clouted him out. Wait and see. Old Jim won't lose much time getting down here with the story. I didn't hurt him very bad."

And in that prophecy Buckley was right. That very evening Malone heard the story in a dozen versions across the Palace bar. In only one particular were all narrators in accord. It was Steve Blaine who had robbed Old Jim. Speculation was rife as to why Young Steve had committed this act. Men recalled that Steve was drunk at the Dominion Day dance. But that was two months ago—a man couldn't pack liquor enough to stay drunk for two months! Sally Adams had turned him down, and he had robbed Old Jim to get even. His claims on Deep Creek had petered out, and he robbed the old man and skipped out with what he could get.

Corporal Downey came in, looked the crowd over, and inquired for Steve Blaine. Malone obtained curt corroboration of the story from him. Later he drifted over to the Tivoli, and, mixing unobtrusively among the grave-faced sourdoughs, he heard it from the lips of Old Jim himself. Unlike the blatant chechakos, neither Old Jim nor the sourdoughs offered explanation. It was just a thing that a man like Young Steve wouldn't do; but he'd up an' done it. No man doubted Old Jim's word.

"Corporal Downey's in charge of detachment now," said Camillo Bill. "Downey's smart. The chances is, the police'll git him."

"Here's a hundred ounces says they won't!" offered Old Bettles. "Stevie was borned in the hills."

CUTER MALONE suppressed a grin. Here was a set-up—a

sure thing bet, the kind of a bet upon which a man of Malone's stripe liked to lay his money. Of course the police would pick Steve up! Knowing nothing of the robbery, he would return to his cabin and walk right into their hands. Or should he hear of it, the first thing he'd do would be to hit for Dawson to clear himself of the charge. In either event, the police would pick him up.

Camillo Bill covered the hundred, and Malone challenged Old Bettles. "You ain't got no more dust that says the police won't pick him up?"

Bettles eyed the burly proprietor of the Klondike Palace with disfavor. "Why sure, Cuter. Five hundred ounces of dust. Er, mebbe that's more'n you'd care to lay down on anything that wasn't a frame-up."

"It's a hefty bet all right," admitted Cuter. "Yer feelin' kind of flush since you cleaned Buckley out, eh? I'll take it. It's more'n I've got on me. I'll have to go to the safe." The man stepped out, and ten minutes later he reappeared and tossed some heavy little sacks onto the bar. "There she is, Bettles. An' this is one bet you can't win with no bluff."

"That's right," grinned the oldster. "But we got to set a time limit. What I claim, if they don't collar him in a month, they never will. An' I don't aim to tie up no five hundred ounces indefinite."

"Give 'em till Chris'mas," argued Malone. "If they ain't picked him up by then, you can shove that dust in yer pocket an' call it a Chris'mas present from me."

"Chris'mas she is then," agreed Bettles. "I'll hang my sock right there over the bar, an' I'll be down here bright an' early Chris'mas mornin'."

"They'll have Young Steve locked up long before that," grinned Malone. "But jest so you won't be disappointed, Bettles, I'm orderin' Santy Claus to shove a fat quart of good licker down that sock. I'll pay fer it out of yer five hundred ounces—when they bring Steve in."

LATER, AS Malone made his way back to the Palace, a grin of satisfaction hovered behind his heavy black mustache. "Buckley done a good job," he muttered. "Old Jim Adams believes it was Steve that robbed him, an' the rest of the sourdoughs believes old Jim—an' they're a damn hard bunch to fool."

Suddenly Malone stopped dead in his tracks as an idea born of his own muttered words flashed into his brain. Good God— what if Buckley hadn't fooled Old Jim! The thick lips clamped hard as the thought expanded. Adams must have been sure that it was Steve who robbed him, or he'd never have accused him. Maybe it was Steve! Maybe Sally Adams had turned Steve down, and he'd taken it out on the old man! Then Buckley knocked Steve off, buried his body, and re-cached all the gold in Steve's cache, and come on into Dawson with Old Jim's dust, and the story of robbing the old man on the trail. That way he'd bought his alibi cheap. He had come across with the two hundred and forty ounces—twenty-five percent of Old Jim's dust—and he was holding out all the dust in Young Steve's cache—and from what folks said that would be plenty! And—with Young Steve dead and planted somewhere, the police could never pick him up, and Bettles would collect the five hundred ounces! He, Cuter Malone, stood to lose two hundred and sixty ounces of dust! Buckley had played him for a sucker!

Thought of the loss sickened the avaricious Malone. The more he thought of it, the more convinced he became that Buckley had doublecrossed him. His story about Steve's being away from his shack wasn't so good, come to think about it. What would a man with three good claims on a crick be doin' somewheres else? He'd be right on his claims shovelin' gravel— that's where he'd be! An' Buckley had a good forty thousan' dollars of Steve's dust cached away—an' left him, Cuter Malone, holdin' the bag! The pig-like eyes glittered beneath their fat lids.

"Alibi!" The word rasped from between clenched teeth. "I'll alibi him!" The next moment he was hurrying toward the Klondike Palace.

A hurried glance about the big room showed Buckley seated with four chechakos at a stud table. Passing around behind the bar, Malone opened the safe and scanned the record of deposits and withdrawals of dust. There was Buckley's deposit—seven hundred ounces. He had retained twenty ounces for working capital out of the seven hundred and twenty he had left after paying Cuter two hundred and forty ounces of the nine hundred and sixty he had taken from Old Jim Adams. There was the entry—and there was the gold. Cuter's eyes lingered for a moment on the nine new moosehide sacks ranged on top of a row of similar sacks in the big safe. That was the Buckley gold—he remembered that the little sacks Buckley had tossed onto the table in the little back room had been new sacks.

Returning the book to its place, Cuter closed the safe and, the fat fingers of one hand closing about the Derringer in his side pants pocket, he strolled over to the stud table and waited till the conclusion of a deal. Catching Buckley's eye, he motioned with a jerk of the head toward the door of the little back room.

"Want to see you a minute," he spat out the words in the side-mouthed delivery of the professional bartender.

"Anything important?" countered Buckley frowning.

"Plenty important," retorted Malone as he turned away.

"Deal me out," Buckley said tersely and, pausing at the bar to cash the chips, he followed the proprietor into the little back room.

Malone closed and locked the door and, standing with his back against it, eyed the gambler who turned to face him. "Where's Steve Blaine?" he asked abruptly. "Er—what I mean—where's his dust?"

Buckley stared in surprise. "Why, I told you I don't know where Steve is! I couldn't locate his dust."

"Yeah, that's what you told me. You damn doublecrosser! Come clean!"

"What do you mean?" A note of fear blended with the

surprise in the gambler's voice as he stared into the narrowed glittering eyes.

"I mean it was a damn slick story you thought out, about you robbin' Old Jim Adams, an' him thinkin' it was Steve Blaine done it! You might of got by with it an' held out all Steve's dust on me, if I hadn't went over to the Tivoli an' got the story first hand off'n Old Jim hisself—"

"Good God!" cried Buckley, his eyes wide. "Don't Old Jim think it was Steve that robbed him?"

"Think!" rasped Cuter. "He knows damn well it was Steve! Listen—Old Jim didn't hit straight fer Dawson when he come to. He hit up Deep Crick after Steve—an' he run onto Clem Worling. Clem's a sourdough that located on Deep Crick on account of Steve's strike—an' he's know'd Steve sence he was a kid. An' Clem told Old Jim that he'd saw, an' talked to Steve the day before, an' that Steve was headin' down the crick. You was follerin' Steve, an' seen all that—an' then you claimed it was you, an' not Steve Clem talked to! Then after Steve knocked Old Jim out an' robbed him, you killed Steve an' took Old Jim's dust, an' slipped back, an' changed Steve's cache, which you'd located when you was up there! You can't fool them old timers— an' I'd ort to had sense enough to remembered that when you told me yer yarn."

"You're crazy as hell, Cuter! Everything happened just as I told you. What put that fool notion in your head?"

"I'm crazy all right—fer fallin' fer yer damn lies in the first place. Now let me tell you one—an' this one ain't no lie. 'Till you come back here with Steve Blaine's dust, you ain't got no more alibi than a fish. If Downey er any other police comes here to check up on you whilst you was gone, neither me nor none of the boys will know a damn thing about where you was, nor what you was up to."

"But," cried Buckley, "I can't bring Steve's dust here. I tell you, I never found it. I wish to God I had! You can't go back on the alibi, Cuter. Where would I be if Steve showed up?"

MALONE LAUGHED, a nasty, grating laugh of derision. "If Steve showin' up is all you had to worry about, Buckley, you'd be easy in yer mind. Steve won't never show up—an' no one knows that as well as you. When the police can't find him they'll git to wonderin' where he is. Then's when your worry will begin. If that dust of Steve's ain't fetched right here in this room as quick as you kin git out an' fetch it—I'll slip the word to Downey who it was killed Steve Blaine. An' not only that, I'm goin' to tell off Zinn to go with you to Deep Crick to fetch back the dust. I wouldn't trust you as fer as a steamboat kin jump. You'd pick up Steve's dust an' high-tail to Alasky with it, an' leave me with the lousy little jag of dust Steve got off'n Jim Adams. An' what's more, that seven hundred ounces you got in the safe is frozen assets as fer as you're concerned! I'm holdin' onto that till you show up with Steve's dust. I bet Bettles five hundred ounces that the police would pick Steve up. That was before I figgered out that he never would show up, 'cause he's dead."

"I tell you," cried Buckley, his face paper white in the lamp-light, "that Steve isn't dead! He's liable to show up any minute! Then where in hell will I be if you don't alibi me?"

Malone shrugged. "Where'll you be if he don't show up?" he sneered.

"You mean," cried Buckley, "you're holding up my seven hundred ounces? The stake I—"

"Yeah," sneered the other, "the stake you played me fer a sucker with—" The thick hand that grasped the Derringer jerked from Malone's pocket as Buckley leaped toward him. But it was just the fraction of a second slow, owing to the heavy diamond setting of the massive ring catching upon the cloth of the pocket. A hard-driven fist thudded against the point of Malone's heavy jaw, and the big man pitched forward to sprawl grotesquely across the table top as the Derringer thudded upon the floor.

CROSSING SWIFTLY to the door, Buckley unlocked it, and

stepped into the saloon, pausing to turn the key in the lock behind him. Slipping the key into his pocket, he sauntered casually to the bar, presented a slip to the bartender, and received therefor nine little sacks of gold—new sacks—the sacks he had removed a few days before from the packsack of Old Jim Adams. Then very leisurely he sauntered toward the door, and vanished into the night.

VIII

OLD JIM ADAMS GOES HOME

AFTER HIS USUAL three or four days in Dawson Old Jim Adams returned to French Creek. The five day trail ordinarily sufficed to wipe out all trace, in his tough old body, of the night-long sessions with the sourdoughs; so that he was wont to arrive at the cabin fit and fine, with a twinkle of fun in his shrewd blue eyes, and a humorously preposterous excuse in answer to Sally's tolerant chiding for the delay. "Now, Sally, damn if a b'ar didn't run me off'n the trail an' into a hole in a mount'in an' havin' only my jack knife it took me four days to dig through to t'other side." Or "I'd of fetched home three, four days quicker, Sally, only I took out after a moose an', not havin' no rifle, I had to run him down, an' by the time I ketched him he was wore plumb down till there wasn't a square meal in his hind quarters." Or, "I'd of got back a couple of days sooner only I run onto a Siwash which a steamboat had run over him an' cut off his leg, an' I set down an' whittled out a wooden one fer the pore devil. It takes time—whittlin' out a leg that'll work as good as a reg'lar one. Jest you try it, sometime."

Sally missed the merry twinkle in the eyes that faced her across the table as the old man seated himself after washing up at the bench beside the door.

"Well," she asked, the shadow of a smile playing at the corners of her lips, "what was it this time, Daddy? Did someone tie a knot in the trail?"

"No," answered Old Jim gravely, "this time it was different."

Sally Adams knew her menfolks—she knew and appreciated the sterling worth of the sourdoughs who wrested raw gold from the creeks and the mountains. And she knew and tolerated their faults and their foibles. She knew, now, that something serious had happened, and she knew that in due time her father would tell her.

Old Jim finished his meal, lighted his pipe, and tilted his chair back against the log wall.

"Wimmin," he observed casually, "is sometimes right."

"Yes?"

"Yeah. Take it, now, sizin' a man up. Sometimes they might come closter'n what men would."

"Think so?"

"Well onct in a while they might. Take Stevie, now—"

"What about Stevie?" The words leaped to the girl's lips, and Old Jim frowned slightly at the eager look in the brown eyes.

"Well, you was right; an' we was wrong."

"What do you mean?"

"Steve Blaine—Old Steve—was a good man. He'd go to hell fer a friend, any day. An' Stevie he looked like a chip off the old block. You're the only one I ever heard say a word agin him. When you lit into him about usin' Sam Buckley like he done, last winter, I didn't hold with you, because knowin' Sam fer a damn tin horn, I figgered he couldn't git no more'n what was comin' to him—no matter what it was. An' besides I figgered you was jest sort of teasin' Stevie, anyhow. An' agin when you got mad an' come away from the dance an' come on home on account of Stevie gittin' drunk an' dancin' with them other gals, I figgered it was like any woman would be apt to do. I rec'lect yer ma ustn't to hold with such carryin's on. A many a time she's up an' raised hell when I done sim'lar—but it didn't amount to nothin'. She always got over it, an' after a while we'd even have a good laugh over it. But next time it happened she'd fergit she'd ever seen nothin' funny in it—an' she'd raise hell all over agin. Women's curious that-a-way—they ain't consistent. An', of course, I figgered you was like the rest of 'em."

"But," urged the girl, "what about Stevie? Is—is he still in Dawson?"

"No—he ain't in Dawson," retorted the old man savagely. "But he will be when the police gets hold of him."

"The police!" cried the girl. "What have the police got to do with it? What's Stevie done?"

"He done plenty. He robbed a man on the trail."

"It's a lie!" cried the girl, her eyes flashing. "You know as well as I do that Stevie Blaine never robbed anyone! Who claimed Stevie robbed him—that miserable Sam Buckley?"

"No. Not Sam. Me."

"You! What do you mean?"

"Jest like I say. I was headin' down the trail a little ways below the Deep Crick Fork, when all to once somethin' hit me a clout in the head, an' I went down on my knees. I was kind of stunned an' dizzy, an' I looked around an' there was Stevie raisin' the club to finish me off. I yelled at him—an' that's the last I remember till I come to. I got a good look at the club he used—it was a leather blackjack. When I come to Stevie was gone, an' so was the nine hundred an' sixty ounces of dust I was packin' to Dawson."

"Did you see his face?"

"What of it wasn't covered up, I did. He tied a handkerchief over the lower half of it. But it was Stevie all right. He had on that red an' black mackinaw—the one he got off'n that chechako in Forty Mile. I'd know that coat anywhere. An' Stevie's pacs—new ones, with the hobs in a pattern. I back tracked 'em to his shack. Goin' up Deep Crick, I seen Clem Worling, an' he told me that Stevie had headed down the crick the day before, an' he'd spoke to him. Stevie told Clem he was in a hurry, an' he'd see him later. Clem says Stevie ain't be'n around his shack none fer goin' on two months. An' we seen where he'd spent a night in the shack—the night before Clem seen him. I seen, too, that Clem was right—his diggin' hadn't be'n worked in quite a while."

"But where has he been? In Dawson?"

"No. The boys says he pulled out right after the Dominion Day dance, an' he ain't be'n seen sence—till Clem seen him hitting down Deep Crick. He bought them new pacs at the A.C. Store Dominion Day. We checked up on the pattern the hobs made in the mud. Downey's got all the police in Dawson huntin' him. One come on up with me as fer as Deep Crick. He's goin' up an' hang around Stevie's shack, in case he'd show up. It was Stevie, all right—there ain't no two ways about it."

"It wasn't Stevie!" cried the girl hotly. "And there *are* two ways about it! Stevie never robbed any man, least of all you! Why, he loved you like his own father!"

"He took a hell of a way of showin' it," replied Old Jim dryly. "He better not show up where I can throw a rifle down on him. I'll shoot the damn robber on sight."

"But I tell you he never did it!" reiterated the girl, stamping her foot. "There's something wrong! Why would Stevie leave his claim? Something's happened to him! Someone else was wearing his coat and his pacs. I'll bet that miserable Sam Buckley's at the bottom of this. He's about Stevie's size!"

Old Jim shook his head. "Nope," he replied stubbornly. "It's hard to take, but it wasn't no one but Stevie. Clem Worling knows Sam, an' he knows Stevie. Stevie spoke to him on his way down the crick. You couldn't fool Clem. An', besides, Sam Buckley was in Dawson. He was there when I was tellin' the boys."

"It wasn't Stevie!" insisted the girl, tears welling from the brown eyes. "You could talk till you were black in the face, and you could never make me believe it!"

"Well, I'll be damned!" exclaimed Old Jim, eyeing his daughter in disgust. "Wimmin's contrarier'n a man would believe—if he never seen one! Here you up an' raise hell with Stevie over things that don't amount to a damn—an' then when he does somethin' plumb ornery an' criminal, you stick up fer him! What kind of a way is that? What wimmin uses fer brains is more'n I know. There ain't no reasonin' about 'em!" And, without waiting for a reply, the outraged oldster strode from the room and spent a couple of hours puttering aimlessly about his sluice. When he returned to the cabin it was empty, and the remains of the midday meal were still on the table.

IX

SALLY TAKES THE TRAIL

RIFLE IN HAND, Sally Adams walked swiftly along the weed-choked trail that cut across the ridges to Deep Creek. She swallowed once or twice as she remembered that last summer, and the summer before, this trail had not been weed-choked. She could not for the life of her have told why she was heading for Deep Creek—nor what she would do when she got there. Something terrible had happened to Stevie, and she was going to get to the bottom of it. The police and the sourdoughs would arrest him—shoot him, maybe—for something the girl knew he had never committed. And somewhere was Stevie—needing help! Or—maybe—dead. She would get to the bottom of it—if it took years and years! She would run down the man who was responsible for it, if the trail led clear across Alaska! The police would stop at the border—but not she! International boundaries meant nothing to her. Her jaw set, and her fingers clasped more tightly about her rifle. She would pick up the trail, and would follow it to the end—and at the end they would find a dead man! Then they could take her and hang her if they wanted to. She hoped they would, because somewhere in the dim beyond—if there is any beyond—Stevie would be waiting for her.

The ground was rising more rapidly now. She was ascending the ridge on the crest of which was the post office stump. She was surprised that she had arrived there so quickly. Ten miles, and it seemed no time at all since she left the cabin. She quickened her steps—could it be possible that Stevie had left a note there for her? Why hadn't she looked in the stump before? He might have written her something of vital importance—might even have contrived to slip an appeal for help into the stump—hoping that she would find it. And now—it might be too late! Up the steep slope she charged, urging her feet to frantic speed as her panting lungs pumped great gasps of life-giving air. At the top she half ran, half staggered to the stump. It was empty. Wearily she leaned against the stump and stared with dull eyes at the trail beyond—the trail to Stevie's cabin—a trail weed-choked and overgrown, as the trail she had just followed.

Utterly exhausted by the forced climb, the girl sank to the ground, buried her face in her arms, and sobbed, and sobbed.

How long she lay there she did not know. She must have slept, for when she raised her head, the sun was low in the west. Already the chill of autumn was in the air, and she shivered. Suddenly she sat erect—her eyes searching the crest of the ridge to the westward. A slight sound had reached her ears—the sound of a snapping twig. Again she caught the sound. Something was moving along the ridge—coming toward her. A moose, maybe, or a bear. Then her eye caught a flicker of movement, and the next moment from behind the cover of a wind-gnarled spruce a hundred yards away stepped a man. Instantly the girl flattened herself, and rolled into shelter of a huge rock fragment, from which point of vantage she gripped her rifle, and waited, her eyes on the man who approached slowly along the ridge.

He carried a light pack on his back and a rifle in his left hand. His right grasped a long staff upon which he seemed to lean as he walked. As he drew nearer, Sally saw that he walked with a limp, and that an inch-long growth of beard covered his face to the eyes. He was not a prepossessing looking man. Some chechako who is lost, thought the girl, as she watched his halting progress. She would wait and put him on the trail to her father's cabin. Old Jim would look after him till he was better able to travel.

THE MAN was close now, and the girl saw that his clothing was ragged, a great tear in his shirt sleeve revealed a bare upper arm and shoulder. She was about to speak, when suddenly her muscles grew rigid and her eyes tense. The man was moving faster, his blue eyes fixed eagerly upon the post office stump, not five yards from where the girl crouched behind a rock fragment. He walked straight to the stump, stooped, and peered within! Then he stood erect, and she saw his profile against the sky as he turned and gazed for a long moment down the trail to French Creek. He shook his head wearily, and a deep sigh escaped him.

"I might have known—"

"Stevie!" Sally's rifle clattered among the rocks with a ring of steel.

The man whirled at the sound, and the next instant the girl was before him, her two hands on his shoulders, and the liquid brown eyes gazing up into his own with a light he had never before seen in any eyes. His fingers relaxed from the staff, instinctively his arm closed about her waist, and for a brief instant he held her close as words poured in a torrent from her lips:

"Where have you been, Stevie? You're hurt! What's happened? Oh, tell me!"

"But—but—Sally—I don't understand."

The girl scrutinized the eyes of blue that were regarding her with devouring intensity. "You mean," she cried, a sudden apprehension leaping into her brain, "that you've been—been wandering around? That you don't know where's you've been?"

The man's lips parted in a smile, and any fear as to his sanity vanished with his words. "I know where I've be'n all right. I meant that I—I thought you'd never speak to me again after me actin' like I done—dancin' with all them girls, an' buyin' em drinks, an' such—"

A silvery laugh drowned the words. "If you'd picked out *one* of 'em and danced with her and bought her drinks, I never would have spoken to you again! But you danced with 'em all, Stevie. And you bought them all drinks. You were just showing off! You were mad at me because I teased you about Sam Buckley. And—don't forget, Stevie—you told me I looked like hell!"

"You did, too—in them togs! God, Sally, when I looked at you rigged out like—like them others—it made me see red! I was so mad I got drunk. It was me throw'd them baseballs at the dance. I—I hoped I'd hit you with one of 'em! You rigged out like that—an' dancin' with that damn Sam Buckley! An' I figgered I'd show you I didn't give a damn, so I danced with every girl I could get holt of. Next day I was sick, an' plumb disgusted with everything, an' I hit out fer Deep Crick."

"But—where have you been? And how did you get hurt?"

"By the time I'd got to my shack, I was over bein' sick, but I didn't take no heart in my work—what with the trail to your place all grow'd up to brush. I was shovelin' out dust—plenty of it. But seemed like I didn't care. Then a Siwash came along an' showed me some big nuggets he'd found on a rocky crick way back in the mountains. He was an old Siwash that my dad an' me helped out one winter on Forty Mile when his family was starvin'. He hadn't forgot it, an' he offered to take me back there an' show me the crick. So I cached my dust where no one would find it an' went along with him. I was glad to get away from Deep Crick—so clost to you—an' not ever seein' you, an' all. The further I got away, the better. I figgered to come back later, an' sell the Deep Crick claims. We went east till we was clean up against the divide, an' we prospected this crick. It was a funny kind of a proposition—all rock. There wasn't no place where a man could sink a shaft. The gold was all coarse stuff, an' you had to pry it out of cracks with the blade of your huntin' knife, or find it layin' under loose rocks in the crick bed.

"There wasn't so much of it, anyway, an' we had to keep movin' from place to place along the crick, an' it kept gettin' harder an' harder to find. Then one day I slipped an' fell off'n a rock ledge, an' broke my leg. The Siwash set it an' tied splints on it, an' tended me like a baby till the bone knit. When I was able to walk, I gave him the gold we'd found an' hit back. That's all there is to tell."

"Not quite all, Stevie," smiled the girl. "You haven't told me why you came here—to the post office stump—instead of going straight to your cabin."

"Why—it was because—you see, Sally, layin' up there in the hills with my leg broke, I had time to do a heap of thinkin'. An' always I was thinkin' about you. At nights, I'd dream about you—an' sometimes in them dreams it was like it used to be—with the post office stump an' all. I kept dreamin' there was a note here for me—that everything was all right—like it used to be. In the mornin' I'd know it wasn't nothin' but a dream—an' you'd never have nothin' more to do with me. I wasn't blamin' you. I seen how I'd played the fool there at the dance. I seen how, if I'd kept my head an' hadn't got mad when you carried on about Sam Buckley, that everything would have come out all right. You'd have found out, sooner or later, that Sam wasn't nothin' but a tin horn. But I figgered the dance had settled my hash fer good an' all. It was too late. But I kept dreamin' that dream about a letter from you in the stump. I hadn't never believed in dreams. But some folks do, an' I got to thinkin' maybe they was right. I sure got to hopin' they was. But they wasn't." The man paused as a look of burning intensity flashed into his eyes and once again his arm closed about the girl's waist and he drew her toward him with crushing force. "There was somethin' waitin' fer me here, a thousan' times better than any letter! Sally, girl—suppose we jest forget everything an' get married an' settled down on Deep Crick! Ferget all about me bein' a damn fool—an' you dressin' like one—"

"Steve Blaine—that's a perfectly lovely evening gown!"

"Yeah," grinned the man, "an' when we get married, we'll send it down to one of them dance hall girls fer a weddin' present. It ain't no rig fer Deep Crick. It won't keep out the cold in winter, nor the mosquitoes in summer. Let's get goin', Sally. I guess Old Jim'll loan me his razor."

The last words had been uttered with the man's lips buried in the mass of raven hair. When the girl raised her eyes to his he saw that they were wet with tears.

"Oh, Stevie," she faltered, "we—you can't go to French Creek. Daddy would—would kill you!"

"What!" The word rang sharp, like a pistol shot.

"Oh, I do love you! I've never loved anyone but you—and I've been horrid! I'll marry you, Stevie—in spite of all of 'em! In spite of daddy and the police—"

"Police! What in thunder you talkin' about?"

"They're hunting you, Stevie! There's one at your cabin, right now—waiting for you to show up. I was going over there and I stopped to rest. That's why you found me here."

IN HURRIED words the girl told Steve of her father's trip to Dawson with the dust, and what he told her on his return. "And, somehow," she concluded, "I can't help but think that that miserable Sam Buckley is at the bottom of it!"

Steve nodded thoughtfully. "He might be," he agreed. "Sam was sore at me because I wouldn't take him back to Dawson last winter, an' if he's found out that claim I bought cheap from him is prob'ly worth real money, it would burn him up. Whoever done it must have be'n to my shack, to have my mackinaw an' pacs. The pacs was new an' hurt my feet, an' I knew it would be cold in the mountains, so I left the mackinaw behind an' took a parka."

"You go on back home, Sally. I'm goin' to light out an' find the man that robbed your dad. How much was it you said he lost? An' how was it put up?"

"Nine hundred and sixty ounces. And it was in twelve new sacks. I made 'em myself. You'll know 'em if you see 'em. Turn 'em wrong side out and look at the seams. I ran short of sinew, and sewed 'em with red silk."

"Don't worry. I'll get 'em!"

"But," objected the girl, "you can't. The police are looking for you. The first one that sees you will arrest you!"

Steve grinned. "There ain't none of 'em that would recognize me, like this. Not even Downey. I'll slip down to Dawson an' mingle with the riff raff, an' no one'll pay any heed to me. I'll be jest one more chechako that ain't made a go of it. I've got a hunch that I can pick me up an earful around Cuter Malone's."

"But you're lame!"

"Well, there ain't nothin' in the books against a chechako bein' lame."

"It's a long trip, Stevie—and you'll suffer so!"

"Never mind the sufferin'. It ain't so bad now—an' gettin' better every day. I've jest come through ten days of rough country an' no trails. From here on, it's easy. I'll jest slip on over to Deep Crick an' have a look at my cache. It might be that whoever was up there found it. Anyway, I'll want some dust in my pocket. Don't say nothin' to your dad about seein' me. When I get the man that robbed him, I'll come up to French Crick an' give him hell fer believin' his own eyes."

"But there's a policeman at your cabin!"

"He'll be easy to dodge, seein' I know he's there. So long, Sally. You better get what use you can out of that dance hall dress. I'll be comin' back, sometime!"

Crushing her to him, Steve smothered her retort in a long kiss. When he released her, the girl rubbed her lips vigorously with the back of her hand.

"You get a shave before you come back, Steve Blaine! I'd just as soon kiss a hair brush! And—oh, Stevie—be careful! Won't you, dear?"

"Don't you worry about me, sweetheart," laughed the man. "Run along now; go fast, or it'll get dark on you."

X

STEVE GOES TO DAWSON

DAYLIGHT FOUND STEVE Blaine concealed among the rim rocks, peering down upon his own little cabin in Deep Creek valley. An hour passed, and smoke began lazily to ascend from the stovepipe. Another hour, and a man in the uniform of the Royal Northwest Mounted Police stepped from the doorway, strolled aimlessly about for a while, and headed down the creek.

Steve smiled. "He'll go down an' kill time chewin' the fat with Clem Worling," he muttered. "It's a good thing I ran onto Sally, or I'd have walked right in on him."

Descending to the valley by the same trail used by Buckley, he slipped into the scrub. A quarter of a mile upstream, he dropped to his knees and removed a stone roughly fitted into the mouth of an aperture in the rock wall. Reaching in, he withdrew two fat, heavy little sacks which he thrust into his pocket. Assuring himself that the cache had not been tampered with, he replaced the stone, limped rapidly back, and climbed the steep trail to the rim where he regained his staff and his rifle and struck off toward the Klondike, paralleling the course of the creek.

Three days later, in the guise of a busted and beaten checha-ko, he was given room in a poling boat by three prospectors who were drifting down to Dawson. Two of these were ac-quaintances of long standing, and Steve realized with satisfac-tion, that if these men did not know him the chance of his being recognized in Dawson was slight indeed.

In the A.C. Store, McGowan the manager failed to recognize him as he bought a shirt. And, crossing the street, he mingled for an hour unheeded among the sourdoughs who had been his lifelong friends.

Corporal Downey came in, chatted for a few minutes with the sourdoughs, and went out. Steve had known and liked Downey ever since the young officer had come into the territory, and he stood in the doorway and watched the trim, uniformed figure disappear in the direction of detachment. He wondered whether Corporal Downey actually believed that he had robbed Old Jim Adams. It was amusing to move about unrecognized among the sourdoughs—but it was different with the police. Suddenly he realized that the rôle of a fugitive was distasteful. He wished he could go to Downey and tell him where he had been. "Well—why not?" The words leaped unconsciously to his lips as he stood gazing toward the police buildings. A moment later he was limping down the street in the wake of the young officer.

Corporal Downey was just seating himself at his desk when Steve stepped into the little office. Across the room, two constables off duty from town patrol were playing cribbage.

"Something we can do for you?" asked Downey, as Steve approached the desk.

"You the boss?"

"I'm commanding detachment."

"Could I have a word with you, private?"

Corporal Downey eyed the uncouth newcomer sharply for a moment, and motioned to the constables who picked up their cards and cribbage board and stepped into the barrack room, closing the door behind them.

"Sit down," invited Downey, indicating a chair drawn close to the desk.

Steve hunched the chair closer and looked the young officer in the eye. "I hear you're huntin' Steve Blaine," he said, "fer robbin' Old Jim Adams."

Downey nodded. "That's right. Do you know where he is?"

"Yes. An' I know he never robbed Old Jim."

"Can you prove that?" The question snapped sharply from the young officer's lips, a glint of sudden interest lighting his eyes.

"Not yet. But I want the chance to try. I want the chance to find the man that done it."

Downey frowned. "You mean, you want a job with the police?"

"No—only the chance to find the man that robbed Old Jim. When I find him, I'll turn him over to the police."

"How do you know Steve didn't rob Old Jim? Who are you anyway?"

"I'm Steve Blaine."

Corporal Downey's jaw dropped as he stared, wide-eyed, into the face masked behind the short, heavy beard. "Stevie!" he cried. "My God, what's happened to you? Where have you been?"

For half an hour Steve talked rapidly and Downey listened. "An' so you see," he concluded, "I want the chance to find the damn cuss that done it, an' tried to put the blame on me."

Corporal Downey drummed on the desk top with his fingers as he regarded the man before him. "It was hard for me to believe you'd done the job, Stevie," he said. "But Old Jim was mighty positive in identifyin' you as the robber. An' Clem Worling said he saw you goin' down Deep Crick the day before, an' hollered at you, an' you hollered back."

"Old Jim identified me by my mackinaw," reminded Steve. "He said the robber's face was masked."

"But it wasn't masked when Clem Worling saw him."

"Clem claimed he hollered at him. A man can holler a long ways further than he can see a man's face—especially if the man is hurryin' past. Besides, knowin' that mackinaw, an' expectin' me back any time, he'd naturally think it was me."

Downey nodded. "That's true," he agreed thoughtfully. "An' if we could locate that Siwash you'd have an alibi. But you know how it is, Stevie, white men don't go much on Siwash testimony."

"I know," answered Steve. "That's why I want the chance to find the robber. I could do more good than the police, in this case. No one will recognize me, and I can hang around the Klondike Palace, posing as a chechako on the bum, and sooner or later I'll pick up something. Those birds shut up like a clam when a uniform shows up. Every wrong man in the Yukon hangs around the Palace."

Downey grinned. "Till we get something on 'em. Then they hit for Halfaday Crick."

"Are you goin' to let me do it?" persisted Steve. "You can't believe I robbed Old Jim! Hell, man, why would I rob anyone? I've got three claims on Deep Crick that I wouldn't take a million for!"

After a long moment of silence, Downey spoke. "I believe what you've told me, Stevie. I never more'n half believed you done it, anyhow. It wasn't reasonable. I'm convinced, now, that you didn't. With the disguise you've got—that limp, an' them whiskers, you could have hung around Dawson from now on, an' no one would have spotted you. If you'd done it, you'd never have come to me. I'll tell you what I'm goin' to do—an' I wouldn't do it unless I'd known you, an' your dad before you. I'm goin' to give you thirty days to find your man. I won't call my men off you—it's a cinch none of 'em'll spot you, if I couldn't. An' I'll detail a man to go out an' get your Siwash. At the end of thirty days you come here an' give yourself up, an' we'll go to bat on the evidence. I believe you can beat the case. But if you can find the man that did it—go to it, an' good luck!"

"Thanks, Downey," said Steve. "If I can't find him in thirty days, I'll never find him." He paused and grinned broadly. "It's a load off my mind to feel that I'm not dodgin' the police. Those rookies of yours don't count."

"Get out of here!" grinned Downey. "Or I'll pinch you for speakin' light of the force!"

XI

IN THE KLONDIKE PALACE

LEAVING DOWNEY'S OFFICE, Steve made his way down past the saw mill and out onto the trail to Moosehide, the Indian village that straggled along the bank of the river below Dawson. Before reaching the village, he turned from the trail and made his way to a shack before the door of which a young Indian was working over some fish nets.

"Hello, Owl Man!" he greeted, pausing at the corner of the shack.

The Indian regarded him with a stare of indifference from the block upon which he was seated, grunted unintelligibly, and proceeded with his net mending.

Steve grinned, and tried again. "Mebbe-so white man come 'long Forty Mile Kink, find Siwash canoe all smash to hell. Mebbe-so white man jump in the river an' pull Siwash out before ice cakes smash him all to hell, too."

The young Indian was upon his feet before the last sentence was finished, his black eyes staring with a peculiar intensity into the eyes of the speaker. The next moment, Steve's arm was seized roughly and he was hustled into the shack, as the Indian's glance swept the scrub that surrounded the shack.

"Stevie!" he uttered. "W'at de hell! W'er' you be'n? You no go Dawson! De poliss she hont you! Jim Adam she tell de beeg dam lie 'bout you steal hees gol'!"

Steve laughed. "I thought, at first, you weren't glad to see me—"

"To hell!" interrupted the Indian. "I'm ain' know you! I'm t'ink you wan dam chechako comes to hire me tak heem out in hills fin' gol'. Chechako no good. No fin' no gol'; no kin pay. You got de w'at you call w'iskers on de face—look like ol' Bettles. Me—I'm ain' fergit you pull me out Forty Mile Kink. I'm say som'tam I'm pay you back. Owl Man no fergit. W'at you want me do?"

"Nothin'," grinned Steve, "except to let me shack up with you here for a while. The police won't bother me. They don't know who I am. I'm goin' to find the man that robbed Old Jim. I'm goin' to hang around Cuter Malone's for a while—maybe a couple of days, maybe a month. If anyone asks about me, tell 'em I'm a chechako that's boardin' here with you. I want to cache most of this dust here, too. I don't want but a little of it on me."

Steve tossed one of the little sacks he had taken from his cache onto the table, and reaching for a dish, poured most of the contents of the other into it. "You take care of it, Owl Man, an' rig me up a bunk here. I'm goin' now."

AN HOUR later, Steve limped to Malone's bar, called for a drink, and paid for it out of a limp sack. Then he shuffled across the floor, seated himself in a chair near a table at which four men were playing stud, tilted it against the wall, and dozed.

Malone's Klondike Palace was the catchall for the riff-raff of Dawson. Here foregathered the chechakos, new to the gold field, bent on one final spree before heading out into the hills, spending their money at the long bar, and among the tawdry women who swarmed the broad dance floor. Here, also, gravitated the down-and-outers—the beaten men, who had played the game and lost. Men broke, and discouraged, hoping vaguely for luck to turn—for someone to grubstake them for another fling at fortune. And men who accepted defeat, and just lived on from day to day, mooching drinks, subsisting God knows how, awaiting—they knew not what.

Also to the Klondike Palace gravitated the scum and the dregs of all the North—thieves, tin horns and petty rogues swept into the country on the crest of the big stampede, to prey upon the drunken and the unwary. Among these, in the rôle of a down-and-outer, Steve Blaine spent his nights. In the daytime he slept in Owl Man's shack.

WHEN SAM BUCKLEY failed to show up on the second night, Steve slipped out, explored his shack, saw that his packsack and blankets were missing, but found nothing to indicate his whereabouts. Jim Adams had told Sally that Buckley was in Dawson when he arrived there and reported the robbery. Why had he left? And, above all, where had he gone? Half-convinced of the man's guilt, Steve could not account for his absence. Had his own cache on Deep Creek been robbed, he could well believe that the man had hit for the outside. But the nine hundred and sixty ounces he had taken from Old Jim would never satisfy him when there were such easy pickings among the chechakos in Dawson. Nor could Buckley believe himself suspected of that robbery, in the face of Old Jim's insistence that it was Steve Blaine who had robbed him.

A week passed, and part of another—and still Sam Buckley didn't show up. Chechakos came and went. Beaten men drifted in from the hills and sought the grudging sanctuary of the Klondike Palace.

To vary the monotony Steve paid occasional visits to the Tivoli to mingle unrecognized among the sourdoughs. It was there he learned of the stud game in which Old Bettles had cleaned Buckley out on a bluff, and of Buckley's sojourn at Eagle until Moosehide Charlie had told him that the sourdoughs bore no grudge. He gathered that the robbery of Old Jim Adams occurred within the week after Buckley returned from Eagle.

In the Tivoli, also, he learned of Bettles' bet with Cuter Malone, and he grinned to himself as he pictured Cuter's rage when he should learn that the man whose delivery to the police meant five hundred ounces in dust to him had been a nightly hanger-on at his bar.

Try as he would, Steve could think of no reason for Buckley's continued absence from his usual haunt. If he had got Old Jim's dust, why wasn't he playing it against the chechakos? Could it be that Cuter or some of his minions had known of the robbery, and had knocked Buckley off for Old Jim's dust? It might well be that Old Jim's gold was lying there in Malone's safe—within a few feet of him—in the little moosehide sacks that Sally had stitched with red silk. In vain Steve tried to contrive some means of gaining access to that safe—but even as he planned he realized the futility of it. He even thought of asking Corporal Downey to search it under authority of the law, but dismissed the idea as impracticable. Downey would demand much stronger evidence of guilt than a mere hunch.

Ten days of the time allotted him by Corporal Downey had passed, and Steve realized that he had accomplished exactly nothing in clearing up the robbery. The rest and inaction had done wonders for his injured leg. For several days he had walked with no perceptible limp.

A STUD game was in progress and, his chair tilted against the wall close by, Steve apathetically watched the run of cards. Less than three weeks, and he must give himself up—and Cuter Malone would pocket five hundred ounces of Old Bettles' dust. It was too bad—Steve had known Old Bettles ever since he had known anybody.

The stud game broke up in the early hours of the morning, and feigning sleep, Steve watched one Zinn, who remained at the table, spread the cards for solitaire. A notorious and a sinister figure, this Zinn. One of Malone's trusted lieutenants. I wish I knew what he knows, thought Steve, as he studied the sharp featured profile through nearly closed eyelids. He knows who robbed Old Jim all right—and he knows what has become of Buckley, too. Steve played with the idea of kidnapping Zinn, taking him out into the hills and making him talk. The man was a rat. The isolation and the solitude of the high hills would terrorize him—he would squeal like a rat to be freed.

Ways and means floated through Steve's brain. It was a dull night in the Palace. A small group of chechakos stood at the bar engaged in endless and maudlin debate as to the merits of various creeks of which they were entirely ignorant. The dance hall piano was silent, the pasty faced man who answered to the name of "professor," was languidly arranging sheets of music on his rack, while a bevy of girls lolled listlessly about the instrument. Over near the huge cannon stove a dozen derelicts slept in chairs, or stretched out on the floor. Zinn studied his cards.

The hands of the clock above the bar were together at three, when Cuter Malone stepped from behind the bar and joined Zinn at the card table. Steve feigned sleep.

"I got a tip on Buckley," said the proprietor in a husky undertone.

"Where's he at?"

There was a pause, during which Malone had evidently questioned Steve's presence. Then the voice of Zinn:

"Oh, that damn bum! He's dead to the world. Be'n hangin' around here two, three weeks. Holes up daytimes with the Siwashes down around Moosehide. Where's Buckley at?"

"Halfaday," answered Malone viciously. "An' you an' Anvil Johnnie have got to go up an' get the doublecrossin' cuss!"

"Why not tip off the police that he killed Steve Blaine, an' tell 'em where he is?"

"What the hell would that get me? Listen—he's got the dust on him that Steve Blaine took off'n Old Jim Adams. An' he's got the dust that he lifted out of Steve's cache after he knocked Steve off—an' believe me, it's a-plenty! I claim a cut on that dust—an' if the damn cuss had played square that's all I'd of claimed. But he tried to gyp me, claimed it was him robbed Adams, an' that he never seen Steve Blaine, an' never located his cache! Before I figgered out what come off, I bet that five hundred ounces with Bettles. But with Steve dead, I'm bound to lose. I already told you about cornerin' Buckley in the back room, an' tellin' him what's what—an' that I was holdin' out on Adams's dust till he come across with my cut of Steve's. He busts me one on the jaw, an' gits his dust off'n the bartender, beats it—an' leaves me holdin' the bag. Curley handin' over five hundred ounces of my dust to Bettles, come Chris'mas!"

His brain in a whirl, Steve sagged in his chair, feigning sleep, hoping that neither Malone nor Zinn could hear the thumping of his heart.

"You want me an' Anvil to fetch Buckley clean back here, er jest make him come acrost with yer cut of Steve's dust?"

"Cut hell!" growled Malone savagely. "The time fer that egg to square hisself with a cut is past! I'm goin' to have every damn ounce of Adams's dust, an' Steve's too! I'll learn the damn snake to doublecross me, an' bust me in the jaw besides! Listen—you an' Anvil slips up to Halfaday an' grabs off Buckley, an' slips him acrost to Ladue Crick. There's an old cabin there, ten mile above the big bend. Hold him there, an' you stay to guard him, an' send Anvil down to let me know you've got him. Then I'll come up there. I've got ways of makin' a man talk!"

"How'n hell am I goin' to git to Halfaday? I never done no back country travelin' to speak of."

"Anvil knows the trail. He knows about that cabin, too. You go along—see? I got to have a man along that Buckley can't buy off. I'll make it good an' worth yer while. An' I ain't afraid you'll try any monkey business—I know too much. There's a boat at the landin' now. Her captain was in a while back an' he's pullin' out fer Whitehorse at seven. You could save time by goin' as fer as White River with him."

"Seven o'clock!" protested Zinn. "Hell—it's a quarter to four now! I've got to hunt Anvil up, an' then we've got to git us a trail outfit an' a canoe, er whatever it takes to git up there with. We can't never make it. What the hell's yer sweat? There's another boat due tomorrow. What difference does a day make? I'll go 'long with Anvil, but I'll be damned if I'll go this mornin'! I ain't even got no clothes but these hen skins."

"All right, all right!" growled Malone. "Tomorrow'll do. I s'pose there ain't no hell of a hurry—only I'm jest itchin' to git to work on that doublecrossin' skunk!"

XII

ON HALFADAY CREEK

FIFTEEN MINUTES LATER Steve's feet were pounding the trail to Owl Man's shack. Sam Buckley had robbed Old Jim—and Buckley was on Halfaday Creek with the old man's gold on him! By what process of reasoning Malone had concluded that Buckley had killed and robbed him, Steve did not know—nor did he care. Nor did he stop to figure what he would do when he reached Halfaday. He knew, vaguely, the location of the creek—a tributary of the White River, close against the International Boundary between the Yukon and Alaska. And he knew the reputation of its inhabitants, the little band of outlawed men who dug their gold and minded their own business far from the police surveillance. Rumor had it that a strict code, if not of morals at least of conduct, was ruggedly enforced by one Black John Smith, ably assisted and abetted by Old Cush, the trader. The sourdoughs would tell you—and the police, too—that there was no crime on Halfaday.

AT SEVEN o'clock, when the steamboat cast off and headed upriver, Steve stood at the rail and watched Dawson merge slowly into the landscape. At the mouth of the White River, seventy miles above Dawson, he was set ashore with his stampeding pack and canoe, and began the laborious ascent of that shallow and turbulent stream.

Eight days later, he drew his canoe from the water, ascended a steep bank, and pushed open the door of a long log building that stood close to the bank. Swinging his pack from his shoulders, he advanced to the bar where a huge man with a jet black beard appeared to be in earnest conversation with a somber-faced man, evidently the proprietor. Both turned to face the newcomer, the somber-faced one behind the bar lowering a pair of steel-framed spectacles from forehead to nose.

"Hello," greeted Steve. "Is this Cushing's Fort?"

"This is the place," admitted the solemn one, setting out a bottle and glasses. "Have one on the house."

The three poured their liquor, the black-bearded giant cleared his throat, and indicated the man behind the bar with a jerk of his thumb. "That there's Cush hisself an' in person. An' my name is Smith—Black John, they call me, so folks wouldn't conclude my whiskers was white, er mebbe green." He paused, and pointed toward a tin molasses can that stood at the end of the bar against the log wall. "Jest reach in an' help yerself," he invited.

Steve's eyes shifted from the speaker to the can. "Help myself to what?" he asked with a smile.

"To a name," answered Black John. "It's like this—folks, takin' 'em by an' large, as a orator would say, ain't got no imagination to speak of. Wherefore an' hence, they all want to claim their name is Smith. It was all right with us, Smith bein' a handy enough name, an' we managed to tell 'em apart by addin' a nickname. Besides me, there's One Armed Smith, Long Smith, Shorty Smith, Squint-eyed Smith, One Eared Smith, Peg Leg Smith an' so forth. But at last it got so that we run out of nicknames. When you stop to figger that there ain't only a certain amount of physical peculiarities, an' a certain number of parts that can be missin' off'n a man, you'll see that any further influx of Smiths would be confusin'. So about a month ago me an' Cush hit on a plan that works out good. Cush found a hist'ry book which a feller left behind when we hung him an' copied all the names out of it, an' then switched 'em around puttin' the wrong front ones to the hind ones, an' wrote the names on slips of paper, an' put 'em in the name can there, an' shook 'em up. Of course, they ain't nothin' but synthetic names, as a chemist would say, but they answer the purpose, relievin' us of more or less confusion, an' takin' the mental strain of thinkin' up some name besides Smith off'n the newcomers."

Smiling broadly, Steve reached into the can and drew out a slip of paper. "John Quincy Washington," he read.

Black John and Old Cush nodded gravely. "Pleased to meet you, Jack," said Black John, extending his hand.

"Yer welcome on Halfaday, Worshington," iterated Cush.

THE DOOR opened and a man stepped into the room. Behind his short, heavy beard Steve's face set hard. The man was Sam Buckley.

Black John greeted him with a curt nod. "Cush is buyin' one," he said. "Let me make you acquainted with John Quincy Washington." He turned to Steve. "Shake hands with Alexander Burr," he said.

Not wishing to antagonize Buckley, nor to arouse his suspicion, at least until he had formulated some plan of action, Steve thrust out his hand. As Buckley took it, Steve thought he gave a perceptible start. Raising his eyes to his face he found it impassive as a mask. A moment later they had turned to the bar. Black John bought a round, and Steve followed with another. As Buckley ordered a round, he tossed a little sack upon the bar. It was a new sack of moosehide, and Steve knew that if he could turn it wrong side out, he would find that the seam was stitched with red silk!

"Did you locate a claim?" asked Black John.

"Not yet," answered Buckley shortly. "Hunting one now. Just stopped in for a drink. See you later."

"Take Burr, now," said Black John, when the door had closed behind the man. "He come to Halfaday with intentions to make his livin' off'n cards. That's all right with us. Cards should ort to be a good occupation, providin' a man's luck held better'n the average all the time or he could rightly guess the bulk of the time, what the other feller had in his hand. But such luck consistent, an' such guessin', ain't fell under my observation to date.

"Burr done well fer his'self fer about a week till one day when only me an' him an' Cush was in the saloon here, I happens to mention to him, casual, that we've got morals an' ethics, not to say downright laws, on Halfaday. I p'ints out to him that murder, thievin', in all its forms an' technicalities, claim jumpin' an' general skullduggery ain't neither condoned nor put up with. They're not only punishable, but punished, I tells him—after due ad-joodication in miners' meetin'—by hangin'. Card cheatin', I mentions, comes under the head of skullduggery—an' also I p'ints out that under such rules of procedure as obtains on the crick consistent good luck on a man's own deal is primo facial evidence of skullduggery an' as such, is hangable."

Steve grinned, and ordered another round. "Did he quit playin' cards?" he asked.

"As a means of livelihood, yes," answered Black John. "He plays now an' then evenin's, but he puts in his time huntin' him a claim er perfessin' to. I mistrust, however, he spends it mostly hangin' around Shorty Smith's shack. Shorty's a man of low moral stamina, bein' too lazy to work. I shouldn't wonder if the damn cuss was livin' off'n the proceeds of some misdeed."

"That reminds me I've got to look around for someplace to stay."

"Yer welcome to throw yer stuff in my shack while you look around," offered Black John. "Yer a minin' man, by the looks of you. Leastwise, you never got them callouses on yer hands playin' no dance hall pyanner, nor yet dealin' cards—not that cards hadn't ort to be dealt, an' pyanners played."

"Thanks," answered Steve. "I'll take you up on that. How does the gravel run, around here?"

"Oh, jest about so-so. Most of the boys takes out a little better'n wages. If they don't, they move along till they do. There's plenty room on the crick."

THAT EVENING, with the dishes washed, Steve filled his pipe and sat down on the edge of his bunk and watched Black John clean and oil his rifle.

"Seein' I'm stayin' with you," he said abruptly, "it's no more'n right to tell you that I'm on the run from the police."

Black John received the information with equanimity. "Lots of folks is," he opined. "Alaska, Yukon, er the States?"

"Yukon."

"Mine's Alaska. A major, an' three common soldiers. I stuck 'em up fer a payroll."

"The hell of it is," said Steve, "I didn't do the job they're after me for. Someone wearing my mackinaw rapped Old Jim Adams over the head an' robbed him. Old Jim saw the coat an' reported to the police that I'd robbed him."

"H-u-m," grunted Black John. "Rap him on the head with a blackjack?"

"Yes," answered Steve, his eyes widening. "How did you know?"

"Who—me? I don't know. But speakin' of blackjacks, if they ain't to rap a man over the head with, what the hell are they good fer? Was you meanin' Old Jim Adams of Forty Mile?"

"Yes—only he's located on French Crick now. Got a mighty good proposition there. Do you know him?"

"Hell—yes! Know'd Old Jim fer years. Wonder what ever became of that little gal of Jim's? There was a sourdough! I mind the time we stampeded up the Koyukuk. Old Jim left her at the Fort Yukon mission, figgerin' she'd be in the way, on the winter trail. Well, sir, it must be three, four hundred mile from there to Coldfoot, an' it was around seventy, eighty, below, an' Old Jim's little gal no more'n about ten year old, an' we went like hell, 'cause there was only sourdoughs on that stampede—an', by God, when we got to Coldfoot, damn if there wasn't that little gal of Jim's awaitin' fer us to ketch up! Yes, sir—she'd held up a tribe of Siwashes an' stole a dog outfit, an' the store at Rampart fer her grub! After that Old Jim let her stay. It would be too bad, he figgered, to send her back, after the trouble she'd went to."

Steve laughed. "I've heard different versions of that yarn so many times there must be some truth in it."

"Truth!" exclaimed Black John. "It's as near the truth as I ever come in my life! Ask Old Bettles! He was there. So you know the gal, do you?"

"I ought to," said Steve earnestly. "We're goin' to be married as soon as I can locate the damn scoundrel that robbed her dad!"

"So, that's the way of it," grinned Black John. "Well, young feller, I'll say yer due fer a hardy wife. What does she think about this robbery business?"

"She knows damn well I never done it!"

Black John slanted him a glance. "An' Old Jim's claimin' you did 'cause he don't want her to marry you, eh?"

"No—he does want her to. Or did till this robbery. No, Old Jim honestly believes he saw me—that it was me that robbed him."

"Hum," mused Black John. "It would be a man about yer size, then."

"Yes," answered Steve, "I've got a hunch it was—a gambler."

Black John nodded thoughtfully. "Ondoubtless it was," he agreed. "From the evidence you've presented, a reasonable man couldn't hardly draw no other conclusion. An' besides which, gamblers is folks which a man might expect 'em to revert to robbery, as a lawyer would say."

"If I could run across this fellow an' get holt of one of his gold sacks I could prove it on him. Sally Adams made those sacks out of new moosehide—an' she sewed 'em with red silk, bein' out of sinew."

"That's right," agreed Black John. "An' if you'd find out he was wearin' a blackjack, it wouldn't hurt yer case none, neither."

"Is he?" cried Steve.

"Who?"

"Why—er—"

"There ain't no use lettin' the cat out of the bag, till after the horse is stole," opined Black John oracularly. "In the mean time, if I was you, I'd jest kind of keep my shirt on an' look around a little. Like I said—there's some good pay dirt on Halfaday. An' sometimes the dirtier it is, the better it pays. But—we don't like fer no one to do nothin' that would fetch the police in on us."

Steve smiled. "I'm layin' my cards on the table," he said. "I've got a lot of friends—Buck Hammond, an' Old Bettles, an' Corporal Downey are among 'em—yes, Downey, even if the police are huntin' me, right now. So I don't, somehow, feel like I was talkin' to a stranger when I'm talkin' to you."

Steve caught a twinkle in the keen eyes, and behind the black beard teeth flashed white. "Yeah," replied Black John, "an' I know'd Old Steve well. I was sure sorry to hear that he—"

"What!" cried Steve. "You know me, then! I figured that these whiskers—"

"It's a well known fact," interrupted Black John, "that a man that's got 'em don't look like a man that ain't. Them whiskers would ondoubtless fool anyone that had know'd you before you grow'd 'em. But a man can't expect too much of whiskers. You couldn't expect to fool me an' Cush with 'em—we never seen you before you grow'd 'em. An' jest by way of observation, I've got a hunch that they didn't fool Alexander Burr, alias Sam Buckley, none, neither."

"Well—I'll be damned!" exclaimed Steve.

"So'll most folks," grinned Black John. "But it ain't nothin' to worry about."

"But—how did you spot me? And Sam?"

"Well, neither Old Jim nor the police kep' very quiet about him gettin' robbed an' who they thought done it, did they? We're quite a piece back from the river, but news has got a way of filterin' in. Likewise, we heard that Old Bettles had busted Tin Horn Buckley on a bluff, an' that Buckley had disappeared. When he shows up here with plenty of dust it ain't none of our business so long as he refrains from dealin' off the bottom of the deck, an' such like."

"Do you know Cuter Malone?" asked Steve abruptly.

"Like a book."

"I believe that after Buckley was busted, he an' Cuter framed it for Buckley to rob me, an' that Cuter was to come in for a cut. Buckley didn't find me, so he robbed Old Jim. He kicked in with Malone's cut, an' then Malone somehow got the idea that Buckley had knocked me off, an' robbed my cache an' was holdin' out his cut on that job. It seems that Malone accused Buckley of this, an' Buckley got scaired an' skipped out with his share of Old Jim's dust. I've be'n hangin' around Malone's tryin' to get a line on the robbery, an' the other night I heard Malone tell this to one of his side-kicks named Zinn. He just got the tip that Buckley was here, an' he ordered Zinn an' another to come up here an' kidnap Buckley an' take him to a cabin over on Ladue Crick. Then Malone intends to go up there an' make Buckley talk."

"Well," opined Black John with a grin, "that had ort to be satisfactory all around. You wasn't aimin' to tip Buckley off, was you?"

"No—but I want to get Buckley back to Dawson! Those sacks of Old Jim's can be identified. Downey gave me thirty days to find the robber. I've got twelve days left. I've got to clear myself of that robbery!"

"How was you aimin' to git him back?"

"I knew how you men up here feel about the police, so I didn't want to tip them off that Buckley was here."

"We're obliged. But if Downey had come, hisself, it would of be'n all right. The Yukon wanteds would of slipped over acrost the line, an' he would of be'n welcome to take this here Alexander Tin Horn Buckley Burr anywheres he wanted to. I deem him a man of lax morals, an' as such he can be got along without on Halfaday. But seein' you didn't fetch Downey—what was yer next bet?"

"Well, I figured I'd hang around till Zinn an' his pardner took

Buckley over to Ladue Crick, an' then while one of 'em went back to bring Malone up I'd slip in an' take Buckley away from the other, hustle him down to Dawson an' turn him over to the police for robbing Old Jim."

Black John nodded. "Simple an' sensible. I know this here Zinn. He's as low down an' ornery a skunk as ever lived. He's done Cuter's dirty work fer quite a spell. I could tell you things that would make yer hair curl. I favor yer scheme, except that when you foller 'em over to Ladue Crick, me an' mebbe one or two of the boys'll go 'long. You see this here abduction of our feller citizen, Mr. Burr, constitutes the crime of kidnappin', an' can't be winked at nor condoned, if an' when it is consummated on Halfaday. So we'll fetch Zinn back here an' call a miners' meetin' an mete him out a little justice on the end of a rope that's be'n due him fer a hell of a while. He won't hang hard—an' it'll give him a chanct to die upright, if he ain't never lived that way. I'm sorry we can't wait till Cuter comes up there an' fetch him along fer similar treatment but it wouldn't be right, nor neither ethical. In the first place, torturin' Buckley to make him talk couldn't rightly be considered no crime. It wouldn't even be a misdemeanor. An' in the second place, it wouldn't be committed on Halfaday, nohow. Many a man has got in trouble tryin' to cover too much territory. I hold agin the userpation an' expansion of jurisdiction, as a congressman would say, knowin' damn well his colleagues would think he was askin' fer an appropriation to build a fish ladder up a mountain because the trout in his district was missin' the sunrise. I'm dry—let's go over to Cush's."

Chuckling, Steve followed as the big man opened the door of the cabin and led the way through a dense spruce thicket. "It might be," said Black John, as they emerged into the clearing, "if yer luck runs good, then I'll drop in on you an' Mrs. Washington sometime an' talk over old times on the Koyukuk. French Crick, you said?"

"We'll be on Deep Crick—it runs into the French. Ask Old

Jim—he'll tell you. An' you bet your life you'll be welcome whenever you show up!"

XIII

A FIGHT ON A SANDBAR

A DOZEN OR more men were in Cushing's saloon as the two entered. Striding to the bar, Black John ordered a round of drinks, pausing to introduce Steve as John Quincy Washington, to the assembled prospectors, most of whose names seemed to be Smith. Grinning at the look of perplexity on Steve's face, he continued. "You'll git 'em straightened out, if you stay long enough. If you don't it won't make no difference—one's about as good as another, anyhow. These gents all got here before we invented the name can."

The men grinned and drank, some drifted over to the card tables, and others remained to drink at the bar. Black John sat in a stud game, and declining an invitation to join, Steve looked on for a while, and then sauntered to the bar and engaged in conversation regarding likely locations on the creek.

Half an hour later, someone touched him on the arm, and he turned to see a short, thick-set man at his elbow.

"Buckley wants to see you," the man whispered slyly. "Says it's fer yer own good—his'n, too."

"Where is he?" asked Steve, glancing about the room.

"Outside—says it's best you an' him ain't saw talkin' together. Foller me."

Steve hesitated. Was this some ruse of Buckley's to get him alone? What could he have to say—for the good of them both? What could he say? The scrub crowded thickly about the clearing that surrounded the fort—maybe Buckley intended to serve him as he had served Old Jim Adams. The short man gained the door and passed out without looking around. Steve was no coward, and the clearing lay almost as light as day under the full moon. He would step into the clearing—but no farther. Unnoticed, he made his way to the door and stepped out into the night. Suddenly it seemed that the ground flew up and dealt him a smashing blow in the head. A fountain of brilliant stars blazed before his eyes and—

WHEN STEVE came to it was daylight and he was lying close against the scrub on a sand bar. His head ached fiercely, and he was conscious of a dull, annoying pain in his arms and legs. He tried to shift his position, and discovered that his hands were tied behind him, and that his feet were bound tightly together. A creek rushed noisily past the bar and drawn up onto the sand he could see a canoe. He heard voices and turned his head to see two men crouched beside a camp fire. The movement caused him a low moan of pain and the men glanced toward him. They were Sam Buckley, and the short man who had enticed him from the saloon.

Buckley arose and walked over to him. "Come to, eh? It's about time. We thought maybe we'd have to pull on without giving you any breakfast. Roll over on your belly and I'll untie your hands. I'll trust you while you eat, with your hands loose, as long as I know you haven't got any weapons on you."

As the man talked, he knelt and untied the babiche line that bound Steve's hands. Sitting up, Steve wriggled his stiffened fingers as the blood tingled through the starved veins.

"How about my feet, Sam?" he asked. "They're numb from the ankles down, an' damn near froze."

"They won't freeze," grinned Buckley, "an' a man can't run far on numb feet. I'd hate to have to shoot you for trying to make a get-away. I want to deliver you on the hoof." The short man handed Steve a plate of food and a cup of scalding coffee as Buckley continued. "So, they crowded you so close you had to hit for Halfaday, eh?'

"Yeah," answered Steve indifferently. "Where you takin' me, Sam?"

"Dawson, of course. A man named Corporal Downey wants to have a little talk with you."

"What good'll that do you? There ain't no reward."

Buckley laughed. "There's a reward all right, a damn good reward—for me. You see, after you robbed Old Jim Adams, Cuter Malone got it into his head that I knocked you off, and copped Old Jim's dust, and yours too. He insisted on a cut, and when I told him I didn't know what he was talking about he pulled a gun on me and told me that he was going to send Zinn along with me to get the stuff. I knocked him down and beat it. He's got too damn many murdering gents on his payroll to suit me. Before I turn you over to the police, I'm going to show you to Cuter, so he'll see you're not murdered—and then Dawson will be safe for me again." The man paused, and added with a meaning look, "There's nothing for me on Halfaday; but with you convicted of robbing Old Jim, there'll be a hell of a lot for me on French Crick."

"How did you recognize me?" asked Steve, ignoring the taunt.

Buckley grinned, and pointed to a small crescent shaped scar near the base of Steve's right thumb. "I sat across the table from that scar for five months on Deep Creek. I might not have recognized you if you hadn't offered to shake hands."

"So, you think I robbed Old Jim, do you?" asked Steve.

"Hell—everyone knows you did."

"But," answered Steve, "I didn't. An' no one knows that but you—an' me."

Buckley grinned. "They'll let Old Jim tell 'em all about that at the trial. Come on—put your hands behind you and we'll get going."

TRUSSED HAND and foot, Steve was lifted into the canoe amidships along with the duffel, and the two shoved off, Buckley paddling the bow. The descent of Halfaday was fraught with much labor, the creek having numerous shallow rapids that necessitated portaging, and while the packs were light, Steve was a load for both men, neither being expert in the art of packing.

At noon, the two dumped their prisoner onto a sand bar at the foot of a rapid, and Buckley turned to the other. "Build a fire, Shorty, and we'll eat. I'm damn near all in. We'll feel better for an hour's rest."

The short man's brow drew into a frown. "It would be better to keep on goin'," he objected. "We hadn't ort to camp this noon. If Black John should miss this here party, he'll shore as hell take out after us. Long as a man minds his own business on Halfaday he's all right, but when he goes hornin' in, stealin' other folks, an' such, he's out of luck if Black John ketches him."

"Black John won't catch up with us," said Buckley. "We've made good time, and he wouldn't start till morning—if he starts at all, which I very much doubt. What the hell does he care about Steve here, or what becomes of him? Even if he does miss us all, he'll think we pulled out together to do some prospecting."

Shorty appeared not satisfied. "We ain't made no time to what them boys would make, if they took after us. They'll be travelin' light—an' not carryin' no prisoner around no rapids. It ain't that he'd prob'ly give a damn about this here party, as such. It's the principle of the thing that Black John looks at. He's hell fer principles! The way he figgers, if folks was allowed to be stole off'n Halfaday whenever anyone tuk a notion, it would make it mean fer the boys—them not knowin' who might be next. I'm tellin' you, the man that bucks Black John ort to git him an iron neck—hangin' seems to jist come natural to him!"

"I'll take a chance," growled Buckley. "I'm too damn tired to paddle another stroke without a rest, and something to eat. Trouble with you fellows up here, Black John's got you buffaloed."

"Yeah," answered Shorty, as he started for the scrub with the ax, "but, at that, I'd ruther be buffaloed than hung."

"How about untyin' my hands?" asked Steve, as Buckley carried the cooking outfit from the canoe.

"Plenty of time when grub's ready," retorted Buckley. "I can't bother to watch you and the cooking, too."

Steve lay idly watching the preparations for dinner, and devoutly hoping that Shorty's prediction would come true. His view of the rapids upstream was cut off by the scrub, and their roar, he knew, would drown any sound of approach from above. If Black John would only come!

Suddenly, his eye caught a blur of motion at a bend of the creek, some fifty yards downstream. Intently he fixed his gaze on it, and made out the bow of a canoe, nosing slowly around the bend. The craft halted abruptly with more than half its length exposed, then slowly and silently it slipped back around the bend. Steve's pulse quickened. He had caught a glimpse of two men in the canoe. A glance told him that neither Buckley nor Shorty had seen it. Who could they be? Surely not Black John—he would be coming downstream! Zinn and Anvil Johnnie? If so, they had made much better time than Steve gave them credit for. Whoever it was had no intention of being seen by the men on the bar. Minutes passed, tense minutes for Steve who strained his ears to catch, above the roar of the rapid, the sound of a snapping twig or swishing branch that would tell that the two from the canoe were approaching afoot. He wriggled into a position that gave him a view of the scrub, and of the two who puttered about the fire.

His pulse quickened as, after what seemed an interminable period of waiting, he saw a tremble in the young spruce close to the edge of the scrub and not more than fifteen feet from the kneeling figures at the fire. The next instant the low trees at the edge of the scrub swished violently, and two figures catapulted from the dense cover and hurled themselves upon the kneeling figures at the fire. Grunts and curses and the thud of blows sounded from a confused blur of writhing bodies and flying sand. Then a scream, shrill and terrible, rent the air as Anvil Johnnie rose to his feet, his two hands tearing at the hilt of the hunting knife that was buried to the guard in his chest.

Still screaming, he staggered across the sand to crash almost at the water's edge, red blood gushing from his mouth, choking the screams to a gurgle.

Zinn and Buckley were thrashing about, now in the fire, now out, locked in a struggle in which neither seemed able to gain an advantage. Gaining his feet, Shorty pranced about the pair, shouting foolish advice to Buckley as he lashed viciously out with his heavy pacs whenever an opening seemed to give opportunity to land a kick on Zinn. Not until he had landed two telling blows on the person of Buckley in his excitement, did he heed the gambler's frantic yells to get the rifle from the canoe. He was too late. With Buckley slowed up by the exertion of the struggle, and dazed by the vicious kicks, one of which had caught him squarely in the side of the head, Zinn found time to go for his gun. As Shorty turned, rifle in hand, from the canoe, the six-gun in Zinn's hand roared, and Shorty, a look of puzzled surprise in his eyes, sank into a grotesque heap on the sand.

THERE WAS no more fight in Buckley. Slipping a pistol from the gambler's armpit holster Zinn rose to his feet and glanced at the two dead men. He eyed Buckley with a twisted grin. "Looks like a horse apiece," he said, balancing a six-gun in either hand, "an' a pair of sixes to beat. If you can't beat 'em, Buckley, you lose."

"What the hell's it all about?" mumbled Buckley, his eyes on the guns.

The twisted grin broadened. "Cuter wants to see you—that's all. These babies are the invitation to his party. Are they good?"

"I want to see him, too," growled Buckley. "It looks as if you'd played the damn fool, Zinn. There was no need for the rough stuff."

"Yeah? Well, mebbe. Mebbe not. I've got you—that's the main thing."

"Let's be pullin' for Dawson," said Buckley nervously.

"Not Dawson. Ladue Crick."

"Where in hell's Ladue Crick?"

"Not so fer from here. It's where Cuter's holdin' his party—jest you an' me an' him. It'll be quite a party, Buckley—it'll last all your life. But first he'll make you talk."

"What do you mean?" cried the other, the color suddenly leaving his face.

"Cuter, he kind of wants to know what you done with Steve Blaine's dust."

Buckley grinned. "Still thinks I bumped Steve off, and grabbed his dust, does he?"

"He sure does."

"Well—I didn't, and I can prove it."

LYING CLOSE against the scrub and entirely unobserved by Zinn, Steve cleared his throat. Zinn whirled and the next instant Steve found himself looking into the muzzles of two six-guns. For a long moment the two guns covered him, then suddenly they were lowered. A scowl darkened Zinn's face. "You!" he cried. "What the hell are you doin' here? Come here!"

"I can't," grinned Steve. "I'm tied up. Buckley was goin' to pass me off fer Steve Blaine, so Cuter would think he didn't kill him."

"That is Steve Blaine!" cried Buckley, who had listened with bulging eyes. "He was on the run from the police, an' I kidnapped him!"

Zinn grinned, broadly, and Buckley reiterated, "I tell you he is Steve Blaine! Anyone down at Dawson can swear to it!"

A laugh of derision greeted the words, as Zinn turned his sneering eyes on Buckley. "You damn fool—I know Steve Blaine! I've saw him a dozen times! You can't fool me—an' you wouldn't of fooled Cuter, neither! He knows him! Why this bum has be'n hangin' around the Palace fer a hell of a while, right in under Cuter's nose—an' the police, too. They'd of spotted him in a minute if he was Steve Blaine—an' besides, Blaine's got three good claims! What in hell would he be hangin' around Cuter's fer like a bum—moochin' drinks, an' layin' up with the Siwashes down to Moosehide?"

"But I tell you," cried the almost frantic Buckley, "that he is—"

"Cut it out!" snapped Zinn.

"We've got to take him along, I tell you! Cuter'll kill me to make me tell where I hid Steve's cache—and I've got to prove he isn't dead!"

"Yeah," sneered Zinn, "he'll kill you, all right—fer bustin' him on the jaw—an' skippin' out with Jim Adams's dust that you had in the safe—but before he kills you, you're goin' to sweat a hell of a lot of blood. I've saw Cuter work before. He's got some tricks that a man would have to see to believe. Red hot gun bar'ls is only part of it."

Sweat stood out on Buckley's forehead in little beads. "I tell you—"

"You ain't tellin' me nothin'," interrupted Zinn. "I'm tellin' you! Come on now—git in that canoe, in front. An' any monkey work, an' I'll begin trimmin' you with these six-guns. Cuter wants you alive—but he didn't say you couldn't be shot up a little around the edges."

Buckley turned to Steve in a frenzy of terror. "Tell him, Steve! For God's sake, tell him who you are!"

Steve grinned, and turned to Zinn. "Say, pardner," he said, "how about me? You ain't goin' to leave me here, are you?"

Zinn scarcely accorded him a glance. "Yeah—you stay here to keep them company." He jerked his head in the direction of the two dead men. "I got my hands full tendin' to him."

"But untie me, anyway!"

"Untie—hell! I'd ort to shoot you fer knowin' too much—but you ain't goin' no place from here, nohow. If you git tired starvin' to death, roll in the river an' drown."

He turned to Buckley who stood the picture of abject terror, and prodded him in the ribs with a pistol. "Come on, step along. Git in that canoe!"

XIV

BLACK JOHN TAKES A HAND

IT WAS NEARLY one o'clock when Black John Smith shoved back his chair, cashed in his chips at Cushing's bar, and called for a round of drinks.

"Where's Jack?" he asked, his eyes searching the room.

"Jack who?" asked a voice at his elbow.

"Why, Jack Washington. John Quincy Washington, accordin' to the name can. He's stoppin' with me till he looks around a bit."

"I ain't saw him in quite a while," said the man. "I thought he was playin' stud."

"No, he didn't set in the game. Prob'ly went over to the shack an' rolled in. An' I'm goin' to do likewise."

The men drank, and as Black John returned his glass to the bar he caught the eye of Old Cush, who had leaned over to mop at an imaginary spot with the bar rag. "Worshington," he said, in an undertone, "went out at nine forty-two. He follered Shorty Smith out, after Shorty had spoke to him, private."

"Shorty Smith!" whispered Black John, his brows drawing into a frown. "It's some scheme of that damn tin horn's! Why in hell didn't you tell me?"

"I did," answered the somber-faced Cush, and moved off down the bar to serve a customer who was demanding refreshment.

Black John left the room abruptly and hurried to his cabin. It was empty, and a hasty survey showed that Steve's pack and rifle were on the bunk where he had tossed them. The moon hung low in the west as, rifle in hand, the big man closed the door of the cabin, and headed up the creek for Shorty Smith's shack, a mile away.

Receiving no answer to his thumping upon the door, he pushed it open, struck a match, and held it to the wick of a tin lamp. He saw at a glance that the place had been deserted. The blankets were missing from the two bunks, cooking utensils and pack sacks were gone, and Shorty's rifle was nowhere to be seen.

Twenty minutes later, Black John re-entered Cush's saloon, stepped to the bar and pounded upon it with his fist. "I want three men to foller me an' fetch their rifles," he said. "Shorty Smith an' that damn Alex Burr has pulled their freight, an' I've got reasons to believe they've took Jack Washington along with 'em, contrary to his right to be left where he's at. The case calls fer investigation, an' if skullduggery has be'n committed, the prisoners, if any, will be fetched back an' dooly tried by miners' meetin'."

A dozen men volunteered, and Black John selected three. "I'm pickin' out only Alaska boys fer this job," he explained. "We might have to foller these damn skunks quite a ways before we ketch 'em, an' it might make it mean if any Yukon wanteds was to git that fer from the line."

"We can't start till daylight, John," ventured one.

"The hell we can't! The moon'll give light fer an hour yet. They've got about five hours start, but if they have to pack a man over them portages, we'll overtake 'em before they hit the White. When it gits too dark to see, we'll camp an' cook breakfast. That way, we won't lose no time."

AT NOON next day the four men, carrying two canoes around a rapid, halted abruptly and peered through a thin screen of scrub at two men who stood on a sand bar. One of these men was prodding the other in the ribs with a pistol, evidently ordering him into a canoe that lay at the water's edge. At a signal from Black John, the canoes were lowered noiselessly to the ground, the men crept to a more advantageous position, and four rifles were trained upon the men on the sand bar.

Black John filled his lungs. "Hold everything!" he bellowed, his voice carrying above the roar of the rapids.

One of the men whirled, a pistol in each hand, to stare at the four leveled rifles.

"Drop them guns!" roared Black John, and the two pistols thudded upon the sand.

The four stepped out onto the bar, "Hello, John!" exclaimed Zinn, putting a vast heartiness into his tone.

"Hello, Zinn." Black John's eyes were taking in the details of the scene. "Up to yer old tricks, eh?" he asked, his eyes on the dead men.

Zinn pointed to the body of Shorty, crumpled against the canoe. "He knifed my pardner, there, an' I clipped him off jest as he was pullin' his rifle down on me," he explained.

Black John nodded. "You done commendable. Shorty couldn't be considered no loss."

Apparently greatly relieved by the words of approbation, Zinn launched into effusive speech, which was immediately cut short by Black John. "One thing to a time," he said curtly. "We'll take up your case, later." He turned to Buckley, who seemed even more relieved than had Zinn. "Where was you headin' fer?" he asked, crisply.

"Dawson!" answered Buckley.

Black John nodded and stooping he cut the ropes that bound Steve's hands and feet. "How about Washington, here? Was he goin' to Dawson, too? An' Shorty?"

"It was damn important that I take him back to Dawson. Shorty was helping me. I can explain—"

"It won't be necessary," interrupted Black John. "Fer as I kin see, there ain't no reason Washington shouldn't go to Dawson. But with you it's different. Yer suspected of stealin' some an' sundry of sacks of dust out of Cush's safe."

"It's a lie!" exclaimed Buckley. "I was never anywhere near Cush's safe! How in hell could I have stolen any dust out of it?"

"The ways of thieves is devious," opined Black John. "Where's yer pack?"

Buckley pointed to a packsack amidship in the canoe. "It's there," he said. "Go through it, by all means. I suppose you know what kind of sacks you're lookin' for."

"Yeah," answered Black John, lifting the sack from the canoe, "I sure do."

Opening the pack, the huge man removed several articles of clothing, and uncovered nine new moosehide sacks.

"Whose dust is this?" he asked, eyeing Buckley truculently.

"Mine! That dust was never in Cushing's safe."

BLACK JOHN tossed one of the sacks to Steve, who untied the string, and turning back the mouth a trifle, carefully examined the seam. Then he handed the sack back to Black John who flashed another question at Buckley. "Is them your sacks the dust is in?"

"Of course they are."

"Where'd you git 'em?"

"Whose business is that?" snapped Buckley. "But if you want to know—I made 'em!"

"An' how did you make 'em?" persisted Black John, examining the seam.

Buckley grinned. If Black John expected to catch him there, he would find himself out of luck. During his partnership with Steve on Deep Creek, he had become an adept in fashioning the little sacks. "How in hell would a man make 'em—cut 'em out of moosehide an' sew 'em together—"

"What with?"

"Why—sinew—of course. What the hell are you driving at?"

Black John retied the sack and tossed it into the pack. "I guess these ain't the sacks Cush lost," he said. "Fact is, they're the ones, er part of 'em, that was stole off'n Old Jim Adams." Picking up the two pistols that Zinn had dropped into the sand, Black John thrust one into the front of his shirt, and handed the other to Steve. "This here might come in handy on yer trip to Dawson," he said. "Mr. Burr, here, seems anxious that you an' him was to go there, an' we won't be hinderin' you none. What I claim, turn about is fair play, an' seein' he had you tied up part of the trip, you'd ort to tie him up fer the balance." He turned to one of the men who had accompanied him. "Here, Spike, you claim you use to be a sailor. Tie Mr. Burr's hands an' feet—an' while yer at it, slip that blackjack out of his hind pocket an' give it to Washington. It might come in handy fer evidence."

Like a flash Buckley whirled and started for the scrub, only to plow into the sand with Steve on top of him, and the erstwhile sailor soon had him trussed like a turkey.

"There you be," grinned Black John to Steve as Buckley, cursing like a maniac, was lifted into the canoe. "You'd ort to reach Corporal Downey before yer time's up, an' you kin tell him that if he needs any corroborative evidence at the trial, he kin count on us four to prove that them sacks was in Buckley's possession, an' that he claimed they was his property. Also that the blackjack was found on him—er, in fact, anything else he'd like to have proved that would be of help in the case. We always like to accommodate a friend. Tell him we're all Alaska boys, with nothin' on us in the Yukon—an' we'd jest as soon testify at the trial."

As Steve stepped toward the canoe, Zinn started to follow.

Black John laid a detaining hand upon Zinn's arm. "Where was you goin'?" he asked.

"Why—back to Dawson, of course! Cuter Malone sent me and Anvil there up to get Buckley an' fetch him over to a cabin on Ladue Crick. He wanted to talk to him about somethin'!"

"You mean, he hired you to come up to Halfaday an' kidnap one of our citizens?"

"Call it that, if you want to," grinned the man. Then his

expression suddenly changed as he caught a glint in Black John's eye. "What do you mean?" he asked uneasily.

"Meanin' that we're plumb moral up here on Halfaday. Crime ain't permitted. It's punishable by hangin'. Kidnappin's a crime."

The man's face went suddenly white. He had heard about the rugged justice that obtained on Halfaday. "But God—you wouldn't hang me for kidnappin'—him!"

"Damn if I know, Zinn. There ain't a man I know of that needs hangin' as bad as you do—onless it's Malone, an' he ain't here. Off hand, I'd say we're goin' to hang you fer somethin'. But you kin rest easy that we won't hang you on no trumped up charge. It'll be all fair an' regular, after a trial by miners' meetin' in which you'll be give all the breaks that's comin' to a damn low-lived skunk like you. Seein' you've objected to bein' hung fer kidnappin', an' takin' due cognizance of the case, I'm inclined to agree with you. My conscience wouldn't be clear if we was to hang you on that charge. You see, bein' as you hadn't, in fact, got off'n Halfaday with yer man, it couldn't rightly be called a kidnappin'. I'm changin' it to illegal possession, instead. That comes under the head of skullduggery, an' as such, is hang-able. That'll be one charge. But we always like to have at least two, so if a man gits turned loose on one, we've got an ace in the hole. Killin' Shorty will be winked at. It was prob'ly, as you said, self defense—an' no one would give a damn if it wasn't. But how about him?" He paused and pointed to Steve. "You had a couple of guns in yer hand when we come up, an' you had him all tied up—"

"I didn't tie him up. That was Buckley. I wasn't goin' to do nothin' with the damn bum. I was goin' to leave him where he was at."

"Tied up?"

"I didn't tie him. It wasn't none of my business!"

Black John nodded. "The other charge will be murder," he announced. "Leavin' a man tied hand an' foot like that, in a place like this, is tantamount to murder, as a lawyer would say."

"But—you can't convict me of murder! Hell—the man ain't dead!"

"That ain't your fault. He would of be'n, if we hadn't come along. You've heard of accessories before the fact—well, this here is murder before the fact. Now if you kin convict an accessory before the fact, it's a damn sight more reasonable to convict a principal before the fact. It would be faulty logic to suppose an accessory could be more guilty than a principal."

"But," shrilled the man, thoroughly terrorized as, at a signal from Black John, the three followers closed about him, "the man ain't dead! I tell you, you can't hang me!"

Black John shook his head dolefully. "Mebbe not," he admitted. "But—fetch him along, boys. We'll go on up to Cush's, an' see."

FORECLOSURE ON HALFADAY

OLD CUSH, PROPRIETOR of Cushing's Fort, the combined trading post and saloon that served the little community of outlawed men that had sprung up on Halfaday Creek close against the Yukon-Alaska border, folded the month-old newspaper he had been reading and, reaching onto the back bar, set out a bottle, two glasses, and the leather dice box as Black John Smith stepped into the room and crossed to the bar.

Picking up the box, the big man shook three sixes. "I'm leavin' 'em," he said. "Three sixes in one is above the average."

Cush gathered the dice into the box and rolled out three aces. "Yer allus talkin' about averages an' the like of that, but what I claim dice shakin' is like anythin' else—sometimes you win, an' sometimes you lose. Sometimes a pair of treys would win, an' sometimes five sixes could git beat. It's accordin' if yer lucky er if you ain't." He returned the dice to the box, shook them out again, and eyed the big man across the bar. "There's a pair of fives. Accordin' to this here law of averages of yourn, they ain't no good to leave in one, be they?"

"W-e-e-l-l, off hand, I'd say that the mathematical probability of—"

Cush interrupted him with a scowl. "I don't want to stand here an' listen to no sermon which wouldn't mean nothin' when you got it preached. I'm leavin' them two fives. Go ahead an' beat 'em if you kin."

Black John picked up the box, rolled out the dice, and regarded a pair of fours with disfavor. Cush made an entry in his day book, and shoved the bottle across the bar. "That proves yer law of averages ain't worth a damn, an' never was. It's like I says—if yer lucky you win, an' if you ain't, you lose. Take old Pat Finnigan, now—"

"What's Pat got to do with it?" Black John interrupted.

"Pat, he's more proof that this here law of averages yer allus hollerin' about is the bunk. Pat, he shows up along in January with a poke of dust in his pocket. He's broke come spring, an' he wants I should grubstake him fer a trip out in the hills. He's old, an' he don't know the country, an' he don't know nothin' about prospectin', never havin' done nothin' sence he hit the country but chop cordwood fer the steamboats. So I turns him down on the grubstake, but I lets him have a pick, an' pan, an' shovel, an' a month's grub on his promise that if he don't strike nothin' he'll work it out doin' chores around the fort.

"He hits up this crick, which everyone else has passed up, 'cause it don't look no good. He's on the run fer somethin'—you kin bet on that. An' the reason he hit the crick is 'cause it's clost to the line so if a police shows up he kin step acrost into Alasky. That's three months ago—an' you know the rest. He goes four mile up it an' starts shovellin' twenty, thirty dollars to the pan right out of the grass ruts—jest like Carmack done on Bonanza. So he names his crick Lucky Crick, an' all the rest of the boys on Halfaday hits up there an' prospects the crick from the mouth clean to the head of it—an' not a damn one of 'em even hits a color! Red John an' Short John got back last night. They was the last ones to quit, an' they claim there ain't another payin' location on the hull damn crick. Now what I claim—if yer law of averages was worth a damn, how come some old cuss like Pat would hit some crick which everyone with any sense had passed up, go half ways up it, an' start shovellin' dust out of the grass ruts, in a place that don't look no more promisin' than any other part of the crick? An' all the other boys that's good prospectors tears up the gravel fer four mile each way from him, an' don't strike a damn color! What's yer law of averages got to say about that?"

"It's an incontrovertible fact that inherently—"

"You kin swaller all the rest of the big words you aim to spit out, like you allus do when you git cornered, 'cause I ain't listenin'. An' not only old Pat hits the richest location in these here parts, but he's got it all fer hisself, 'cause I turned him down on that grubstake. Cripes, if I'd of took him up, half that claim would be'n mine! Pat, he's jest nach'lly lucky—an' no averages about it."

Black John grinned. "He's lucky, all right. I'd forgot he named his crick Lucky Crick. The boys all call it Finnigan's Crick."

"Why the hell wouldn't they? Not a damn one of 'em had no luck on it—only Pat. An' that there other crick that runs along side of Finnigan's Crick, jest over the ridge from it, ain't no better. The boys prospected it, too. Struck a few colors, here an' there, but nothin' as good as what they had here on Halfaday. Chances is, there ain't even one good location on it. The boys all give it up, all but that there young Joe Tuttle—him that married Bill Emmet's gal. Joe, he's got faith in that crick, an' so's Ada. They come in there three, four months ago an' be'n prospectin' it ever sence. Red John, he was talkin' to 'em the other day, an' Joe told him they was jest about makin' wages. They built 'em a little shack jest over the ridge from Finnigan's, an' they're sinkin' a shaft there. Red John says Joe told him he figgers that mebbe Finnigan's pocket stretched clean acrost in under the ridge, an' he might hit it on this other crick. Red John says the ridge ain't very high nor very wide there. Joe an' Ada ain't recorded no location yet. They're jest prospectin'."

BLACK JOHN nodded. "Yeah, I was through there not long ago. They're a nice couple—them young folks. Joe, he's a hard workin' fella, an' Ada Emmet, she's a sourdough born. I'd like to see 'em make good."

"Why, shore," Cush agreed. "But they ain't goin' to do no

good where they're at. They better hit out an' find 'em another crick."

"Gold's where you find it," Black John reminded. "They might hit it lucky. Finnigan did. An' his crick don't look a damn bit better than the one they're on."

"An' who the hell's takin' me name in vain?"

Black John turned at the sound of the voice and smiled into the twinkling blue eyes of the little old man who advanced toward the bar. "Speak of the devil, an' up he pops."

"Divil, er not—it's me that's here, wid a poke o' dust 'twould choke a moose. 'Tis me birthday, an' I'm takin' the day off to celebrate."

"Your birthday, eh? How'd the old world look a hundred years ago today?"

"'Twas a damn fine day. I didn't git here till twenty-five year later. I'm siventy-five year old today, an' I was born on me mother's twinty-fifth birthday. So I know a hundred year ago today was a damn fine day for the world, when a woman like her was born into it."

The big man's smile widened. "You're all right, Pat. That's as fine a tribute as I ever heard. Fill up, Cush is buyin' one."

For answer the little man produced a moosehide poke which thudded heavily on the bar. "The drinks is on me."

One Armed John stepped into the room carrying a string of fish. Cush scowled at him from behind the bar. "Take them damn fish outa here! I sure ain't a-goin' to have the bar slimed up—nor neither yet the floor!"

Old Pat glanced at the one armed one. "Hold on!" he cried. "What's them fish worth?"

One Armed John held them up for inspection. "They's some nice ones here—I jest ketched 'em. I'd ort to git half an ounce."

"Half an ounce—hell! I'll give ye an ounce. Take 'em out back an' tell Cush's klooch to fry 'em up fer supper. Ye've saved me life—er mebbe only me soul. Hadn't ye showed up wid them fish, I'd had to go hungry, or else git tossed into hell fer eatin' moose meat on a Friday. When ye git shet of the fish, I'll give ye another ounce to go up an' down the crick an' tell the boys to come on in to Cush's, an' help me celebrate me birthday. Tell 'em the drinks is all on me, an' tonight we'll have a stud game—an' tell 'em I hope I lose."

"Hope you lose?" asked Cush, as One Armed disappeared, "why would anyone hope he'd lose in a stud game?"

"'Tis like this—if I'm reasonably diligent wid me drink, be supper time I'll be feelin' fine. After supper we'll play stud. If I lose I'll hit out fer home in the mornin', still feelin' fine. If I win, I'll have to stay around mebbe a day or two blowin' in me winnin's, an' it's gittin' so, lately, that a two, three day's drunk is hard on me guts. I wouldn't feel good fer a week."

BLACK JOHN laughed. "Why not bank your winnin's here with Cush, or carry 'em back to the crick an' cache 'em? Cripes, man, if you'd really get to work on that location of yours, you could lay out a hundred thousand er so fer pipe an' tap that little lake back in the hills an' sluice out enough dust to fill the safe here in six months time. Or if you didn't bank it, you could cache enough there in the rocks to make you a millionaire."

"An' what's the good of it? I'm an old man. So far as I know I've got nary kith nor kin in the world to leave it to. Why should I work like hell fer six months an' shove it in Cush's safe, so when I die ye boys could divide it amongst ye, or else blow it in drinkin' an' playin' stud? Nussir, if there's any drinkin' an' stud playin' wid my dust, I'm a-goin' to be in on it meself! An' as fer cachin' it—why should I tear out the bone to bury a lot of dust somewheres in the rocks? Hell, it's in the ground a'ready! Let whoever's goin' to spend it after I'm gone dig it out. Like now, I ain't got a worry in the world. If I had a cache, I'd be worryin' fer fear someone might rob it. But wid the dust layin' there in the gravel, there can't no one dig a hell of a lot of it before I'd ketch 'em at it. Take it like now, if I need some supplies, er felt like doin' a bit of drinkin' an' card playin', all I got to do is work fer half a day wid me shovel an' pan, put the dust in me poke, an' come down here to Cush's."

"Seems like sound philosophy, at that," the big man agreed.

"'Tain't no philosophy about it. It's jest common sense."

"If I was you I'd record that location, though."

"Well, you ain't me—so I ain't recorded it. Why the hell should I record it? 'Twas pure luck made me start diggin' there where I did, an' hittin' the only pocket on the hull damn crick. But it worn't luck that put me on that crick. Nussir. I hit up that crick 'cause it run right up agin' the line where if the police come huntin' me I could step over into Alasky. I shot Gus Huber, an' if the police would find his body, they'd have me dead to rights. An' if I'd record me location they'd know where to find me. Me an' Huber took a contract to git out a thousan' cords of wood fer the steamboats. We put up a shack an' went to work. I didn't know much about Huber, then. But by Chris'mas time I know'd plenty.

"Mike O'Leary was workin' a claim on a crick a couple of mile from our shack. His daughter Mary lived wid him—as likely a lass as a man would want to see. Gus Huber was a big broth of a lad, mebbe risin' of thirty. 'Twas not long before he'd tuk to walkin' acrost to O'Leary's of a Sunday, an' now an' agin of a moonlight night. At first I didn't blame him fer that, fig-gerin' he was courtin' Mary an' how mebbe they'd be gittin' married. One night I twigged him about it—an' 'twas then I found he'd an evil mind. He winked and grinned a wicked grin. "Give me a little more time," he says, "an' I'll git what I want widout marryin'."

"'If that's what ye're up to, Gus Huber,' I says, 'ye'll not git away wid it, I'll tell Mike O'Leary to warn Mary to have nothin' more to do wid you.'

"'One word out ye,' he says, 'an' it'll be yer last word. Ye mind ye're own business an' I'll mind mine.'

"Gus, he was bigger than me, so I shet up, but I made up me mind to keep an eye on him, fer I wanted no harm to come to the girl.

"Come Chris'mas time me an' Gus hits for Dawson for to celebrate a bit. We draws what money we had comin' on the contract, an' Gus he tries to hold out on me an' we have a row there in the Tivoli, an' some of the sourdoughs hears it. Later Downey claimed someone heard me threaten him. Mebbe I did, but when he came acrost wid my share the row was over.

"We're in the Klondike Palace, one night, an' I take on a bit of a load an' git sleepy. So I crawls in one of them booths there in the dance hall an' takes me a snooze. When I wakes up I hears someone talkin' in the next booth. I recognize Gus Huber's voice. 'She's a knock-out fer looks,' he's sayin', 'an' ye'll have to pay high fer her.'

"'How do I know she'll work in?' says another voice. 'An' how you goin' to git her here?'

"'She'll work in, all right. She's livin' on a crick wid her old man near where I'm workin'. It won't be long, now—an' when the time's right, somethin's goin' to happen to the old man—an' then I'll fetch her in.'

"'Okay,' say the other one, 'but mind ye, I'm lookin' her over before I put out a damn cent.'

"They gits up an' steps out of the booth, an' I peeks out of my booth an' sees Gus an' Cuter Malone walk to the bar.

"The next day we hits back to camp, an' come Sunday, Gus shaves an' steps out the door. 'Where ye goin'?' I says. 'Where d'ye s'pose?' says he, wid a grin an' a wink. 'I s'pose ye're headin' fer O'Leary's,' I says, 'but ye better change ye're mind.' Wid that he whirls on me wid an ugly look in his eye. 'You mind ye're own business, ye old fool,' he says, 'an' ye'll live longer.' An' then he turns around an' heads into the bush.

"**I PICKS** up the old carbine we've got there an' follers him out an' when he's crossin' a bit of slashin' I lets him have it. 'Tis a still mornin', an' wid the black powder cat'ridges we had that old carbine roared like a cannon. I stud there a long time smellin' the powder smoke an' starin' at the spot where Gus Huber had dropped, mebbe it's fifty yards away. 'Pat Finnigan,' I says to meself, 'ye've killed a man.' 'Twas a turrible feelin' come over me standin' there in the bush an' I was wishin' wid all me heart that Gus Huber was alive agin. Then I thought of Mike O'Leary an' Mary there on the crick—an' what would have happened to them—an' the feelin' passed, an' I was glad I'd shot him. 'But the police will call it murder,' I says, an' a feelin' of fear come over me. I'd seen 'em hang O'Brien fer murder in Dawson—an' I seen meself in O'Brien's shoes, standin' there on the scaffold waitin' fer 'em to spring the trap. 'Let 'em call it what they will,' I says. 'Twas a good deed—an' ketchin' comes before hangin'.'

"'Twas then I noticed it had started to snow. I walks over to Gus an' looks down at him. I seen where the bullet had ketched him in the back of the head but hadn't gone on through. First I thought of splittin' his head an' gittin' the bullet, an' droppin' it along wid the carbine an' the rest of the cat'ridges through a hole in the ice in the river. 'Cause I know'd if the Mounted Corporal ever found Gus, an' got that bullet they'd know it come from that old carbine of mine, them knowin' 'twas the only one like it in the country. But I had no stummick fer splittin' his head open an' messin' around amongst his brains fer the bullet.

"The snow come down faster, fine snow, almost like fog, it was. I went back to the shack an' fetched the sled an' loaded Gus onto ut, an' drug him to the river. I chopped a hole in the ice an' shoved him through it. Then I went back to the shack. The wind come up, an' fer two days the blizzard roared, an' when 'twas over there was big drifts along the river, an' the snow laid deep in the slashin'.'"

The old man paused, ordered another round of drinks, and resumed. "'Tis hell how things works out. 'Tis the next Sunday, an' I'm settin' there in the shack readin' a magazine Gus had fetched down wid him from Dawson. But I didn't take no comfort in it. There was murders an' shootin's an' killin's of one kind an' another—an' some of 'em looked like they was pulled off pretty smart—but every damn time the shuriff, er police, was smarter, an' the one that done the killin' got ketched, an' evidence enough agin him to hang him higher'n hell. It's a wonder the ones that writes them stories don't give a killer a break, now an' then. The more I read the jumpier I got, an' when all to onct someone give a yell outside the shack, I damn near jumped through the roof. I opens the door, an' there's Mike O'Leary an' Mary. 'Come in,' I says, hearty, bein' glad I'd have someone to talk to. They done so, an' Mary, she looks around. 'Where's Gus?' she says. 'I looked fer him to come over last Sunday, an' agin today, so when he didn't show up, I was afraid he might be sick er somethin'.'

"'No,' I says, 'Gus ain't sick. Leastwise,' I says, 'he worn't sick when he went away.'

"'Went away!' she says. 'Where did he go?'

"'He went down the river a ways,' I says.

"'That's funny,' she says. ''Cause he promised me he'd come over the first Sunday he got back from Dawson an' fetch me a present. He was here last Sunday, wasn't he?'

"'Sure,' I says, 'he was here part of the day. 'Twas last Sunday he headed downriver.'

"'When'll he be back?' Mary says.

"'He didn't say,' I tells her.

"I seen how Mike's eye had be'n sort of rovin' around the shack an' then they swung on me wid a hard look in 'em. An there was a hard sound to his voice when he says, 'I take notice that Gus's packsack is there under his bunk, an' his extra clothes is hangin' there on the nails. D'ye mean to tell me, Pat Finnigan, that he headed downriver in the face of a blizzard, like last Sunday, wid neither pack nor dog outfit? Where downriver was he goin'?'

"'He didn't say,' I says.

"Wid that Mike got up an' stud there glarin' down at me. 'Ye're a damn liar, Pat Finnigan!' he says, an' his voice sounds gritty, like draggin' a sled over gravel. 'Gus warned us a while back that ye'd prob'ly try to come betwixt him an' Mary in some way er another—as if Mary'd look twict at an old coot, like you! But we didn't think ye'd resort to murder.'

"'What d'ye mean—murder?' I says, a cold chill runnin' up an' down me spine at sound of the word.

"'I mean jest what I said—murder!' his voice roarin' the words in me ears. An' wid that, he reaches behind the door an' picks up me old carbine. ''Tis plain as day what happened,' he says. 'Ye git back from Dawson, an' come Sunday, Gus cleans up an' wid Mary's present in his pocket, he hits fer our place, an' ye take this gun an' foller him, an' when ye see ye're chanct, ye let him have ut—shoot him down from behind like a dog. Then the blizzard covers him deep wid snow. But ye'll not git away wid it. Me an' Mary's hittin' fer Dawson to have a talk wid Corporal Downey, an' we're takin' yer gun along. If ye shot him, an' be chanct the bullet didn't go on through, ye're goose'll be cooked when the police find his body. Remember, Pat Finnigan,' he says, 'a murderer always gits ketched. I rec'lect seein' ye there lookin' on when they hung O'Brien—an' ye kin bet ye're last dollar me an' Mary'll be there lookin' on when they're hangin' you!'

"The shack sounded awful still when Mike got through. I could hear the alarm clock tickin' on the shelf. The two of 'em—Mary sittin' on the edge of Gus Huber's bunk, an' Mike standin' betwixt me an' the door, was glarin' at me wid hate in their eyes. I done some quick thinkin'. I seen how me story about Gus headin' downriver in the face of a blizzard widout no pack was a foolish one. An' I tried to take comfort in knowin' that widout no corpse they can't prove no murder. But then I didn't know how far downriver Gus would go. Mebbe, if the current took him clean over into Alasky I'd be all right. But agin, if he'd git ketched in an eddy he might spin around right there at the wood landin' till the ice went out—an' knowin' Gus like I did, I wouldn't put it past the damn cuss to do just that. After all, I thinks, what I done I done to save the girl, so I decided to resort to tellin' 'em the truth. I done so—but it only made 'em the madder. They didn't believe a word I spoke. 'Ye dirty lyin' snake!' Mary cried, her voice high pitched an' quivering wid rage. 'Gus Huber was a fine man! We'd be'n married, come spring, if ye hadn't murdered him in cold blood!'

"'Ye've lied to us onct,' says Mike. 'An' a man that'll lie onct will lie twict—an' keep on lyin'. An' jest to fix it so ye'll not be able to dig pore Gus out from under the snow an' make away wid his body, ye're goin' to Dawson along wid us—an' we're hittin' out right now.'

"'I ain't goin' to Dawson,' I says.

"'The hell an' you ain't!' says Mike.

"'Be God, ye'll go on ye're two feet, er I knock ye out wid this gun bar'l an' pack ye there on me back,' he says.

"Mike, he's bigger'n me, an' he's got the gun—an' there's Mary who's strong as any man. I seen how the odds was agin me, so I agrees to go along.

"So we hit the trail, an' 'tis near midnight, an' black dark when we slant up the bank from the river, there by the old sawmill. Mary's ahead, an Gus is behind me an' when we git to the top of the bank I pretends to slip an' fall down. I grabs Mike by the legs, an' flips him over the bank, an' before Mary kin turn around, I shoves her over, too, an' they go rollin' down through the snow.

"I'm in a hell of a fix. I know'd most of the sourdoughs from back when I took wood contracts around Forty Mile, an' I want to connect up wid 'em. But I don't dast to show up at the Tivoli, where I figgered they'd be playin' stud. So I sneaks around into Bettles' cabin an' lays down on his extry bunk. After a while he comes in, an' Swiftwater Bill wid him. I tell 'em the truth about what come off, an how I done it to save Mary, an' how the two of 'em turned agin me like I was a mad dog, er somethin'. The two of 'em set there an' laughed like it was a hell of a joke on me. But I can't see no joke in me gittin' hung—an' I tells 'em so.

"'They ain't apt to be hangin' you, Pat,' Bettles says. 'The chances is Gus'll slip on through Alasky an' clean down to Norton Sound, come spring.'

"'Ye don't know the damn cuss like I do,' I says. ''Twould be jest like him to spin around in under the ice all winter in some eddy an' then when the break-up comes to pop up right in front of Downey's canoe wid that bullet in his head—an' Downey havin' me gun to fit the bullet in.'

"Swiftwater nods his head. 'Yeah,' he says, 'Gus Haber wasn't no blue chip in any man's game—an' Downey damn well knows it. But still an' all, shootin' him from behind, like ye done, might be considered an infringement of some law, at that.'

"'Me conscience is clear,' I says. ''Twas the only way I seen to save the girl. I'd nothin' to go to the police wid. If I told 'em what I heard in the Palace, both Cuter an' Gus would lie out of it—an' the police couldn't do a damn thing till it was too late. Even with Mike an' Mary turned agin me, I'm glad I done ut.'

"'I claim ye done right,' Bettles says.

"'Me, too,' says Swiftwater. 'If I was you I'd lay low till spring, an' see if they find Gus.'

"'Layin' low would be fine,' I says, 'but I ain't got nothin' to lay low on—an' nowheres to lay, if I had it. Me an' Gus draw'd all the money we had comin' on our contract, an' blowed it in around Chris'mas. I dastn't go back to me shack—an' I ain't got no money for grub.'

"'Ye better hit fer Halfaday Crick,' Bettles says, pullin' a poke out of his pocket an' tossin' it to me. 'There's dust enough in there to feed ye till spring an' a few drinks on the side.'

"'An' I've got a good dog team,' Swiftwater says. 'In the mornin' I'll git an outfit of blankets an' grub, an' hire a Siwash to take you to Halfaday. Ye'll be hittin' out, come dark tomorrow night.'

"''Twas damn white of them boys to help an old man out, an'

them not expectin' to git a damn cent back. But they did git ut back—an' more with it. The dust was in them two pokes I sent down to 'em, when you went to Dawson last month, John."

BLACK JOHN nodded. "Yeah, they didn't want to take it, but I told 'em you was lousy with dust—that you'd hit the richest pocket in the Halfaday country. The fact is, Pat, I knew why you was here all along. Swiftwater sent a letter up by the Siwash that brought you here, so in case the police showed up, I could keep you out of sight. I'm like Bettles an' Swiftwater—I believe you done right in riddin' the country of a low-lived skunk. But here it's July, an' the chances are that if they haven't found Gus Huber's corpse by this time they never will find it. So I figure you'd be pretty safe in recordin' your location."

"Pretty safe ain't safe enough to suit me. I ain't takin' no chances on Gus Huber—if you'd know'd him like I do, you'd know 'twould be jest like him to ketch in some rock er stick in the mud on the bottom of the river, till I got to feelin' I was safe, an' then pop up fer Downey to find. Nussir. I'm settin' pretty like I be. I've got me claim, an' there ain't no one goin' to jump ut. Most of the boys here on the crick wouldn't want to—an' them that would, dastn't, knowin' damn well you'd hang 'em if they did—an' that goes fer anyone down along the river. They all know how you hang folks up here that don't mind their own business.

"Even if the police should find Gus an' find out where I'm at, I'd still be settin' pretty. I'd step acrost the line an' thumb me nose at um. Ye asked me a while back why I didn't git out me dust an' cache it. I'm tellin' ye now, I have got a hundred pound of it cached—over on the Alasky side of the line. Twenty-five thousan' dollars it figgers, enough to keep me as long as I'll ever live—so no matter which way the cat jumps, I'll have all I kin eat, an' all I kin drink, an' all the stud playin' I'll ever want—so what more could a man ask?"

Black John grinned. "I guess you win, Pat," he said. "Well,

drink up. I see Pot Gutted John an' Red John comin' acrost the clearin'. It looks like One Armed John is roustin' out the guests for your birthday party. Here's to you—an' I hope I'll be settin' as pretty as you are when I'm seventy-five."

"Huh," Cush grunted behind the bar, "you won't never see seventy-five—an' even if you do, you won't be settin' pretty—some good lookin' woman will have took you fer all you've got long before that, the way you fall fer 'em. You've be'n lucky so fer—but luck like that can't hold. Me, I know. I'm a four-time loser, myself!"

II

DESPITE THE OLD man's expressed desire to lose in the stud game that evening, the cards decreed otherwise and he won enough dust to finance a three-day spree. On the morning of the fourth day he headed for home fortified with half a dozen good stiff drinks.

Late that same afternoon Joe Tuttle appeared at Cush's and accosted Black John. "Is there a doctor here on Halfaday?" he asked.

The big man shook his head. "Not at present. The last doctor to sojourn amongst us deemed it expedient to step acrost into Alaska one time when Corporal Downey showed up on the crick, an' he ain't been heard from sence. Not," he added with a grin, "that the medical profession would suffer any great loss if he never is heard from. Why? Who's sick?"

"It's old Pat Finnigan. Ada and I heard someone yelling along about noon, and we investigated and found old Pat with his leg wedged in between a couple of rocks. He'd slipped and fallen and rolled part way down the ridge where the trail slants down to his shack. He said he'd been over here for a couple of days celebrating his birthday—and I guess he celebrated, all right. His breath smells like he'd swallowed a distillery. We found his leg broken and made him comfortable. Ada stayed there with him and I went home and made a litter out of a couple of poles and some canvas, and we carried him to his shack and put him to bed. Ada is staying there with him and I came over here to see if I could find a doctor."

"Where is it broke? An' how bad? Is the bone smashed, or splintered, or stickin' out through the skin?"

"No. It's his shin bone, and it's broken about half way between his knee and his ankle. It doesn't appear to be too bad a break, but neither Ada nor I know much about such things, and we didn't want to monkey with it, and maybe do the wrong thing."

"I don't claim to be a doctor, but I've had more or less experience with broken bones. We'll go over an' have a look at it an' if it ain't too bad, I guess we can set it."

Cush set a bottle of whiskey on the bar. "Take that along," he advised. "It'll prob'ly hurt like hell when you git to messin' around that leg, an' a couple of good stiff drinks'll ease it up."

Tuttle pocketed the bottle with a grin. "A couple of good stiff drinks on top of what he's got in him now, and we could cut his leg off without him knowing it."

THE INJURY proved to be a simple facture, and, thanks to the handling of the Tuttles in moving him to his shack, there had been no displacement, and it was a comparatively easy matter to fit the ends of the bone into place and apply splints and a bandage.

It was some six weeks later, while on a moose hunt back in the hills, that Black John dropped in on the old man to see how he was getting along. He found him hobbling about with the aid of a stout cane. "How's the leg comin'?" he asked.

"Fine! I be'n walkin' around on ut fer a week. Another week an' I'll be able to git over to Cush's fer a bit of a drink, an' a game of stud. An' be God, this time I hope I do lose! What I claim, them three, four day drunks is too hard on a man."

"You say you've be'n walkin' around for a week—how'd you manage here alone before you could walk around?"

"I wasn't here alone. Ada Tuttle, she moved over here, an' she tuk care of me jest like she was me own darter. There's two as fine young folks as ever walked in shoe leather! Ada she give the shack a hell of a cleanin' out, an' then she kep' ut clean, an' she done the cookin', an' fed me me meals, an' Joe he come acrost the ridge every day an' cut the wood an' fetched it in, an' carried the water."

"How they doin' over there?" Black John asked.

"They ain't doin' no good, an' it's a damn shame. They've got faith in that crick, an' they're stickin' wid it. They build their shack right acrost from mine, hopin' this pocket I hit reaches clear acrost in under the ridge. But I'm doubtin' it. I never heard tell of no pocket stretchin' in under no ridge. They're workin' like hell, sinkin' shafts, an' takin' out jest enough to live on—an' they live slim. They ain't recorded their location, yet. They're waitin' to see what they strike. Joe, he ain't no minin' man. His heart ain't in minin'. He wants to make a strike so he kin go back to the States, an' go to some college an' learn to be a doctor."

Black John eyed the oldster. "I believe you told me once that you didn't have no folks of your own, didn't you?"

"Nary kith nor kin in the world that I know of."

"An' you've got a location here that's bound to pay out more dust that you can ever use—why don't you stake young Tuttle to an education? It would be a fine thing to do. He could pay you back after he got going."

"Pay me back! If he ever tried to pay me back I'd smash me cane over the head of um! They've more than paid me back, a'ready—them two. I've offered to do that. But they won't take a damn cent off me. I've begged 'em, an' I've cussed 'em, an' it don't do no good. They've got a pride to 'em—an' they're stubborn as Mulligan's hog. But there's sure one thing I kin do, an' they can't stop me—I kin leave 'em this location, when I'm gone."

The big man nodded. "Yes, you could do that—but hell, Pat, as tough an old devil as you are, you're apt to live as long as they do. Joe'd look like hell goin' to college with a long gray beard."

THE OLD man shook his head. "That's what you think—about me livin' as long as them. But I won't. Nussir. I'm liable to drop in me tracks any minute. It's in here—in me heart. Me father went that way—an' me mother, an' me brother Dan. 'Tis a good way to go. It beats layin' around on a bed an' dyin' fer a month, er mebbe a year, like some does."

"You're right," Black John agreed. "But about leavin' the Tuttles this location—you've never recorded it. If you should drop off sudden, there's nothin' to prevent the first man that can get to Dawson from recordin' it—me, for instance, or any of the boys on Halfaday."

The oldster's face drew into a frown. "Mebbe by this time Gus has soaked long enough to git so water logged he can't pop up. Anyways I'm going to take a chanct an' record it. But I ain't in no shape to make the trip to Dawson."

"We can fix that part, all right. Cush is what's known as a Free Miner's recorder. You can record your location with him an' he'll record it within a reasonable time with the regular recorder. It's a perfectly legal procedure, where a claim lays more than a hundred miles from the nearest recordin' office. Cush an' I are hittin' for Dawson tomorrow. He can record it as soon as we get there. That will put the location on record in your name, but that won't give title to it to the Tuttles when you drop off. It'll go through the hands of the public administrator, and if he can't locate any legal heirs it will revert to the Crown."

"Well, what a hell of a way to do!" the old man cried angrily. "Jest because somewan ain't got a lot of relations to fight over his property when he dies, the Crown grabs it—an' I s'pose the King of England would be over here diggin' in it the minute he hears I'm dead!"

Black John laughed. "We can keep the King out of here, easy enough. All you got to do is make out an assignment transferrin' all right, title an' interest in this property to the Tuttles. An' I'll record the assignment, after Cush records the location. Of course, that would give the Tuttles immediate ownership of the location, but I don't believe you need to worry about that. They wouldn't know that the transfer had been made, an' even if they did, they would not kick you off the property an' take over."

"Hell, no! I'd trust them two, with anything I've got."

"How about me? How do you know I won't record that assignment to myself instead of the Tuttles?"

There was a twinkle in the old man's eye as he replied. "The sourdoughs all claim ye're an outlaw, John. An' from what I've heard, if I was a crook er a dredge company, I wouldn't trust ye over the first ridge. But ye ain't the kind of an outlaw that would beat an old man, nor yet a couple of young folks out of a claim, be a damn sight!"

III

ONE DAY, NOT long after Black John and Cush had returned to Halfaday from a trip to Dawson, during which they had duly recorded old Pat Finnigan's location, and also the assignment of the claim to Joe and Ada Tuttle, Joe barged into the saloon where Black John and Cush were shaking a game of dice for the drinks. "Old Pat's sick as hell," he announced, "an' I'm headin' for Dawson to fetch Doc Sutherland."

"What ails him?" Cush asked.

"It's in his belly. Ada went over there last evening to take him a blueberry pie she'd made, and found him lying in his bunk in terrible misery. He claimed his belly was so sore he couldn't hardly stand the touch of the blanket. Ada took a look and she says it's all swollen up and kind of red looking, and she thinks he's running a hell of a fever because his forehead is hot, and his eyes are kind of bright and funny looking, and he seems sort of out of his head. She set the water pail where he could reach it, and came over and told me, an' then she went back to Finnigan's."

"Sounds like a ruptured appendix to me," Black John said. "If it is you couldn't get Doc here in time to do any good. The old man would be dead of peritonitis before you could get to Dawson."

"Well, I can try!" Joe cried. "I can't just sit around and see the old fellow die without doing something to help him."

"That's right," Cush agreed. "Chances is, if it's only his guts, a couple of damn good drinks of licker'll fetch him around. I'll send One Armed John over with a quart soon's he shows up."

Joe shook his head. "I'm afraid old Pat's number's up. Ada said he was rattling off as fast as he can talk—now about one thing—and almost in the same breath about another. She says he told her he wanted us to work the claim for all it's worth. He claimed there might be a million in it, but first we'd have to tap that little lake back on the ridge and pipe water to it. But hell—we haven't recorded the location, yet. We're just sort of prospecting it—sinking a shaft on our crick, right opposite Pat's in hope that the pocket he struck reaches under the ridge into our crick. Funny he'd say that—about the claim might be worth a million—because before he'd always told us he figured we're wasting our time on that location—said he didn't think we'd ever hit it lucky there."

Black John eyed the younger man. "This time he was talkin' about his claim," he said.

"His claim! How could we work his claim? That's a mighty good claim of old Pat's. I wonder who will get that claim, if he should die?"

"You will," the big man replied. "You an' Ada."

"What?" cried the astounded man.

"That's right. His claim is duly recorded and assigned to you an' Ada. He done it in appreciation of what you two have done for him."

"Cripes!" Joe exclaimed. "What little we ever did for the old man isn't worth mentioning!"

Black John smiled. "That ain't the way Pat Finnigan figured it. The assignment says the location was granted in return for value received. Sometimes the little things a man does count up mighty big in the long run."

"Anyhow, old Pat is still alive, and I'm hitting hell-bent for Dawson to get the doctor," the younger man said, and tossed an empty packsack to Cush. "Throw what grub I'll need for the trip in there and I'll be on my way."

BLACK JOHN glanced at Cush. "Yeah—throw the grub in the pack," he said, and as Cush stepped into the storeroom, he turned to the other. "I'll make the trip to Dawson, son," he said. "If old Pat is as sick as I think he is from what you told me, he'll be dead long before I get there. But I'll do my damndest. I know a shortcut that'll get me there a good three days quicker than you could make it. You go back an' help Ada take care of him. If Pat should kick out, you hit for Dawson so's to head Doc off. No use in him makin' the trip for nothin'."

"That's mighty white of you. I sure hate to bother you—but it would be kind of hard for Ada—there alone with him."

"Who the hell's botherin' me! I'd go as far as you would to help the old man! An' besides," he added, with a wink, "it might be I could make some slight profit on the trip if I can find a stud game. I feel a streak of luck comin' on."

The other smiled. "I guess you've helped a lot of folks, from what I hear."

The big man returned the smile. "Yeah—helped some—an' hindered others. It's accordin' to the way things shape up."

"I sure hope old Pat pulls through," Joe said. "But in case he don't make the grade—gee! With a claim like that Ada and I could do all the things we've planned to do if we ever made a strike. I'd planned to study medicine. And Ada—just think of it—poor kid, she's lived here in the Yukon all her life. Back there, living in the city, she could have things she never even dreamed of! And believe me, she's earned everything she'll ever get! She's worked hard, and she's never lost faith. But about piping the water down from that lake? Old Pat always claimed that if he'd tap that lake for water he could clean up a million in a short time. He measured off the distance he'd have to pipe it, and the last time I went down to Dawson, he had me find out about what the cost of the pipe and labor would be. Sorenson, at the A.C. Co. figured out it would run right around a hundred, or a hundred and ten thousand dollars. That seems like a lot of money, but do you know, while Sorenson was figuring on it, Mr. Petticord happened to come in.

"He glanced at the figures, and told me to tell Pat that when he got ready to put in the pipe, he would lend him the money to finance the deal cheaper than the bank would. He said he'd heard enough about old Pat's claim from the sourdoughs, so he'd advance the money without bothering to look the location over. He said he understood that the location hadn't been recorded, but he guessed no one would dare to jump it, lying as close to Halfaday Crick as it does—and old Pat being a friend of yours. He said, though, that Pat would have to record it before he'd loan any money on it. Then he'd take a mortgage on the claim for the amount of the loan. So if old Pat shouldn't pull through, now that the location and the assignment are recorded, I can go to Mr. Petticord and get the money. If the assignment is made out to Ada and me both, she'd have to sign the mortgage, too. So if old Pat does die, she better come along with me, when we hit down to head off the doctor."

Black John reached for the bottle and poured a drink. "H-u-u-m," he said, when the other had finished. "Petticord, eh? I presume you refer to Amos D. Petticord, attorney-at-law, dealer in minin' properties, an' loaner of money?"

"Yes, he's the one. He said he'd advance the money cheaper than the bank would."

THE BIG man nodded slowly. "Y-e-a-h. Yeah—I s'pose he would, at that. You know, son, I was just standin' here thinkin'. You an' Ada have got faith in that location you're workin'—there where your cabin's at, ain't you?"

"Sure we have. But I don't expect it'll ever be anything like old Pat's claim."

"Prob'ly not. But you've done quite a bit of work on it, ain't you?"

"Yes, we've sunk a couple of shafts trying to find out if that pocket of Pat's stretched through under the ridge."

"Well then, if I was you, I'd record that location when you an' Ada get down to Dawson."

"Record it! But—why should we record it? That is, if—if old Pat shouldn't pull through?"

"Lots of folks owns more than one claim. But in case old Pat should kick out, I was thinkin' it would be a right nice gesture on your part to record that location, an' name the crick Finnigan's Crick—after old Pat. It would sort of—of keep his name alive—after he's gone."

"But—his crick is Finnigan's Crick!"

Black John shook his head. "Only in the vernacular, as you might say. It's true that it's known hereabouts as Finnigan's Crick, an' in recordin' it Cush used the popular name of Finnigan's Crick—an' that's the way it stands on the grant. But Pat named his crick Lucky Crick, an' that's the way he wanted it. So you see, if you don't name your crick after old Pat and restore the name of Lucky Crick to the one he lives on, the poor old man's wish would be frustrated. If you do as I suggest then his crick will be left as he named it. And at the same time his name will not be lost to posterity."

"Huh," grunted Cush, who had just returned with the pack of supplies, "it wouldn't of be'n lost to prosperity if Pat would of worked it harder!"

The big man ignored the interruption. "Yes sir," he continued, "I believe old Pat would appreciate that—if he could know."

"By God, I'll do it!" Joe exclaimed. "And not only that, I'll get me a couple of nice boards and burn the name, FINNI-GAN'S CRICK and LUCKY CRICK into 'em, and set up a post at the mouth of each crick where they empty into Halfaday so everyone that goes along can see 'em. You know, the mouths are only a few yards apart."

"A damn good idea," Black John agreed. "Well—here's my trail outfit—so I'll be hittin' for Dawson. In case Pat kicks out, you an' Ada hit out for Dawson as soon as you can, so Doc won't be travelin' no farther than he has to."

As Joe turned toward the door, Cush called him back. "Here—take this licker along. Wait, I better make it two quarts. Like I says—if it ain't nothin' but his guts that ailin' him, chances is the licker'll fix him up—an' John'll have his trip fer nothin'—onlest, mebbe, he gits lucky in a stud game."

IV

ARRIVING IN DAWSON, Black John proceeded directly to the hospital where Dr. Sutherland greeted him with a smile. "Hello, John. What's the good news from Halfaday Crick?"

The big man returned the smile. "If a man depended on Halfaday for his good news he'd be in a hell of a fix. The kind of riff-raff that persists in showin' up amongst us, the best news a man could hear would be if one of 'em got hung. The fact is, I'm afraid I've got bad news for you. Joe Tuttle showed up at Cush's the other day on his way down to get you to go up an' doctor old Pat Finnigan."

"What's the matter with Pat, now? I heard he broke his leg a while back."

"Yeah, but it wasn't a bad break, an' I set it for him. He's walkin' around on it, but accordin' to Joe, this is worse. He says Ada went over to Pat's to take him a pie she made an' found him layin' in his bunk with his belly all swelled up an' sort of red lookin' an' hurtin' so bad he could hardly stand the blanket touchin' it. She says he's runnin' a hell of a fever. I sent Joe back to help Ada look after him an' I come on down to get you. To tell the truth, it looks to me like a swell case of peritonitis, prob'ly followin' a ruptured appendix."

The doctor's smile widened. "I don't know why you came clear down here to bother me with it. You seem to be a pretty good medico yourself—you set his leg and got away with it, and according to the symptoms, I believe your diagnosis of his present ailment is correct."

"Oh, shore, the diagnosis is prob'ly okay. But onfortunately a diagnosis ain't worth a damn to Pat. It's proper medical treatment he wants—not diagnosis."

"Guess that's right, but with the symptoms as you described them, it's my guess that old Pat's dead by this time. Probably been dead for several days. However, I'll hit for Halfaday on the bare chance he might still be alive."

"You prob'ly won't get very far," Black John said. "I figured it about like you do—that Pat wouldn't last long, the fix he's in. So I told Joe to hit for Dawson as quick as Pat died, so's to head you off. I wouldn't be surprised if you'd meet him on the river before you hit the mouth of the White. No use in you makin' a run clean up there for nothin'."

"Good for you. You going back with me?"

"No, now I'm down here I figure it's my duty to instruct a bunch of them onregenerate sourdoughs in some of the finer p'ints of stud. An' on top of that I figure I might be of some slight service to Joe an' Ada Tuttle in financin' a deal for some pipe. They live on the next crick to old Pat, an' they've be'n might good to him, so a while back, unbeknownst to them, Pat recorded his location, an' then assigned it to them. So if he's dead, they'll be takin' over. An' they won't be satisfied with workin' that claim by the panful, like Pat done. By pipin' water down from a little lake in the hills they can prob'ly clean out that pocket in a year or two. Joe, he'd like to clean up as soon as he can, so he can go down to the States an' study medicine."

The doctor nodded. "Yes, he's talked to me about it—he and Ada both. Joe's a hard worker, and I believe he'll make good. They say they want to come back up here and practice. We could use a few more physicians here in the North—men who savvy the country. I'm glad to know that he can probably finance his education. They say old Pat has a good claim."

"Best one around there. Well, so long, Doc. I'll be slippin' down to the Tivoli."

"So long, John. Before you get in that stud game hunt up Bill Atlee and tell him to throw enough grub in his canoe for a trip to Halfaday, and stop here for me. Bill's a damn good hand with a canoe."

AFTER ARRANGING with Atlee for the doctor's transportation, Black John sauntered into the Tivoli Saloon to find Amos D. Petticord standing before the bar, a bottle and glass before him. The attorney greeted him cordially. "Why, hello, John, old top! Haven't seen you in quite a while. What are you going to have?"

"Well, along about this time of day, a little touch of liquor mightn't come amiss. How you doin'? Or," the big man added, with a grin, "to express it more aptly, as a professor would say—who you doin'?"

The other returned the grin with a wink. "Birds of a feather flock together, they say. Anyhow, they understand each other, eh?"

"Perfectly."

"By the way, this meeting with you is a rather fortunate coincidence. You know young Joe Tuttle, don't you?"

"Yeah, I know him."

"Well, I happened to be talking to the recorder in here the other day, and he told me that old Pat Finnigan had finally recorded his location up there in your country, and has assigned it to Tuttle and his wife. Know anything about it?"

"Yes, I was with Cush when he recorded the location, an' I recorded the assignment for Pat. It's all on the books. Why?"

"Throw that one into you," the other replied, "an' bring your glass along. We'll go over here to a table where we can have a talk."

Picking up his own glass and the bottle from the bar, Petticord led the way to a table at the far side of the room. "I've got a hunch," he said, when they had seated themselves, "that you and I can make medicine." He filled the two glasses from the bottle, and leaned closer. "How'd you like a cut on a damn juicy proposition?" he asked.

Black John considered. "How much of a cut on what kind of a proposition?" he asked.

"It's all open and aboveboard, and perfectly legal."

"Kind of out of your line, ain't it?" the big man remarked with a grin.

Petticord returned the grin. "Yours too—if you want to put it that way. The fact is, we've both operated pretty extensively in our own particlar lines, and have always managed to keep clear of the law."

"Oh, shore. But you ain't answered my question."

"It's like this—I've got to put up a hundred thousand in cold cash—but you don't put up a cent."

"Sounds reasonable, so far," Black John admitted.

"On the other hand, you've got some information I need— and your word is law on Halfaday and vicinity. If it became known that you were interested in an enterprise up there, it would insure the success of the undertaking. That is, in case we obtained title to a rich location in your neighborhood, the fact that you were in on it would render it safe from any inroads or depredations from your gang of outlaws, wouldn't it?"

Black John nodded. "Yes, I could prob'ly guarantee that such proposition would be unmolested."

"Okay. That's where you git in—that and the fact that you undoubtedly have some information I need before investing a hundred thousand dollars in the venture. What do you say to a fifty-fifty arrangement?"

"Sounds reasonable. Let's hear the rest of it."

"In the first place the talk around here among the sourdoughs is that old Pat Finnigan struck it lucky on a crick that runs into Halfaday. They say that Pat, for reasons of his own, refused to record his location, but that no one would dare to jump it for the reason that you have given the word that it wouldn't be exactly healthy for anyone to attempt it. Is that right?"

Black John nodded. "Yes, that seems to be a fairly accurate summin' up of the case, as you lawyers would say."

"So far, so good. Now, in your honest opinion, is this location worth what the sourdoughs seem to think it is?"

"Yup. Maybe a damn sight more. It's one of them lucky strikes—a pocket where the dust got caught behind a transverse rock dike in a bend of an old crick."

"And you corroborate the recorder's statement that the Finnigan location has been recorded, and that an assignment from Finnigan to the Tuttles has also been recorded? Of course, I could verify the facts by going over the records—but your word on top of the recorder's is good enough for me."

"The recordin's were made, all right. You don't need to worry about that."

"Do you recollect what consideration was mentioned in the assignment?"

"Yup—one dollar, an' 'an old man's appreciation of many acts of kindness,' is the way he wrote it out. You see, Joe an' Ada lived on a location of their own on another crick just acrost a ridge from Finnigan's claim. Seems to me they named it Lucky Crick, on account of them havin' faith that they'd make a strike there. But up to now they haven't taken out much more'n wages. They always befriended old Pat any way they could. An' naturally, old Pat appreciated it. To show his appreciation, he transferred the location to 'em—with, of course, the onderstanin' that they won't take it over till old Pat's dead."

Petticord's eyes widened. "Do you mean," he cried, "that the Tuttles don't get possession till Finnigan's death?"

"Yup."

"Was that stipulation stated in the assignment?"

"Nope. It didn't need to be. Finnigan knew them two would never shove him off his claim."

"But legally there's nothing to prevent them from doing just that," Petticord said.

"Prob'ly not—legally," Black John admitted. "But morally there's plenty to prevent it. You might not know it, Petticord—but there's times an' situations when a moral concept makes a damn fool out of the law."

The other frowned. "What the hell are you—a preacher?"

"Not so reputed, I believe."

The other cleared his throat. "Ahem, I'm wondering whether an—er—an appropriate consideration wouldn't induce the Tuttles to oust Finnigan, and take over the claim under their legal rights?"

"Nope."

AFTER SEVERAL moments of silence, during which Petticord toyed with his glass, his brow wrinkled in thought, Black John broke the silence. "You might as well forget what you're thinkin' about, Petticord. Murderin' Finnigan to get shet of him wouldn't get you nothin' but a hangin' on Halfaday."

The other glanced up sharply. "What do you mean?" he asked.

"You know damn well what I mean. It didn't take no mind reader to follow your line of thought. But as a matter of fact, I don't think we've got to worry much about the Tuttles takin' immediate possession of that location. Old Pat was damn near dead when I started down after the doctor, ten days ago."

Hardly were the words out of his mouth before the door opened and Dr. Sutherland stepped into the room, dressed for the trail. Glancing about, he stepped to the table and paused. "I didn't have to go very far, John," he announced. "Bill and I met the Tuttles just as we were shoving off in the canoe. They said old Pat died the day after you left Halfaday. They're over at the hotel, now."

As the doctor left, Petticord's face fairly beamed. "Now that's what I call luck! It seems, John, that fate is playing straight into our hands. Finnigan's dead—and the Tuttles are right here in Dawson. We can get this thing cleaned up in no time. Now, according to what young Tuttle himself told me a while back, there's a lake not far back in the hills from which water could be piped to the Finnigan claim, thus permitting operation on a large scale. Is that right?"

"That's right. Old Pat could have piped that water down for about a hundred thousan', an' be one of the biggest operators in the Yukon. But as long as he was gettin' out enough dust for expenses, he wasn't interested."

"Okay—now here's where we come in. Joe Tuttle is going to pipe that water down. That is, he thinks he is. As a matter of fact, you and I will do the piping—and we'll rake the profit, too. You see, when he was down here a while back, old Pat had him find out how much it would take to pipe that water to his claim. I happened in while Sorenson was figuring it out, and I told Tuttle to tell Finnigan that I'd loan him the money cheaper than the bank would—so now that Tuttle has the claim, he'll certainly come to me for the money to finance the deal. Why, he told me then that if it was his claim he wouldn't lose any time in getting in that pipe line. Here's the way we'll work it—I'll advance the money, and take a mortgage due in six months on the claim. Tuttle will buy the pipe and start it for the claim. If it should so happen that delivery on part of it should be delayed until such time as Tuttle could not possibly get his operation going in time to meet the mortgage payment, then I will foreclose on the claim, we'll move the delayed pipe on up, and start getting out our million. How does that sound?"

"Sounds like a damn good swindle—one it would take a lawyer to think up, an' a damned crooked one, too. You hire a crew of freighters an' I'll put a man in charge of the job. The White is a damn tricky river, an' if a man that knows it was bossin' the job we could be sure of havin' the pipe right where we wanted it—when we wanted it. Red John knows every inch of the river—an' he'd do as I say."

The other smiled. "Okay. Then you'll go in on it?"

"Oh, shore. I ain't no hand to pass up the chanct to make a profit. But just as a matter of precaution, Petticord, you better draw up a memorandum of agreement, statin' that you an' me are equal pardners in Finnigan's location."

"All right. Come on over to my office, and I'll make out the note and the mortgage, and draw up the agreement which we can both sign." In his office the man busied himself at a typewriter. He looked up. "The name of this crick the claim is on is Finnigan's Crick, isn't it?"

"That's right. It's known as Finnigan's Crick."

"And now as to the location of this crick—about where does it flow into Halfaday Crick?"

"About six miles, more or less, above where Halfaday runs into the White."

"And about how far up Finnigan's Crick is the claim located?"

"About five miles. That's the way it's recorded."

WHEN THE man finished, he handed the note and mortgage to Black John. "It just occurred to me that it would be best if you take these documents over to the hotel and get the signatures of the Tuttles. You see, when Tuttle was down here, he happened to mention that he was a friend of yours. He said that you had advised old man Finnigan to put in that pipe line, and that he has a lot of respect for your judgment. I believe that knowing you still approved of the deal would cinch getting his signature on the dotted line. Have them both sign the mortgage and the note, too. As I said—he's got confidence in your judgment."

"Yeah, quite a lot of folks has—one way an' another. All right, I'll slip over to the hotel. Joe'll prob'ly come back with me, an' in the meantime you better get the money an' have it here to turn over to him."

In the hotel Black John accosted the Tuttles, who sadly informed him of Finnigan's death. "Yeah," the big man replied, "Doc Sutherland stopped in to the Tivoli an' told me about it. By the way, Petticord was in there, too, an' when he heard about Pat's death, he told me about his offer to loan Finnigan the money for the pipe line when you were down here that time. He said the offer held for you, too, if you wanted to take it up. I told him I was certain you would, as I judge it to be a sound investment. So he went ahead an' made out these papers, for you an' Ada to sign. I told him I'd take 'em over an' get your signatures, an' then Joe can go back with me to Petticord's office, an' get the cash, without no delay at all."

"Why—thank you, John. We sure do appreciate that. Let's see, where do we sign?"

The big man selected one of the papers. "This here's the note—it calls for a hundred thousan' dollars, an' runs for six months. Just you an' Ada sign there on them two lines. An' this here's thet mortgage as security for the note. You can both sign it, too—there on the lines."

"Gee," Joe said, as he handed back the signed paper, "I never thought I'd some day be signing a note for a hundred thousand! It makes me feel like I'm in big business." Picking up the other paper, he scanned it. "It says here that the claim is located on Finnigan's Crick. Don't you remember—old Pat named his crick Lucky Crick?"

Black John nodded. "That's so—but did you ever hear anyone but him call it Lucky Crick? You did not. Everyone else calls it Finnigan's Crick. That's what it's known as—an' that's the way the mortgage reads. So go ahead an' sign it."

"But I named my crick Finnigan's Crick. You suggested my doing that, so old Pat's name would be remembered. I even made those signboards like I promised with the names burned in, and nailed 'em on posts at the mouths of both the cricks— where they flow into Halfaday only a few yards apart."

"Oh, shore—but don't quibble! Cripes, if folks persists in

callin' both of them cricks Finnigan's Crick old Pat's name'll be remembered twict as long. Anyhow, Petticord'll find out which one is Finnigan's Crick when he gets up there—you don't need to worry about that. All you got to do is sign up, an' come on over with me an' get your money. An' don't go shootin' off your mouth to Petticord about the names of them cricks, or he might think you're tryin' to put somethin' over on him. Them lawyers is suspicious folks, at best. A lot of deals has be'n fouled up by too much talk. The way it is, you'll have the money—that's what you want. An' Petticord'll have the note an' mortgage—that's what he wants. So everything is all jake. An' by the way, you don't need to bother about findin' a crew to freight in that pipe. Petticord will 'tend to that for you. He knows the ropes. He can get it done a damn sight cheaper than you could. An' I'll see to it that you can pick up a crew on Halfaday to lay the pipe as it comes in. Come on—let's go."

Accompanying Black John to Petticord's office, Joe turned over the note and mortgage, and received one hundred thousand-dollar bills. The lawyer smiled as he counted out the money. "There you are, Tuttle. Allow me to congratulate you on your good fortune. It isn't every young man your age that steps right into the middle of a million-dollar proposition. My advice to you is to purchase your pipe at once and have it loaded on the *Hannah*. I understand she is due to pull out tomorrow morning for upriver.

"I will hustle around and procure a crew of freighters and a couple of scows for the trip up the White and have them on the boat. That will undoubtedly prove a tough job of freighting which will necessitate several trips. My friend, Black John, assured me that you can obtain the necessary labor on Halfaday Crick for laying the pipe and building your sluice. If I were you I'd lose no time, but start laying your pipe as soon as the first load arrives on your claim. And I may say here that you are mighty lucky to have a friend like Black John so close at hand. Isn't that so, John?"

"I'll say he is," the big man replied. "Yes sir—mighty lucky."

V

TAKING PASSAGE ON the *Hannah*, Black John and the Tuttles disembarked with their canoes at the mouth of the White River and watched the pipe unloaded from the steamboat. As the first two scowloads headed up the smaller river Black John assured the freighters that he would have a man who was thoroughly familiar with the river meet them at Fish Rapids and take charge from there on. The three then proceeded upriver in the canoes.

Arriving at Cushing's Fort, Black John bid good-by to the Tuttles who proceeded to their own claim. "It'll be two, three weeks before them first two loads of pipe get here," he said, "what with portagin' it around rapids, an' a lot of track-linin' on the fast water stretches. An' in the meantime I'll rustle a crew here on Halfaday that'll start layin' the pipe as soon as it gets here."

"That's fine, John," Joe Tuttle said. "We sure appreciate what you've done for us—and sometime we hope to be able to pay you back. The first thing we're going to do when we get back home will be to tear down that shack of old Pat's and get out the logs for a decent cabin on the claim."

Black John nodded approval. "Yeah, that's a good idea. If you get out your logs before the pipe gets here, the chances is that the boys can help you roll up the cabin, odd times—like while they're waitin' for the next load to come in."

As Black John had predicted, nearly three weeks elapsed before the first two loads of pipe arrived at its destination. A dozen men from Halfaday packed the pipe to the little lake, and proceeded to lay it in place. Then snow came, and a month later the second consignment arrived, hauled in by dog teams recruited from Halfaday. But it was near the end of December before another lot showed up. In the meantime, the men of

Halfaday had not only completed the cabin on the Finnigan claim, but had also rolled up a log bunkhouse of ample proportion for their own housing.

LATE IN January Joe Tuttle stepped into Cushing's saloon one day as Black John and Cush were shaking dice for the drinks. Cush spun an extra glass toward him as he reached the bar. "Drink up," he invited. "This un's on the house."

Tuttle poured his drink and glanced into Black John's eyes. "I'm worried," he announced. "Damn good and worried."

The big man smiled. "What in the devil has a young fella with a million-dollar proposition on his hands got to worry about?" he asked.

"As slow as that pipe is coming in, I'm not even going to get it laid before my six months is up—let alone get out a hundred thousand dollars worth of dust to pay off that mortgage. It's due next month. I've got to go down to Dawson and ask Petticord for an extension.

The big man shook his head. "You can save yourself the trip, son. You won't get no extension on that mortgage. Petticord don't give extensions. He's a man who demands his pound of flesh, accordin' to the strict construction of the law."

Young Tuttle's face went white. "But—but good Lord, John— that claim is good for that hundred thousand ten times over! He couldn't lose any money by granting an extension."

"The way he figures it, he couldn't lose any money by takin' over the claim, either."

"You mean—he'd actually take the claim over, without giving me a chance to redeem it! Why, man, if that pipe had been delivered within a reasonable time, it would have been in place before this, and I'd have had gold enough sluiced out to pay off the mortgage."

"That's right. That's what Petticord was afraid of. That's why he seen to it that the pipe wasn't delivered on time."

"You mean that he knew the pipe wouldn't get there on time?

That he actually planned to have it delayed, so he could foreclose on the property?"

"Shore he did. Them freighters was hand-picked—an' Petticord picked 'em."

"Then it's fraud, or something! By God, I'll fight him in the courts!"

"How you goin' to prove it? Them freighters ain't goin' to squawk—an' shore as hell Petticord ain't. Trouble with goin' into court is, the law demands evidence—an' you ain't got none."

"But—you know it's a fraud—you just told me so. You could testify."

Black John grinned. "I'm only guessin'. An' accordin' to law, a guess ain't evidence. Take a miners' meetin', now—an' if a good guess would serve the ends of justice, we admit it, same as any other evidence. But the law demands facts, an' if there ain't no facts available, justice is left hangin' in midair. By the way, Joe—you moved over in your new cabin, yet, there on Finnigan's claim?"

The other shook his head dully. "No," he answered, "it's all finished and ready—but now I guess we won't ever move into it. My God, John, this will just about kill Ada! Poor kid—she's counted on being able at last to do the things we'd planned to do. I was going to study medicine and then we'd figured on coming back to the Yukon and practice. But I guess now we can forget all that."

Behind the bar Cush scowled. "It's a dam' shame!" he cried. "Believe me, if that damn cuss shows up here when he comes up to take over yer claim, I'm goin' to bust him one right between the eyes with a bung-starter! An' how about you, John? Yer allus outfiggerin' them damn crooks one way er another. Be you goin' to stand around an' see them young folks beat out of their claim?"

THE BIG man cleared his throat. "Petticord is ondoubtless actin' within his legal rights. Who am I to interfere?"

He turned to Tuttle. "About movin' into your new cabin on

Lucky Crick, there's no need to be in any hurry to. The way things is shaped up, I'm bettin' that Petticord will be showin' up to take over his property in accordance with a strict construction of the law on the day that mortgage falls due. He'll prob'ly stop in here on his way up there, an' I'll go along to Finnigan's Crick with him—just to see that everything's legal. We don't stand fer no skullduggery on Halfaday an' vicinity." He paused and glanced into the irate eyes of old Cush. "An' when he does show up, you lay off him, see! Pastin' a man between the eyes with a bung-starter is not only crude an' onmannerly, but it rarely serves the ends of justice."

VI

TRUE TO BLACK JOHN'S prediction, Petticord, accompanied by a husky individual, stepped into Cushing's saloon late in the afternoon of the day before the mortgage fell due. The two approached the bar where Black John stood facing Cush, a bottle, glasses, and the inevitable leather dice box between them. Petticord greeted the big man jovially. "Well, John, it looks like tomorrow is our lucky day! Meet Pete Jarvis. Pete's a prospector who happens to be down on his luck at present, so I hired him to make the trip with me. He's a good hand with a canoe, and he understands panning out gold. They say you can shovel gold right out of the grass roots anywhere on that claim, and I thought I'd have Pete make a few test pannings, here and there. It might give us an idea of exactly where to start to work the claim systematically. And besides, that," he added, with a wink, "he's good and stalwart, Pete is, and I figured he might come in handy if the—er—present incumbent should kick up a fuss about turning over the property."

"Oh, I don't believe Joe'll resort to no violence. He knows the time's up on the mortgage, an' he knows there ain't nothin' he can do about it, in case you won't grant him an extension."

"Fat chance he's got for an extension," Petticord grinned. "All the extension he'll get is just time enough to grab up his personal belongings, and get off the claim."

"Yeah—he was in here the other day, an' I told him I didn't figure you'd grant an extension. But hell, I forgot—Petticord, meet Lyme Cushing. Cush, he's the proprietor of this emporium of good cheer. Cush meet Amos D. Petticord, attorney-at-law, an' his side-kick, Pete Jarvis."

Cush acknowledged the introduction with a surly grunt. "Drink up," he invited sourly as he slid a couple of glasses across the bar, "this un's on the house."

When the glasses were emptied Petticord tossed a bill onto the bar. "We'll fill 'em up again," he said. "I've heard of you, Mr. Cushing. In the future I expect to be spending considerable time hereabouts. I trust that we will become better acquainted."

"Huh. Well, tellin' you about me, Pettyfog, I wouldn't give a damn if I never seen you agin. I don't like lawyers of no kind—an' a crooked one worst of all."

Petticord frowned. "What do you mean—crooked? What is crooked about foreclosing a mortgage when it falls due? Any judge and jury in the world would uphold me in this foreclosure."

"Huh—a jedge ain't nothin' but a glorified lawyer. Gittin' app'inted jedge can't change his nature none. You can't cure a skunk of stinkin' by tyin' a ribbon around his neck. An' as fer a jury—the kind of folks they pick to set on one, they'd uphold anything the jedge tells 'em to."

"But I tell you this is a perfectly legal procedure," Petticord insisted.

"Oh, shore. Lawyers robs folks legal, an' outlaws robs 'em onlegal—but it's the same difference in the long run."

THE ATTORNEY turned to Black John. "I certainly did not expect to encounter a hostile attitude here on Halfaday," he said. "But at least we can ignore it. Now as to the pipe, I assume that your crew has already laid the consignments that have been delivered?"

Black John nodded. "Yeah, it's all in place from the lake almost to the claim. The boys built 'em a bunkhouse up there an' they're hangin' around waitin' for the rest of the pipe to show up."

"Good. And now if I can arrange for accommodations for the night, I think I'll rest up. Unaccustomed as I am to physical exertion, the trip was very fatiguing. It's upstream all the way."

"Oh, shore, but goin' back will be downstream, an' I'm bettin' you'll go hell a-whoopin'. You can camp tonight in One Eyed John's cabin. It's only a little ways."

"But this One Eyed John—won't he object?"

"Nope. He ain't objected to nothin' since we hung him, a while back. He did object to that—but it didn't do him no good."

"I've heard how you hang men, up here. What was this One Eyed John's offense?"

"Oh, he was a damn crook. Tried to beat a young feller out of his claim, so we called a miners' meetin' an' hung him. Come on, fetch your packsacks, an' we'll be gettin' over there."

"At least," Petticord said, as the packs were deposited on the floor of One Eyed John's cabin, "tomorrow's trip will not be very long. I noted a signboard indicating Finnigan's Creek a short distance below here as we came up. Also another board indicating Lucky Creek. The two creeks empty into Halfaday only a short distance apart."

Black John nodded. "Yeah, the two valleys run parallel with only a ridge between 'em. Joe an' Ada Tuttle has be'n livin' in the shack on Finnigan's Crick. When they get ousted out of there, they can move over onto Lucky Crick. They built a good cabin over there—so it won't be as if they didn't have a place to go."

Petticord shrugged. "I don't give a damn where they go when they leave Finnigan's Creek. They could hole up in a tent, for all I care."

Black John turned toward the door. "Well, you boys make yourselves comfortable. I'll stop by for you early in the mornin'."

Returning to the saloon, Black John met Cush's glowering gaze as he advanced to the bar. "What the hell?" he demanded. "That there damn Pettyfog talked like you an' him was in cahoots, robbin' Joe Tuttle out of his claim!"

The big man nodded, and picking up the bottle, filled the glass Cush slid toward him. "Oh, shore. Like I told him down in the Tivoli when he offered to let me in on it, I ain't no hand to pass up a good proposition."

The words fairly exploded from Cush's lips. "Well, of all the damn, dirty, lousy—" He broke off suddenly, his shrewd eyes fixed on the dead-pan face of the other. "Listen, John," he said, "if I thought you was mixed up in beatin' them two young folks outa their location, by God, I'd bust you one right between the eyes with the bung-starter. But you ain't. I know you too well fer that, so I'm takin' back them names I called you 'fore I stopped to think. I git it now. I'd ort to know'd you wouldn't do nothin' onderhanded. So it's Pettyfog yer aimin' to rob, an' not Joe an' Ada! Well, good luck, John! I'd ort to stumbled to it when you told him you'd bet he'd go back hell a-whoopin'. But hey—hold on. If he's tryin' to rob them two, why the hell don't we hang the guy? I seen a kinda funny look come in his eyes when you told him we hung One Eyed John fer tryin' to beat some young fella outa his claim. Why not go ahead an' hang him? Cripes, Finnigan's Crick is a damn sight more contigulous an' subterderin' than a lot of cricks we've hung men fer committin' crimes on! An' besides, we ain't had no hangin' in quite a while. The boys would enjoy one."

Black John shook his head with a grin. "No. It wouldn't be ethical. Much as Petticord needs hangin' I wouldn't feel justified in carryin' out such sentence in this instance. You see, in a manner of speaking, I was instrumental in his comin' here. I smelt a nigger in the woodpile the minute Joe Tuttle mentioned right here in this room that Petticord had offered to lend the money for the development of Finnigan's claim cheaper than the bank would. So when I got to Dawson an' Petticord broached his plan an' offered to let me in on it fifty-fifty, I took him up. The way things is—Joe an' Ada get their pipe at half price. I get fifty thousan' out of it—an' Petticord is left holdin' the bag. What I claim, any right-minded citizen should go to any length to teach these damn crooks that crime don't pay."

Cush nodded somberly. "Yeah—special when them right-minded citizens kin make a damn good killin' teachin' 'em. But at that, John—I wisht I was smart, like you. Seems like I can't never figger them things out—till after you tell me how you worked it. Then it seems easy as hell."

VII

BRIGHT AND EARLY the following morning Petticord showed up at the Tuttle cabin accompanied by Black John and Pete Jarvis. As the two occupants stepped from the cabin, he greeted them with a smile. "Well, folks, I guess you know why I'm here. Time's up on that mortgage, and I'm here to take over the property."

"Listen, Mr. Petticord," Joe said, "won't you extend that mortgage for another six months?"

"Can't do it, young man. A mortgage is a contract and must be carried out to the letter. By its terms I contracted to turn over to you the sum of one hundred thousand dollars, the amount to be returned to me, together with the accrued interest, at the end of a six-month period. In the event of your failure to return this money when due, I was to take over the property. I performed my part of the contract when I turned the money over to you. I therefore demand that you fulfill your part of it according to the letter of its terms. Either hand over right here and now the one hundred thousand dollars plus the accrued interest, or its equivalent in gold, or give me immediate possession of the property."

All the color had drained from Ada Tuttle's face and her voice faltered as she implored the man. "Oh, please, please, Mr. Petticord, give us a little more time! If only the pipe had been delivered on time we would have had the gold to pay you. We've worked so hard, and this is our one big chance. Oh, if you would only renew the mortgage we'll double the interest—even triple it. Surely it would be a good investment for you. The gold is there in the ground—maybe a million dollars worth. Your investment is surely well secured."

"Can't do it, young woman. Sorry—but a contract is a contract, you know. By the terms of the contract, the property becomes mine on this day. And I'm here to take possession."

Joe Tuttle's face flushed with anger. "I was a fool to let you furnish the crew to freight that pipe in here! By God, you never intended it should get here on time! I see through your dirty scheme, now—now that it's too late. I was a damned fool to trust you!"

Petticord scowled. "Your accusation of fraud on my part is preposterous. It is no fault of mine that unavoidable delays caused by unforeseen difficulties prevented the prompt delivery of your pipe. And what's more, I'm not going to stand here and take any more of your insolence! I'm giving you time to gather your personal belongings together and get off this property. Will you go peaceably—or must I have my man here throw you off?" He paused, with a significant glance at the husky Pete.

Joe Tuttle shot him a glance of astonishment. "But—"

Black John cut him short. "Petticord is right, Joe," he said. "Accordin' to the mortgage you've got to turn this claim over to him today. He's refused to extend the mortgage, an' he's demanded that its terms be complied with. So, if you an' Ada will throw your stuff in a couple of packsacks, I'll help you pack it acrost the ridge to your other claim."

"But—"

Again Black John cut him short, this time with a show of angry impatience. "Damn it, shut up! Get your stuff together an' get off this claim before you're throw'd off!"

"That's right," Petticord seconded. "There's no 'ifs' nor 'buts' about it! This is your claim on Finnigan's Crick, isn't it?"

"Why—yes—but—"

"Well," Petticord interrupted, "then it is now mine. Git!"

Without another word the Tuttles stepped into the cabin and reappeared a few minutes later with a couple of well-filled packsacks. Black John swung Ada's pack to his shoulders, and struck out across the ridge, followed by the thoroughly bewildered Tuttles.

At the doorway of the new cabin on old Pat Finnigan's claim he swung the pack from his shoulders, and faced the two. "You owe me fifty thousan' dollars," he said, "an' you can have all the time you want to pay it."

The two regarded him, wide-eyed. "What?" Joe gasped.

"Yup—fifty thousan'. An' you can stay right here on your claim till you get it out. It won't take long, after the rest of the pipe gets here. An' it won't be long before it gets here. It's layin' on the bottom of the river in a shallows—right where Petticord had it hid."

"But—I don't understand!" Joe gasped,

"There ain't much to understand, except that you get your pipe for fifty thousan' instead of a hundred thousan'. An' you pay the money over to me, instead of to Petticord. Petticord has just foreclosed on your claim over there on Finnigan's Crick—an' you've got to get along with this one, here on Lucky Crick. An' there ain't the scratch of a pen against it. You see, son, when you told me in Cush's that day that Petticord was tryin' to horn in on old Pat Finnigan's location, I smelt a rat—an' Petticord was the rat.

"He ain't hard to smell—in fact, he stinks to high heaven. That's why I advised you to name your crick Finnigan's Crick. I'd always suspected Petticord was a damn crook, so when he come to me to throw in fifty-fifty with him in a scheme to beat you out of the Finnigan location, I took him up. I seen the chant to teach another damn crook that crime don't pay. The scheme worked, too—the only difference is that you an' me split Petticord's hundred thousan', fifty-fifty, instead of him an' me splittin' this claim fifty-fifty. So you see, between the two of us we've performed a Christian act—an' made some slight profit on the transaction, to boot."

"It serves him right—the—brute!" Ada cried. "Oh, just think, Joe, the claim is ours—and we owe it all to Black John!"

The big man grinned. "No, not all—jest a measly fifty thousan'. The way this proposition ort to pay out, you won't hardly notice that."

"I guess a lot of people owe a lot to Black John that they never can repay," Joe said, and turned to the big man. "For my part, I'd be willing to let you in on this whole proposition fifty-fifty. That's the deal you made with Petticord."

Black John shook his head. "Nope. Fifty thousan' is my figure. An' I'm stickin' to it."

A DOZEN men descended the ridge where they had been working on the pipeline and proceeded to the bunkhouse. Ada turned into the cabin. "There are the men going in for dinner," she said, turning to Black John. "You'll eat here with Joe and me. I'll have dinner ready in a jiffy."

At the conclusion of the meal, the three stepped from the cabin to be confronted by Petticord and Pete Jarvis. The attorney greeted them angrily: "Look here—what kind of a swindle have you put over on me?" he demanded.

Black John smiled into the man's narrowed eyes. "Just a common one, Petticord—just a common one. Nothin' fancy. Nothin' like the one you tried to put over on Joe, here—to beat him out of Pat Finnigan's claim."

"But Pete, here, has made a dozen or more pannings, from the dump there beside the shaft, from the bed of the creek, and from the ground between the creek and the rims. He has hardly struck a color—and it's common knowledge that you can pan gold from the grass roots anywhere on the Finnigan claim!"

The big man nodded. "Yeah, I've heard them rumors, too."

"You can't put anything over on me," the man roared. "I tell you, I've been swindled! In Pete's opinion that location over there is worthless!"

"W-e-e-l-l, mebbe not exactly worthless, Petticord. But damn near it."

"I believe this is the original Finnigan claim—not that other one! In some manner you have managed to switch claims on me."

"You've got the one your mortgage calls for," the big man replied, "the location on Finnigan's Crick that Pat Finnigan assigned to Joe an' Ada Tuttle. This here is Lucky Crick—not Finnigan's Crick."

"You can't get away with it!" the man fairly screamed the words. "I'll bring an action in equity! I'll have this matter straightened out in the courts!"

The big man's smile widened. "Oh, come now, Petticord. You, bein' a lawyer, should know the old sayin' that he who comes into a court of equity must come with clean hands. I'm wonderin' how clean the court would say your hands was, when it heard what I had to say—an' also what Red John had to say about your instructions to the freight crew about gummin' up the delivery of that pipe." The words were interrupted by the men from Halfaday who, having finished their meal, were emerging from the bunkhouse a few yards away. Black John glanced toward them, as he added, "The fact is, Petticord, that beneath a mighty thin veneer of respectability, you're nothin' but a damn dirty crook. I don't like crooks—your kind. In fact, I frequently go out of my way to try to show 'em the error of their ways—to implant into their warped an' twisted souls the fact that crime don't pay. I would like to purvey this information free, Petticord, but realizin' that a man values a thing higher if he pays for it, than if it was merely handed to him, I know that you will feel that you're gettin' off cheap at a hundred thousan'. So go your way an' sin no more, Petticord. An' just remember not to attempt to retaliate, nor to molest these young folks in the peaceful enjoyment of their property here. If you should ever show up in these parts again, you'll meet the same fate that One Eyed John met. You'll rec'lect it was his cabin you slept in last night—him that I told you we hung because he tried to beat a young fellow out of his claim.

"With that thought in mind, Petticord, I know that you will feel that you're lucky we're lettin' you off cheap at a hundred thousan'."

ALL OR NOTHING

THE YOUNG MAN beached his canoe and stepped out onto the sand spit just as the last rays of the setting sun gilded the high hills on the opposite side of the river. He would camp here tonight, and in the morning would round one more bend and shoot out onto the Yukon.

He drew the canoe clear of the water, carried his blanket roll and heavy packsack to the edge of the bush, kindled a fire, set his tea pail aboil, and sliced half a dozen slabs of salt pork into his frying pan.

All day he had been paddling down the Little Pelican. Fifty miles he had come—yes, George Ruff said it was fifty miles from the big river to his claim near the head of the creek. It had taken them three days of upstream paddling and poling to cover the distance he had just made in one. And now George Ruff was dead—lying there dead in his bunk in his cabin. And he, Homer P. Smith was back on the Yukon with the gold.

A grim smile twitched the corners of the man's lips as he turned the pork sizzling in the pan. All or Nothing—that's what the boys called me in the poker games down at the U. And there in Sauk Centre, after I went to work in the bank—I was always either flat broke or else way up in the chips. All or Nothing—that's me. I'll die either in a palace or a poorhouse. Nothing half way!

He slipped the pork onto a tin plate, filled his cup from the pail, and devoured the meat, washing it down with drafts of strong tea. He washed the dishes, set them aside, rolled a cigarette, and lolled back against his pack. All or Nothing—I've got it all, and George Ruff got—nothing.

Almost unconsciously his fingers explored the imperceptible bulge where three little capsules nestled snugly in the fold where the cloth had been doubled to form the collar of his heavy flannel shirt, as his mind reviewed the events of the past few days. Hydrocyanic—prussic acid, one of the quickest and most deadly poisons known—and it worked. I dropped two of them in George's tea at breakfast, and he didn't last five minutes—just stood up, his eyes wide open, gasped for air, clutched at his throat, and staggered across the floor to crash face down on his bunk. He was dead before I got the stuff in the canoe.

If ever there was a perfect crime, this is it. With all the claims on Little Pelican fizzled out and abandoned, no one saw us shove up the creek, and no one saw me coming down. No one ever saw us together—except maybe there in the Klondike Palace in Dawson—and then we were only a couple of guys sitting there chewing the fat over our drinks. No one paid any attention to us. That was when George told me about the Eureka Dredge setup. He had abandoned his claim a couple of months ago and gone to work for the Eureka Dredge outfit over on Flat Creek—just eight miles across from his claim on Little Pelican. He kept his eyes open—knew right where the strong box was kept—knew when it would have plenty of dust in it—knew just when the night watchman made his rounds. Then he hid a crowbar in the bush, close by, and quit his job. It sounded good—too good to pass up—for a guy who was broke.

He rolled another cigarette. So we hit up to George's claim, crossed over to Flat Creek through the hills, and while I acted as lookout, George got busy. He laid for the watchman, knocked him cold with the crowbar, and jimmied his way into the strong box with it. He dumped the dust into a couple of packsacks and we hit back to his claim. It was dark when we got there, and he figured that someone might suspect him because some of the men on the job knew he had the location on Little Pelican—so we decided to pull out at daylight. Well—I pulled out at daylight—and when the dredge men get there they'll find George—but they won't find the dust. I dumped it into one packsack—all of it—All or Nothing—that's me. And the thing is heavy—close to two hundred pounds—that's—why it's—there must be somewhere around fifty thousand dollars—and it's all mine!

AND, GEORGE—THEY'LL think he died naturally—heart attack, or something. If there are any fingerprints on the crowbar they'll be George's. They won't know anyone was with him, and they'll hunt all over to find where he cached the dust. Good thing I learned about this prussic acid—and a damn good thing I made up those capsules when I worked in that drug store.

Yup—a perfect crime if ever there was one. And now who's the damn fool—brother Bob, or me? And the old man, too—big business man—small town stuff—worked hard all his life—been mayor three, four times—president of the bank—maybe worth seventy-five or a hundred thousand—never had any fun—always raising hob with me for drinking, and gambling, and women. When I got kicked out at the U. he put me to work in the bank. I didn't last long there—six months, and the directors put pressure on the old man to fire me—they didn't like the All or Nothing way I played poker. Some of 'em used to sit in the games we had in the hotel, and they figured that the way I played 'em I might dip into the bank's money. In fact, I was in for a couple of thousand—but the old man shut up about it, made it good, and kicked me out—told me he was through with me—cut me off without a dollar and put Bob in my place. I hit for Seattle, got a job in a drug store, and stayed with it till I made enough in a poker game one night to hit for the Klondike. Bob'll make good, all right—in the same way the old man made good—work hard all his life after marrying some home-town girl, get a good team of driving horses, a red wheeled runabout, or a surrey with a fringe around the top—or maybe one of these new fangled automobiles, raise a bunch of kids—get elected mayor—and when he's an old man he'll have maybe a hundred thousand to show for it. I've got half that much, right now—and I'm only twenty-five! And the way those sourdoughs play 'em there in Dawson I might run it up to a million!

The little fire had died down. He tossed a handful of dry twigs onto the coals, and as they flared up, spread his blankets on the soft sand. Removing his shoes, he picked up the coat he had folded on top of the packsack. As he rolled it for a pillow his eyes suddenly widened as they rested on the inside pocket. The letter! Where's the letter? Feverishly his fingers explored the empty pocket—the two side pockets—the outside front pocket—a crumpled bandana, a package of cigarette tobacco, a handful of matches—nothing else.

He dropped the coat and explored his trousers pocket—no letter. He tossed more wood on the fire, and when it flared up he shook out his blankets. He overturned his packsack, dumping its contents onto the sand—an extra shirt, a suit of underwear, two pairs of socks, and the Eureka Dredge Company's little canvas sacks of gold.

Slowly, as a man in a dream, he returned the items to the packsack. Maybe—maybe the letter had fallen from his pocket when he tossed the coat into the canoe—maybe it had fallen from his pocket when he carried his coat to the fire.

Stepping to a dead birch, he stripped off a slab of bark, rolled it, ignited it in the fire, and carrying the torch, walked slowly to the canoe, scrutinizing every inch of the sand. Holding the torch high he searched the empty canoe—no letter.

Tossing the burning torch into the water, he walked slowly back to the fire and seated himself on his packsack. He tried to roll a cigarette but his fingers trembled so that the paper tore, spilling the tobacco onto the sand. But the letter—where could it be? He remembered reading it and thrusting it into the inside pocket of his coat just before he and George Ruff left Dawson.

Why had he inquired for a letter, anyway? He wasn't expecting any letter—he and George Ruff were heading for the river, and as they passed the post office, he had stepped in and asked for mail. The clerk ran through a packet of letters and shoved one through the wicket—Homer P. Smith. Dawson, Y. T., addressed in a feminine hand. It carried a Seattle postmark. Why did she write to me, anyhow? I never expected to see her again—never want to. Ran onto her slinging hash in a restaurant soon after I hit Seattle, and we roomed together in a cheap boarding house during the four months I worked in the drug store. Then I made my killing and hit for the Klondike to make my everlasting fortune. She wanted to go along—but I talked her out of it—told her it was a tough country, and that if I didn't strike it lucky she'd be in a bad way—told her to stay where she was, and if I made good I'd send for her. And so she wrote me that letter— said she loved me—never loved anyone else. She's no spring chicken! She knows her way around. But she isn't overlooking any bets—just in case I should make good—the little gold-digger! Why did I keep the letter? I never intended to answer it. Why didn't I tear it up as soon as I read it and toss the pieces away? Why did I stick it in my pocket?

HE REMEMBERED hanging the coat over the rail at the foot of George Ruff's bunk when they got to the shack, and he hadn't taken it with him when they set out for Flat Creek to pull the Eureka job. Then, this morning, he had grabbed the coat and tossed it into the canoe on top of the packsack and shoved off.

His hands were still shaking as he attempted another cigarette. He made it, this time—not a good one, but enough for a few deep inhales. When I hung the coat over the bunk rail the inside pocket would be upside down. That's where the letter is, right now—there on George Ruff's floor between the foot of the bunk and the stove—lying there for the first one that comes along to find it—Homer P. Smith, Dawson, Y.T.!

Panic seized him. He would hit back at daylight and get the letter. But—no. It would take at least three days—more likely four or five, to shove upstream alone to George's shack. And he'd probably run into a bunch of Eureka men searching for the cached gold. But—they wouldn't be searching for the cache! When they picked up that letter they'd know that George had a partner in that robbery—and they'd know just who that partner was. "Perfect crime—!" he cried, aloud. "What a botch I made of it!" He remembered, now, that in hitting across through the hills they had crossed several little creeks—the tracks would show that there were two men. Why hadn't he thought of that? Why hadn't he stepped in George's tracks whenever they hit mud or soft sand? Why hadn't he torn that letter to shreds? He'd pull out at daylight—those men might be coming down the creek. But where could he go? He couldn't show up in Dawson. Not with that letter in the hands of the police, he couldn't. He had heard plenty about Corporal Downey in the couple of weeks he had hung around Cuter Malone's Klondike Palace—what a smart cop he was. Some one—even Malone himself might tip Downey off that he had hung around with George Ruff. He had the gold right here in his packsack but where could he go?

Suddenly his drooping shoulders stiffened. What was it he had heard about Halfaday Creek? About the gang of outlaws that hung out there—and about their leader, Black John Smith?

The talk was that the police didn't dare show up there. That's where he'd hit for—Halfaday Creek! He'd hit for Dawson, pull in behind the sawmill, cache the pack in the sawdust pile, slip up to the Klondike Palace, and find out how to reach Halfaday Creek, pick up enough grub to get him there, and pull out before news of the Eureka robbery reached Dawson. Once on Halfaday—forget the police! He had the dust and the police would never pick him up. But even if they should, it wouldn't do 'em any good. He'd cache the dust where no one would ever find it. And they'd never hang him for the murder of George Ruff—

not as long as one of those little capsules was within easy reach of his fingers—right there in the collar of his shirt.

II

BLACK JOHN SMITH crossed the floor and elevated a foot to the battered brass rail as Old Cush, proprietor of Cushing's Fort, the combined trading post and saloon that served the little community of outlawed men that had sprung up on Halfaday Creek, close against the Yukon-Alaska border, set a bottle, two glasses, and the inevitable leather dice box onto the bar.

Picking up the box, the big man rattled the dice and cast them. "Three fours," he announced, "accordin' to the law of averages they should be good for a horse. I'm leavin' 'em in one."

Cush returned the dice to the box, shook them vigorously, and rolled them out. "An' there's three sixes says yer law of averages ain't worth a hoot—an' never was. That's a horse on you—an' here's right back at you." He cast the dice, left a pair of fives, cast again without helping them, and on the third cast added one more five. "Three fives to beat in three," he grumbled. "What does yer law of averages say about that?"

"W-e-e-l-l, off hand, I'd say that the odds is somewhere around ten, fifteen to one that I'll beat 'em."

"I'll take an ounce of that! If an ounce'll git me fifteen ounces it's a good bet if I lose!"

The big man grinned as he picked up the dice and returned them to the box. "You're on. I shall now proceed to demonstrate the fallacy embraced in the dogmatic hypothesis that an obviously losing bet is a good bet under any circumstances." He cast the dice, eyed the pair of fives that showed, returned all the dice to the box, and cast again. "Of course I could leave 'em, shake another five, and tie your three fives, thus annulin' the bet."

"You ain't 'nullin' nothin'! The bet was fifteen to one you'd beat 'em. Tyin' ain't beatin'."

"You're a hard man, Cush," Black John grinned, as he returned the five dice to the box. "However, three sixes, three aces, or any set of fours will do the job. Here they come, Cush—read 'em an' weep!"

"Huh," Cush grunted, eyeing the pair of treys that showed on the bar, "I'll do the readin', all right. But the fact is I ain't wep' none sence I was a kid—so you kin do the weepin' whilst I charge you up with fifteen ounces of dust and a round of drinks in the day book." He made the entry and returned the book to the back bar, filled his glass from the bottle, and shoved his square-rimmed glasses from nose to forehead. "An' that jest goes to show, like I allus told you—eggication ain't worth a hoot to a man, no ways you look at it."

"Oh, I don't know," the big man grinned, as he filled his own glass.

"Yer right you don't! That's why I'm tellin' you. Take like now—you claimed yer law of averages says how I hadn't ort to beat three fours in one—an' I done it. Then when I can't do no better'n three fives in three, you shoot off all the big words you kin think up in what time you've got an' claim yer law of averages says it's a fifteen to one bet you kin beat 'em. You throw three times an' wind up with a pair of treys. I don't know no big words, nor neither I don't know no law of averages—an' I win. Yer eggication cost you jest fifteen' ounces an' a round of drinks."

"However, I still maintain…."

"You kin stand there an' maintain—whatever maintain means—an' I still claim eggication ain't worth a hoot fer a common man. 'Course, if a man's goin' to be a doctor he'd ort to go to some college an' learn enough so's he don't give someone a dost of physic when he needs pain killer—er like if he's got a misery in his guts, the doctor had ort to know which gut to cut out, an' where it's at. An' if a man's goin' to be a lawyer he's got to go to some college an' learn how to lie legal. An' if he's goin' to be a bookkeeper he'd ort to learn how to figger."

"How about preachers?"

"You ort to know. You claim yer pa was one, an' you went to

a preacher's college onct—an' here you turn out to be the biggest outlaw on the country. 'Course I know, an' all the sourdoughs knows, an' the police knows, you don't never rob no one that ain't got it comin'. But it looks like a funny thing to learn in a preacher's college, at that. Looks to me like all you learnt was a lot of big words, an' what I claim, yer worst off than I be, 'cause me not knowin' no big words I use little ones that everyone knows what they mean—an' they ain't half the folks knows what yer talkin' about—even if they listen. Look—here comes someone. He ain't no one I ever seen before—an' that there pack he's got looks heavy. An' don't fergit—I seen it first!"

THE STRANGER crossed the clearing, paused a moment in the doorway, stepped to the bar, and slipped his pack to the floor. He eyed the two with a smile. "This is Cushing's Fort, on Halfaday Creek, isn't it?" he asked.

"Yup. This is the place," Cush replied, sliding a glass across the bar. "Fill up. This 'uns on the house."

The young man filled his glass and glanced into the face of the big man beside him. "And you, I assume, are Black John Smith, the—er we might say, the dominating satrap of this isolated community."

The big man grinned. "We might. But if we did Cush wouldn't know what we were talkin' about."

Cush glowered across the bar. "My gosh! Before we had only one on the crick—now we got two! An' from now on they won't no one know for nothin' about which no one's talkin'!"

Black John's grin widened. "The obvious obfuscation of Cush's observation is entirely inadvertent, I assure you."

"Yeah," Cush growled, "but if I got somethin' to say, I come right out an' say it in little words which anyone, if he ain't a idiot er a ape, would know what they mean."

The newcomer laughed and raised his glass. "Well, here's how. And, by way of introduction, I'll mention that my name is Smith…."

"Not on Halfaday it ain't," Black John interrupted. "Just reach in the name can there on the end of the bar and draw out a new one."

"Name can!" the man exclaimed. "What the devil's a name can? I'm giving it to you straight—my name is Smith—Homer P. Smith."

"Homer, eh? W-e-e-l-l, the Homer part might be considered a mitigatin' circumstance, at that. Mostly every cuss that shows up on the crick claims his name is John Smith. So we outlawed the name. Cush and I mixed up a lot of names out of a history book, an' wrote 'em on slips, an' stuck 'em in that can yonder, so when anyone shows up with the name of John Smith, we invite him to help himself to a synthetic one out of the can. But—Homer. We never had a Homer. I guess maybe we can let it go at that."

"I understand," the newcomer said, "that you're an isolated little community, up here. That anything a man may have done before he got here is nobody's business but his own. And that he is welcome to remain here indefinitely, provided he refrains from committing any crime that might bring the police onto the creek."

The big man nodded. "Your onderstandin' is approximately correct."

"I also heard that, situated as far back from the big river as you are, there is a vast amount of contiguous territory that hasn't been prospected. Down along the Yukon so many chechakos are piling into the country, a man hasn't got much chance of locating a good claim. I was lucky enough to locate one good proposition, but sold out for a decent price, and decided to hit farther back from the river."

"Yeah, there's plenty of contiguous territory. An' a lot of it ain't be'n prospected."

"My idea is to settle down here on the creek and do some prospecting. I have sufficient gold from the sale of my claim to defray my expenses, and also to indulge in an occasional game of stud—a pastime that I understand is favored here at the fort. I passed an empty cabin some four or five miles down the creek. I'm wondering how it would be if I should move in there, at least temporarily?"

"That's Olson's old shack," Cush said. "It's claimed to be unlucky."

"How—unlucky?"

Black John grinned. "I'd say unlucky. Just about everyone that's lived in it has been shot, or hung, or robbed. Of course, in the matter of the shootin's and robberies we've evened up the score by hangin' the culprit. But lookin' at it from the tenant's angle, it's still unlucky. If you contemplate establishin' a more or less permanent residence on the crick, I'd recommend One Eyed John's cabin. It's in good shape, an' a sight closter to Cush's than Olson's."

"But—how about this One Eyed John? Won't he object?"

"He ain't likely to. We hung him a while back."

"Why did you hang him?"

The big man grinned. "Oh, we didn't have nothin' to do one afternoon, so we hung him."

The man laughed. "Okay. I'll take a chance. Fill 'em up again. And here's hoping that you won't find time hanging heavy on your hands in the near future. Where is this cabin? I might as well move in right now."

Black John accompanied the man to the cabin, and when he returned, Cush filled his own glass, shoved the bottle across the bar, and eyed him sourly. "Well, I s'pose yer happy now you got someone here on the crick that kin say near as many big words as what you kin."

"Yeah—Homer might turn out to be a delightful companion."

"Huh—I wouldn't delight in no chechako no matter how many big words he know'd. An' he's a liar, to boot—claimin' he located a good claim on some crick, an' then sold it. Who ever heard tell of someone sellin' a location an' takin' his pay in dust—what with two banks right there in Dawson? Even if he did get paid in dust, he would have cashed it in fer bills an' not packed all that weight around with him. That pack must weigh clost to 200 pounds—the way it hit the floor!"

The big man shrugged. "Maybe he didn't sell the claim in Dawson. He's got plenty of dust, all right. But it's none of our business where or how he got it."

"Yeah—but if he pulls somethin' an' we go ahead an' hang him, I git my half of that there dust! Remember, I seen him first when he come walkin' acrost the clearin'. An', speaking of dust, reminds me you got to take a batch down to the bank. The safe's gittin' so full I can't hardly git no more in it."

"Okay, Cush. Make up a batch of it an' I'll take it down in the mornin'. Last time I was in Dawson those damn sourdoughs took me for somewhere around six thousan' dollars, an' I aim to get it back. I'll slip over to my cabin an' get a good night's rest so I can get an early start in the mornin'."

ONE AFTERNOON, some ten days later, Black John stepped into detachment headquarters of the mounted police in Dawson to be greeted by Corporal Downey. "Hello John! Pull up a chair. What's new on Halfaday?"

"Nothin' new. We're a quiet little community, up there. Cush's safe got to bulgin' at the seams, so I fetched down a batch of dust. How's things along the river?"

"It's be'n fairly quiet for the past month or so—routine stuff, mostly. Had one murder an' robbery, though—an' what might be another."

"What do you mean—what might be another?"

"About a month ago the Eureka Dredge Company's outfit on Flat Crick was robbed of twenty-eight hundred an' eighty ounces of dust. It was a night job. The watchman was brained with a crowbar, and the strong box jimmied. As luck would have it I was on a routine patrol and got there the following morning. I got a good set of fingerprints—both hands—on the crowbar. I checked them with the prints of every man on the job, and they all came clean. I asked a lot of questions, and found that a character by the name of George Ruff had been employed there for a month or so, and had quit a couple of weeks before. This Ruff was known to have had a claim near the head of Little Pelican, only about eight miles across country from the dredge outfit. I remembered Ruff as a character that hung around Cuter Malone's Klondike Palace last winter. Constable Brock picked him up for attempted robbery along toward spring, but we had to turn him loose for lack of evidence.

"On a hunch I hit across to Little Pelican and before I'd gone far I ran onto footprints—the footprints of two men. I ran onto 'em in several places where they had crossed little cricks and left their prints in the mud. The tracks showed that the two had come across from Little Pelican, and gone back the same way. I knew I was on the right track, because the tracks in the mud were deeper and closer together goin' back than they were goin' toward Flat Crick. They were travelin' light goin' over, an' carried fairly heavy packs goin' back.

"When I shoved open the door on the uppermost claim on Little Pelican I found George Ruff. He was dead. Not a mark on him anywhere. He just laid there on his bunk—dead. I found where a canoe had be'n landed on the sand in front of the shack, an' where one man had shoved off in her. Whoever it was that served as lookout for Ruff made off with the dust. Maybe he murdered Ruff—but I'm afraid we can never prove that. It would be a heck of a coincidence, though, if Ruff happened to die of natural causes just after pullin' off that robbery—an' if he did, where is the man who was with him? An' where's the dust? I went all over the shack, but found nothin'. Got some more fingerprints—all Ruff's.

"I debated with myself whether to hit back to Flat Crick where I'd left my canoe, or hit down Little Pelican afoot. It was a good fifty miles to the Yukon, an' I knew that most of the claims on the crick had been abandoned. There was no chance of pickin' up any evidence by way of Flat Crick, but there might be a location or two bein' worked on Little Pelican, and I might get a line on the man with the dust. So I hit down the crick—but every claim on it had been abandoned—not a soul left on the crick. Whoever got away with the dust don't need to worry about gettin' picked up. If there ever was such a thing as a perfect crime—this is it."

BLACK JOHN knocked the dottle from his pipe and refilled it. "Oh, I don't know, Downey," he said. "If there was no marks on Ruff's body maybe he was poisoned. The doctors might find evidence of poison in him even yet. You might find out who bought that kind of poison lately, an' pin Ruff's murder on him, even if you never located the dust."

The officer shook his head. "I thought of that. As soon as I got back I hustled Constables Brock and Breen up there with orders to bring Ruff's body down." He paused and grinned. "What with the weather hot as it was they didn't seem to relish the detail. But they got back with the body an' Doc Sutherland made a post mortem. He found nothin'. Said it might have been poison—but it wasn't metallic poison, like arsenic. He said evidence of a metallic poison an' some non-metallic ones remain in the body for a long time—but others—what he calls organic poisons, are almost impossible to spot after decomposition sets in—an' in Ruff's case decomposition had shore set in. It took me four days to come down Little Pelican afoot, an' another day to get to Dawson—an' it took Brock and Breen five days to get to Ruff's shack, an' three days to get back.

"I don't suppose any John Smiths have showed up on Half-aday lately, packin' about a hundred an' eighty pounds of dust, have they?"

The big man grinned. "Nary a John Smith, Downey."

The officer shrugged. "The heck of it is, whoever got away with that dust is prob'ly right here in Dawson—an' not a damn bit of evidence against him. About the only thing we can do is keep our eyes open for someone that's started on a spendin' spree—an' even then we'd have a time puttin' anything on him—unless we could find some of the Eureka's canvas sacks in his possession."

Black John rose and pocketed his pipe. "Well so long, Downey. Guess I'll slip over to the Tivoli an' see if I can't kick up a stud game. The sourdoughs kind of took me the last time I was down."

TEN DAYS later, as Black John stepped into the saloon at Cushing's Fort, Cush set out a bottle and two glasses. "Y'know, John," he said, shoving his square-framed, steel-rimmed glasses from nose to forehead, "that there Homer ain't sech a bad guy, at that."

"Well—who said he was? If I remember rightly it was you who jumped to the conclusion that he had plenty of heavy dust in his pack, an' that he prob'ly never got it from the sale of a location. Also I remember that you caviled at his use of words of more than one syllable."

"I never done no sech thing 'cause I wouldn't know how to cavil. I don't even know what it means—let alone doin' it. All I says was now they's two cusses on the crick that shoots off a lot of big words fer the confusal of someone which wouldn't know what they mean, even if he would listen. But this here Homer, he knows a lot of little words, too. He mixes in good with the boys, an' they all kinda like him. He drinks quite a bit, but he holds his licker good. An' he shore plays a game of stud. All er Nothin' they call him, 'cause that's the way he plays 'em. He'll play along for a while, an' then when he gits a good size stack in front of him he'll shove 'em all in the pot—'all er nothin' he'll say—an' he's jest as apt to do it on a bluff, as on a good hand!"

"How's it workin' out? Is he losin', or winnin'?"

"I couldn't say for shore. He allus buys a good size stack when he sets in, an' sometimes he loses the hull works, an' sometimes he cashes in big. I had a kind of a headache, one night whilst the boys was playin', an' I got One Armed John to tend bar, an' I slipped over to One Eyed John's cabin an' looked in that there cache in the wall. I figgered he must have a lot of dust in there—but there worn't over a hundred ounces. Either that there pack of his'n wasn't nowheres as heavy as what I figgered that day he come, er elst he'd cached the bulk of his dust in some other place."

Black John grinned. "As a matter of fact, Cush, I had the same kind of a headache you had about Homer's pack, an' I mistrusted he wouldn't use that inside cache—even if he found it. So instead of goin' to my cabin for some sleep when you told me I had to make a trip to Dawson, that evening, I slipped over an' laid at the edge of One Eyed John's clearin' an' I didn't have long to wait till Homer come out with his pack an' cached fifteen canvas sacks of dust. Did a good job, too, for a chechako. Might be no one ever would have found 'em."

Some three weeks later, with a stud game in progress, Corporal Downey stepped into Cushing's saloon, crossed the floor, and brought up beside the table. "Anyone here by the name of Smith?" he asked, maintaining a perfectly straight face, as smiles broke out on the faces of Black John Smith, Pot Gutted John Smith, Red John Smith, Long John Smith, and Short John Smith. "I mean Homer P. Smith," the officer added.

All eyes flashed to the face of the man who sat opposite Black John at the table, a stack of chips before him. His face seemed to pale suddenly as he moistened his lips with his tongue. "I—I'm Homer P. Smith," he said, raising his eyes to the officer's face.

"Can you prove it?" Downey asked.

"Why—yes—I guess I can." He drew out a wallet from which he selected a card which he handed to Downey. "The identification card issued with an accident policy I took out a year or so ago back in Minnesota."

Downey studied the card and handed it back with a nod.

"You—wanted to see me?" the man asked, and he returned the card to the wallet.

"Yes. In the matter of a letter."

"A letter." Smith repeated the word huskily, as his fingers fumbled at the collar of his shirt. "A—a letter addressed to—to me?"

"That's right. To Homer P. Smith, Dawson, Y.T."

The man's fingers moved to his lips and he swallowed several times with an effort, as Downey removed a long envelope from his pocket and handed it to the man, whose eyes suddenly widened as he grasped it. "Why—why—it's unopened!" he cried.

"Yes," Downey said. "I figured you could do that yourself. It came in an envelope addressed to the Dawson Police Detachment. It's from a lawyer in Sauk Centre, Minnesota, and requests the police to try and locate Homer P. Smith and hand him this letter in a matter of importance."

AS DOWNEY talked Smith tore open the letter, stared at it for several moments and rose to his feet, a wild look in his staring eyes. "No! No! O, my God…!" Suddenly his knees buckled and he crashed face foremost to the floor, the letter still clutched in his hand.

As the men rose from the table and gathered around, Downey turned the prostrate man onto his back and noted the wide staring eyes with their dilated pupils, and the white frothy foam at the corners of the lips. "The man is dead," he announced and removing the letter from his hand, read aloud:

"Dear Homer: I got your Seattle address from a letter you wrote a while back to Bill Dubois. I wrote that address and the letter was returned unclaimed. I got in touch with the Seattle police and they reported that you had engaged passage for the Klondike country, so I am sending this to the police in Dawson City, in hope that they may be able to locate you. I advise your immediate return here, as your father and brother were killed in a railway accident in June, and you are the sole heir to the estate, valued of upwards of a hundred thousand dollars.

> Sincerely yours,
> Frank Kells,
> Attorney at Law."

Pot Gutted John was the first to speak. "Well, what do you know about that! That guy gits a hundred thousan' left to him—an' he drops dead!"

"Must be his heart give out on him," Red John opined. "Too much good luck all to onct."

"All er nothin'—that's what he allus hollered when he'd shove all his chips in the pot," Long John said. "An' that's the way it ended fer him—he got it all—then nothin'."

"It wasn't his heart," Downey said, eying the corpse. "He died of poison. I caught the flash of a capsule of some kind in his fingers as moved them to his mouth. Then he swallowed."

"By God, if I'd jest fall heir to better'n a hundred thousan' I wouldn't p'izen myself, by a sight!" Cush exclaimed.

"He swallowed the poison before he read the letter," Downey reminded. "There must be some other reason—some other letter he had in mind, maybe." Stooping, he searched the man's pockets. "No letter there," he said. Then, suddenly, he bent close and sniffed at the dead lips. "Peach pits," he said.

"Peach pits!" Cush exclaimed. "Cripes, they ain't no peaches in this country! An' even if they was no one would eat the pits."

"His eyes looked just like George Ruff's eyes looked when I found him dead, back there in his shack. An' there was foam on his lips, an' I got that same whiff of peach pits when I bent over him. There must be some kind of poison that smells like peach pits. I'll ask Doc Sutherland. Trouble was, by the time the boys got Ruff's body down to Dawson it stunk so Doc couldn't have smelt no peach pits. Ruff was poisoned, all right—an' this Homer P. Smith was the bird that fed him the poison—

I'd bet my life on that!" He paused and turned abruptly on Black John. "Where has this man lived since he hit Halfaday?"

"In One Eyed John's cabin."

"Okay. Come on over there. I want to look around."

INSIDE THE cabin Downey stepped to the wall and pulled on the bit of string that showed between two logs. "I remember this cache," he said, as Black John looked on. When the loose section of log was removed Downey thrust his arm into the aperture and drew out two small moosehide sacks of dust. "Maybe forty, fifty ounces," he said.

The big man nodded. "Yeah, Homer had his ups an' downs playin' stud, same as anyone else."

"Shore—but I know this Homer was Ruff's pardner on that Eureka robbery. He poisoned Ruff in his cabin an' made off with those twenty-eight hundred and eighty ounces. He must have had damn bad luck with his stud playin' if this is all he had left."

"That's right," Black John agreed, "I couldn't say. I was gone better'n three weeks takin' the dust from the safe down to Dawson."

Downey nodded, and eyed the big man narrowly. "Yeah—an' I remember askin' you if any Smiths had showed up on Halfaday lately, an' you said no."

"You asked if any John Smiths had showed up. This man's name is Homer."

"An' you wouldn't, I s'pose, know whether this Homer had another cache somewhere, would you?"

"Downey—if I was to try an' locate every cache on Halfaday, I wouldn't get no work done from one year's end to another. But how come you shoved way up here just to deliver a letter—not even knowin' this Homer P. Smith was here?"

"I didn't come up here just to deliver the letter. I'm on a routine patrol up to Father Cassatt's mission, an' when we couldn't locate this Smith in Dawson, I stuck the letter in my pocket—just in case."

"What I claim," Black John observed, "this Homer got that dredge company dust—they're the ones to worry about it—not me. Come on over to Cush's an' I'll buy a drink."

The officer shrugged as he slipped the two small pouches into his pocket. "Guess the only thing to do is to ship this dust down to that lawyer in Minnesota to add to the Smith estate. I shore can't figure it out—here I've be'n thinkin' that whoever got that dust had pulled off the perfect crime. But from what we know, now—it wasn't so perfect after all."

Leelanau Historical Society

Celebrating 150 Years of Leelanau History

Leelanau County was officially established in 1863 when the State of Michigan was a young 26 years old. People were attracted to the natural resources from the beginning—first as a way to earn a living and build a home, and later to enjoy recreation away from the cities. Early settlers arrived on the islands beginning in 1839, while Native Americans populated the Leelanau peninsula until pioneers began exploring the area in 1847. For the next 45 years, the villages known today—and some that are abandoned—were settled. North and South Manitou Islands and the Fox Islands officially joined the county in 1895.

The Leelanau Historical Society was launched in 1957 by a group of residents dedicated to collecting and preserving Leelanau's history. Leland, first established in 1853 and later the county seat, seemed the natural location for the Society. When the old county jail became available in 1959, the museum found its first home. Through generous donations and grants, a new museum was built in 1985 and later expanded.

Today, the collections and archives contain more than 11,000 items. Visitors to the museum learn about Leelanau life and maritime history from exhibits, educational programs and publications. The Society continues to collect, document and preserve items relating to Leelanau history.

203 East Cedar Street, Leland, MI 49654

Tel. (231) 256-7475

info@LeelanauHistory.org

http://www.leelanauhistory.org/

THE
HALFADAY CREEK
LIBRARY

JAMES B. HENDRYX

James B. Hendryx's classic series returns to print! The author of more than 50 novels and anthologies, he's best known for his characters set around the outlaw community of Halfaday Creek in the Yukon. Set during the Gold Rush of the late 1890s, Hendryx penned over a hundred stories featuring these characters over the span of 25 years for a variety of pulp magazines.

Now, Altus Press has committed to return these to print. Using the original pulp magazines as the source material, along with the illustrations from their original pulp magazine appearances, these uniform edition books will be augmented with rare material taken from the James B. Hendryx archives held by the Leelanau Historical Society in Leland, MI.

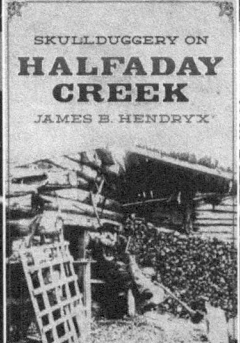